"Colton Denni  **nd**
my counter this minute," and
smacked him on the shou

Ouch. The tiny wom a wallop.

He put Jamie down and turned. "Oh come on now, Magpie. I was just caught up in the excitement of the news."

"Yeah well, catch up on *that* side of the counter. You're going to violate my health codes."

He looked down at himself—dusty, faded jeans that may have been worn one season too long, a relatively clean, long sleeve flannel over a black T-shirt, and cowboy boots caked in dried mud. Okay, she might have a point. Not that he would ever tell her that. One thing Maggie did not need to hear was that she was right, again.

Besides, it was much more fun to tease her.

"I'm not that dirty."

She rolled those pretty green eyes of hers. "You've got hay stuck in your jeans."

A quick glance revealed a short stalk stuck in the waistband of his wranglers. Not surprising. Working on a horse ranch, you were bound to get a stray piece of hay here and there.

"Why, Magpie, were you eying my unmentionables?"

She snorted, a very unladylike snort, but adorable as hell.

"Oh please. You probably put it there on purpose to draw attention *to* your *unmentionables*. You're a shameless flirt, Colton Denning, and you know it."

"What's wrong with a little harmless flirting? Especially when it's with such a pretty lady."

Love on the Sweet Side

by

Mariah Ankenman

The Peak Town, Colorado Series

Love on the Sweet Side

COPYRIGHT © 2016 by Mariah Ankenman

Cover Art by *Kristian Norris*

The Wild Rose Press, Inc.
PO Box 708
Adams Basin, NY 14410-0708
Visit us at www.thewildrosepress.com

Publishing History
First Yellow Rose Edition, 2016
Print ISBN 978-1-5092-0768-8
Digital ISBN 978-1-5092-0769-5

The Peak Town, Colorado Series
Published in the United States of America

Dedication

To Mort and Bonnie,
who showed me what true love really is;
and to my Prince Charming,
who keeps me believing
that dreams really do come true.

Chapter One

Someone is going to die!

Maggie Evans gripped the black, cordless phone tight in her hand, knuckles white, temper red-hot. Someone had screwed up, *again*. When she found out who that someone was, she was going to kill them.

Dulcet tones filled her ear, but the melodic hold music did nothing to calm her simmering rage. *They should use speed metal when placing people on hold.* If the tune matched the mood then maybe the customers wouldn't get so pissed off at the blatant attempt to soothe them.

Nothing about this situation was soothing.

"Pansy's Wholesalers. How can I help you?"

Finally! It had only taken them twenty minutes to get to her. She glanced at the clock in an attempt to suppress her growl. "Yes, I'm calling about my recent order of mascarpone."

"What seems to be the problem?" the cheery, high-pitched voice on the other end of the phone asked.

"It hasn't arrived. It was supposed to be delivered this morning at six a.m., and it's still not here." And it was well past three in the afternoon.

Normally, she was a very easy-going person. Mistakes happened, trucks got delayed, she understood that, but this was the *fourth* screw up from this company in the last six months. That wasn't happenstance; that was shoddy business.

"Oh dear, let me check on that for you, ma'am. Do you have your order number?"

She rattled off the eight-digit number from the receipt printed when she had placed the order and could hear the woman on the other end of the phone tapping away on a keyboard.

Trying to rein in her frustration, she took a deep breath. She'd get this straightened out. Everything would be fine. Her mascarpone cheese would get delivered. She would make her famous tiramisu cupcakes. The blogger would give her a good review, and everything would be just fine…

"I'm sorry, Ms. Evans, but it appears the order was cancelled."

…*or not.*

"What do you mean the order was *cancelled*?"

"It says right here that someone from your bakery called yesterday and cancelled the order."

Impossible. "Who called?"

"We don't have a record of that, ma'am."

She was getting really tired of this "ma'am" business. "Look, the only person who does the ordering or the cancelling around here is me. I'm the owner, operator, baker, and pretty much everything."

The only other person who worked at the bakery was her part-time help, Jamie Thompson. The young girl mostly worked the counter and certainly never handled any type of ordering *or* cancelling.

"You must have made a mistake."

The woman's high-pitched voice dropped an octave, cheeriness replaced with defensive disdain. "There's no mistake, Ms. Evans. Our records indicate a call came in yesterday from your establishment requesting the order be cancelled."

"Did they have my order number?"

"I did not take the call, but they must have if they cancelled the order."

"Well, if you didn't take the call, how can you be sure they had my number?"

The woman blew out a huff of indignation.

Join the club, lady. She was pretty pissed herself.

"We don't cancel orders without processing numbers."

Right, just like they didn't switch a delivery time from five in the morning to five at night. Or mistake an order of flour for an order of cayenne pepper. She ran a cupcake shop. What the hell would she need fifty pounds of cayenne pepper for?

"Look, I need that mascarpone."

"Then I suppose you shouldn't have cancelled the order."

Evidently, the woman wasn't gunning for customer service agent of the year.

"I told you, I didn't cancel it!" Maggie gripped the phone harder, wishing it was possible to reach through the lines and strangle someone.

"Well, someone from your establishment did, that's all I can tell you. Is there anything else I can help you with today?" the agent asked politely, but it sounded like she shared her strangle-through-the-phone-line sentiment.

Letting out a sigh of resignation, Maggie glanced at the calendar on her office desk. "How soon can I get a new delivery of mascarpone?"

"One moment please."

If the lady put her on hold again, she was going to go *Sweeney Todd* on her ass and start making cupcakes with a secret ingredient: customer service representatives.

"June twentieth is the next delivery date available."

"But that's over four weeks away!"

And the blogger would be at her shop in just two.

"Well, ma'am, the brand you ordered comes from Italy, and the company only produces a finite amount of specialty cheeses."

She knew that. It was why she had specifically ordered the mascarpone from that company. They produced the best mascarpone in all of Italy, probably the world. She needed the best so her cupcakes would be the best. A chef was only as good as his or her ingredients. How many times had that been drilled into her at culinary school?

"Your order has already been shipped back to Italy, and their next batch does not arrive in the states for another month."

Yup, someone's going to die. Unfortunately, it looked like it was going to be her dreams of the perfect tiramisu cupcake.

"Would you like me to place the order?"

"No." What she'd like was for something to go right for a change. "I'll just have to prepare something else."

"Thank you for choosing Pansy's Wholesalers for all your wholesale needs. Have a great day."

The customer service agent ended the call with what, Maggie assumed, was the company sign-off. *"Have a great day?" Not likely after that conversation.*

Four screw-ups in six months, that was just too

much. She needed to find a new distributor for her ingredients. After this recent brush with the company, she'd had enough. Customer service was something she prided herself on, and she expected it from other businesses, as well. Pansy's left a lot to be desired in that department. She had filed a complaint after the last two mishaps, and she would file another one after this. What was the saying—three strikes and you're out? Well, four balls and she walked.

Right to another distributor.

Now, she just had to figure out what to make for the blogger. She had been banking on her tiramisu cupcakes. They were divine and decadent. At least that's what the reviewer from the *LA Times* had said when he visited the restaurant she'd worked at in Los Angeles.

But she wasn't in LA anymore. She was in Peak Town, Colorado. About as far from the glitz and glamour of LA as one could get. A place where people didn't lock their doors. Where the sidewalks rolled up after ten p.m. A town where no one had even heard of mascarpone, let alone carried it at the grocery store.

Things were what they were, and she couldn't change them. She just had to pull it together and come up with another recipe to knock the blogger's socks off.

In two weeks.

Maybe her grandmother had a fantastic recipe. Gran had started the cupcake shop after all.

The bell above the front door chimed as someone entered.

"Hey, boss. Where are ya?"

Maggie smiled at the informal call of her eighteen-year-old part-time worker.

"In my office."

Her office was really just the back corner of the shop, separated from the kitchen and front area by a thin piece of plywood to afford some semblance of privacy. A small desk was pushed against the wall and a large filing cabinet filled with paperwork and recipes was wedged into the corner. Not much, but it was all hers.

"I've got news." Jamie's voice bubbled with excitement.

The young girl rounded the corner, ponytail bouncing and brown eyes filled with glee. Her exuberance could only mean one thing.

"I got in!" She held up a large, white envelope with the Harvard seal stamped in the top left corner.

Springing up from her small office chair, Maggie grabbed Jamie's arms, jumping up and down in excitement with her young employee who had worked so hard to get into her dream college. "That's amazing." She gripped the girl in a tight embrace. Pulling back, she gave her arms another squeeze. "Do your folks know?"

Jamie rolled her eyes. "Dad's down at the bar buying everyone drinks, and Mom's calling everyone she's ever met to tell them."

"They're proud of you. It's quite an accomplishment to get into an Ivy League school. I'm proud of you, too."

Youthful cheeks blushed. "Thanks. It's not really that big a deal."

"Oh yes it is. In fact, I'm giving you the afternoon off. Go celebrate."

"Are you sure? I thought you had an order coming

in today."

A groaned escaped. "Ugh, I will not damper your delightful news with tales of the dumb ass distributor."

"Oh no, did they screw up another order?"

Jamie had started working for her two weeks after she took over the shop and knew all about the problems with orders over the past few months. Now, she was headed to Harvard. Well, technically not until the fall. Maggie was so proud and happy for her, but it meant losing her only employee in a few months.

Cancelled orders, her only employee leaving, and absolutely no idea what to make for the blogger, she was beginning to think this day couldn't get any worse.

The bell over the door chimed again.

"Hello? Magpie, you in?" a deep, sexy, familiar voice called from the front of the shop.

Oh crap. She'd spoke too soon.

Colton Denning stepped into Cupcakes Above the Clouds and inhaled the sugary sweet smell wafting from the rows and rows of cupcakes displayed behind the glass counter. The shop had been a Peak Town cornerstone for over thirty years. He remembered coming here after school with his brother, Dade. The owner, Mrs. Browning, would always give him and his brother a Devil Chocolate cupcake with rainbow sprinkles for helping her take out the garbage. Nothing was sweeter than Mrs. B's cupcakes.

"Be right there, Colt."

Except for the new owner, Mrs. B's granddaughter, Maggie Evans.

He leaned against the counter, waiting for her to come up front. The shop wasn't all that big, so it only took a moment.

Long, dark brown hair held back in a tight French braid, mossy green eyes, and a bright smile on her beautiful face, Maggie Evans stepped out from the back and headed toward him. He watched the slight sway of her hips, remembering a time, years ago, when she had been all skin and bones. The years had certainly been kind to her. And though they were friends—best of at one time—he wasn't above noticing what a sexy woman she had become. What man with a pulse wouldn't notice?

Her worker followed close behind, a bounce in her step and wide grin on her young face.

"Hey, Jamie. You working today?"

"Nope." The teenager smiled. "Maggie gave me the afternoon off because I got some great news."

He had a suspicion of what it could be, but she was so excited he wanted to let her share. "Well, don't keep me in suspense, sugar."

"I got in!" Joyful glee radiated off her youthful face as she waved a white envelope in the air.

He whooped out a yell, jumped over the counter, and grabbed her up in a bear hug. Everyone in town knew the ambitious girl had been hoping to get into Harvard. She was smart as a whip, so he wasn't surprised she'd made it. Still, it was a great accomplishment—the first person from Peak Town to go to an Ivy League school.

"Congratulations, sweetheart!"

"Colton Denning, get out from behind my counter this minute," Maggie admonished and smacked him on the shoulder.

Ouch. The tiny woman packed quite a wallop.

He put Jamie down and turned. "Oh come on now,

Magpie. I was just caught up in the excitement of the news."

"Yeah well, catch up on *that* side of the counter. You're going to violate my health codes."

He looked down at himself—dusty, faded jeans that may have been worn one season too long, a relatively clean, long sleeve flannel over a black T-shirt, and cowboy boots caked in dried mud. Okay, she might have a point. Not that he would ever tell her that. One thing Maggie did not need to hear was that she was right, again.

Besides, it was much more fun to tease her.

"I'm not that dirty."

She rolled those pretty green eyes of hers. "You've got hay stuck in your jeans."

A quick glance revealed a short stalk stuck in the waistband of his wranglers. Not surprising. Working on a horse ranch, you were bound to get a stray piece of hay here and there.

"Why, Magpie, were you eying my unmentionables?"

She snorted, a very unladylike snort, but adorable as hell.

"Oh please. You probably put it there on purpose to draw attention *to* your *unmentionables*. You're a shameless flirt, Colton Denning, and you know it."

No denying the truth.

"What's wrong with a little harmless flirting? Especially when it's with such a pretty lady."

"Go peddle that charm somewhere else, cowboy, and get back on the other side of my counter."

"You are just no fun, Magpie."

He appeased her by hopping back over the counter.

Jamie followed, opting to go around to the small opening separating the kitchen from the dining area rather than jump over the three-foot ledge.

"Thanks for the day off, boss."

Maggie smiled. "You deserve it. And don't go home to study. Go out, have fun, get a little wild."

The young girl rolled her eyes the way teenagers do when adults try to sound cool. He remembered giving his parents a few of those himself back in the day. Some things never changed.

"I promise to be totally reckless tonight."

"Good. Don't do anything I wouldn't do," Maggie called after her as her college bound employee left the shop.

"I thought you wanted her to have fun?"

She glanced at him, her brows pinched together in confusion. Time for his favorite past time: tease the cupcake maker.

"You told her to have fun, but then said not to do anything you wouldn't do."

"Your point?"

He reached out with his finger and tapped the end of her small, button nose. "You don't do anything except work."

She huffed out a breath of annoyance. "That's not true."

"Uh huh."

"I do lots of stuff."

"Oh yeah, like what?"

Her mouth opened, but the sexy baker said nothing. He chuckled, pleased with himself at her exasperated look. He had no idea why it was so fun to get her all riled up, but he thoroughly enjoyed it.

"See, you're no fun."

Maggie's teeth clenched together. Her arms crossed over her chest defensively as she scowled at him. "I am so fun."

He laughed. "And way too easy to tease, Magpie."

She uncrossed her arms then placed her hands on her hips instead. "I'm twenty-eight now, Colton. I think I'm a little too old for nicknames."

Maybe, but he'd given her that nickname years ago when she used to come out for the summers to spend time with her grandmother. She'd been so tiny and skittish. The littlest thing would startle her, like a bird. He started calling her Magpie one summer, and it just kind of stuck. He liked that he had a special name for her. One that no one used, but him.

"Did you come in here for a reason or just to annoy me?"

Deciding not to tempt his fate, he stopped his teasing. He wouldn't put it past her to dump a bowl of cupcake batter on his head.

She'd done it before.

"Dade sent me to pick up his order."

"Oh right. He called it in this morning."

Turning, Maggie walked to the large refrigerated cooler along the sidewall of her shop, opened the door, and reached in to pull out a large cardboard box.

"Two dozen vanilla cupcakes with mint-chocolate frosting. A treat for the hands or do you guys have a group today?"

He and his brother ran the family horse ranch where they boarded horses for several people in town who didn't have enough room on their own property for the animals. They also offered riding lessons and group

11

trail rides. The Denning Ranch had been in the family for three generations. He and Dade had helped their mother and father run it growing up. Since their parents retired to Florida five years ago, the brothers had hired on a few hands to help out. He loved the work. Couldn't imagine doing anything else with his life.

"A small bonus for the guys. It's a little too cold out for people to want to ride yet."

It was mid-May, but springtime in the Rocky Mountains could be in the sixties one day and a snowstorm the next. At the moment, the temperature was holding in the mid-fifties. Warm, but still too cold for most folks to want a long trail ride. They did most of their riding business in the summer. The boarding helped pay the bills the rest of the year.

"I'm sure they'd rather a real bonus than cupcakes."

He gave her his best lady-killer smile. "Ask any man around and they'll tell you they'd rather have one of your delicious cupcakes than anything else."

She blushed, the color rising up her cheeks, making her even more beautiful.

"Flattery will not get you free cupcakes, Colt."

He placed a hand to his chest. "You wound me, Magpie. I was just trying to give you a compliment." But he would never say no to a free cupcake.

"That ego of yours couldn't be wounded with a twenty foot pole. Sixty-three dollars." She rang up the order on the old till.

He pulled out some cash and handed it to her, making sure their fingers brushed during the transfer. She shivered at the contact; it was barely noticeable, but he saw it. He didn't know why, but he liked getting a rise out of Maggie Evans.

She passed him back his change, being very careful not to touch him, he noticed, as she dropped the cash onto his outstretched palm.

"Tell your brother I say hi."

He grabbed the box from the counter, balancing it in one hand. "Will do. You gonna come out and ride Maple anytime soon?"

The beautiful brown Arabian they used for trail riding had been on the ranch for two years and had a sweet disposition. Whenever Maggie came out for a ride, she always chose Maple. Though, she hadn't been to the ranch very much since moving back to town, and that bothered him. They'd once been such good friends.

He missed her friendship. He missed her.

"I don't know." She worried her lower lip with her teeth. "I've kind of got some stuff going on right now."

All the protective instincts rose inside him at her worried tone. He placed the box back on the counter. "Everything okay?"

Maggie waved a hand in the air. "It's fine. Just shop stuff."

"Anything I can do to help?"

"No. I'm fine, Colt. Thanks."

She was always fine. One thing he knew about Maggie Evans was that she liked to take care of everything herself. It was an admirable quality, but sometimes he wished she would let someone else share her burdens. When she took over the cupcake shop, after her grandmother died, she went through a mountain of red tape. He offered to help, but she had refused, opting instead to spend countless days and nights on the phone and taking hours-long trips into the city to get everything straightened out.

The woman was too independent for her own good.

Picking up the box once again, he reached out with his other hand and bopped her on the nose with his finger. She smacked his hand away, but he could see the hint of a smile she was trying to hide. Good; he hated seeing her upset.

"You see? No fun, Magpie."

"Yeah well, you have enough fun for the both of us."

Colton laughed as he left the shop, the chime of the bell ringing in his ear and the sweet smell of cupcakes wafting after him. Yup, teasing the sexy cupcake maker was just about his favorite thing to do.

Chapter Two

Maggie watched Colton amble out of her store. The man actually ambled, not walked, ambled. She took a deep breath to steady her nerves, but all it did was cause her to inhale the smell of sweet, sugary cupcakes and delicious, sexy man. Like hay and horses.

Why the hell did that turn her on?

Oh right, because it was the smell of Colton Denning. The man she'd had a crush on since she first came to Peak Town to visit her grandmother over twenty years ago.

She shook her head. Thinking about the first time she met Colton made her remember why she had fallen for him in the first place. A few of the local kids had teased her when a very large horse scared her. She had never seen a horse outside the movies and didn't realize how big they were. Colton had yelled at the other children, shaming them for picking on her just because she had never seen a horse in real life. He saved her from a lot of teasing. In kid world, that made him her hero. Every summer after that, when she wasn't with her grandmother, she was at the Denning ranch playing, riding, and following Colton and Dade everywhere.

Much to her dismay, Colton had always seen her as more of a kid sister. The summer she turned fourteen, she had come back to find him dating Natalie Brake, a cheerleader at his high school. Her poor teenage heart had broken. That was the last summer she came out to see her grandmother. She'd still called Gran and kept in touch, but she hadn't been able to bear to see Colton and Natalie together.

Gran had come out to see her a few times, too, but Maggie hadn't come back to Peak Town. There'd been school to finish and then she had college, finals, and the hassle of finding a job. It was hard to get a day off as a baker, let alone a week to go out of state. Sadly, she just couldn't find the time until eight months ago. For her grandmother's funeral.

Pushing away regrets and memories, she glanced up at the clock and was surprised to discover she only had a couple hours left until closing. Time to pull it together. She had two problems to deal with in the here and now. She needed a new distributor for the shop and a new recipe for the blogger. It had to be a good one, too. If she was going to keep her grandmother's shop open, she needed more business, and that meant needing great exposure.

No time for trips down memory lane or sexy cowboys who didn't even notice her. Men only brought heartache. Maggie had learned that lesson enough times.

****

"Ow! *Mother Fletcher*," Maggie exclaimed as her head connected with the shelf.

The musical tones of her cell phone blaring out Sister Sledge's "We are Family" had startled her from her crouched position on the closet floor. She would have ignored the call, but that ring tone was attached to only one person.

She crawled out of the closet, rubbing a hand over

her throbbing head as she grabbed her cell off the bedside table. "Hey, Lizzy."

"The new pastry chef is a nightmare!"

The overdramatic tone in her best friend's voice made her laugh.

"I'm serious, Maggie. The guy managed to mess up chocolate cake the other day. How the hell do you mess up chocolate cake?"

"I'm sure it wasn't that bad."

Lizzy's snort sounded loudly through the phone. "Oh it was, believe me. It was hard as a rock when it came out of the oven, and I think he mixed up the salt and sugar quantities, because it tasted like a salt lick. I am so getting fired."

She smiled; exaggeration was her best friend's middle name. Her parents were both involved in "The Biz" as they called it in Hollywood. Her father was a producer and her mother was a B list actress. Both had been disappointed when Lizzy decided not to follow the family tradition of the Hollywood life and instead pursued a career in business management. Still, blood was thicker than water, and the dramatic woman had a tendency to be a bit sensational, but in a fun way.

"I never should have hired him for the restaurant. Of course, if *someone* hadn't abandoned me, I wouldn't have needed to hire a new pastry chef."

"I didn't abandon you. I started a new chapter in my life."

Her friend sighed heavily over the phone. "I know, and I'm happy for you. I just miss you."

"I miss you, too."

"So, how's the land of cows? Meet any cute cowboys yet?"

Her mind wandered back to Colton and how he had looked in those tight, ass-hugging jeans today. She would never understand why the youth of today wore jeans so baggy they fell to their knees. A man's butt displayed in a tight pair of pants just made you want to grab and smack it.

"You hesitated. You *did* meet a cowboy! Tell me all about him."

Laughing at her friend's exuberance, Maggie shook her head. "I didn't hesitate. I'm just distracted."

"By cute cowboy butt?"

Her nosy friend knew her weakness.

"No. I'm looking for my grandmother's special recipe box. I've searched the entire apartment, but I can't find it anywhere."

"Why do you need her recipe box?"

Lifting the bed skirt, she glanced underneath. Aside from some dust bunnies and a sock that was in serious need of washing, it was empty. No recipe box. Where the heck had Gran put that thing?

"I need something for the blogger. Something special to really knock her socks off," she replied.

"I thought you were making your tiramisu cupcakes?"

Maggie stood with a grunt. "I was, until my distributor decided to be an incompetent jerk."

Perhaps the recipe box was in the bathroom. It was a long shot, but the only room she hadn't checked so far. Going down the hall, she explained her situation to her best friend. It felt good to vent her frustrations to someone, and being the manager of one of LA's most prestigious four-star restaurants, Lizzy knew all about dealing with incompetent people.

"Isn't this like the third screw up they've made?"

"Fourth," she said, entering the bathroom and scanning the medicine cabinet. Aspirin, bandages, tampons, makeup, but no recipe box.

"You need a new distributor."

"I know."

Crouching down, she opened the sink cabinets. Nothing except her cleaning supplies. No recipe box. "Dammit! I can't find this thing anywhere!" She hadn't really expected to find it in the bathroom, but she'd hoped.

"Want help?"

"Sure," she said dryly. "Hop on a plane and travel over a thousand miles to help me find a box."

"Very funny," Lizzy said. "Where was the last place you saw it?"

Maggie closed her eyes. She pictured her grandmother opening the box and showing her the dozens of colorful three by five cards, all handwritten with various colored ink. A lump caught in her throat as she imagined her grandmother's face. She hadn't seen much of Gran in the past few years before her death. Guilt churned in the pit of her stomach. She had been a terrible granddaughter.

"Maggie?"

Opening her eyes, she tried to snap out of her self-wallowing. "Sorry. I was just thinking about Gran. I should have spent more time with her."

"Oh, sweetie. She loved you. You brought her out here as often as you could."

"I should have come back here to see her."

"It was hard for you to leave the restaurant. She understood that. Plus, she always enjoyed the trips to the beach."

She smiled as she remembered her grandmother lying on a lounge chair during one of her trips. Basking in the Malibu sun, Gran had declared it to be a little slice of heaven.

"She always did say the coast was the next best thing to her cabin." A light bulb went off in her head. "Her cabin!"

"What about her cabin?"

"That's the last place I remember seeing her recipe box. She was teaching me how to make lemon bars when we went out there for the weekend the last summer I was here."

It had been years ago, but since the box wasn't in the shop or Gran's upstairs apartment—where Maggie currently lived—it had to be in the cabin.

"Do you think it's still there?"

"It has to be." It only stood to reason. "I'll head up there tomorrow after I close the shop."

It was only about an hour up the mountain. She could drive there, get the box, and be home in time for a late dinner.

"Well, I'm glad your problem is solved. Meanwhile, my pastry chef is poisoning half of Hollywood. Happen to have any four star restaurants looking for a new manager out in Podunk Town?"

"It's *Peak* Town." She chuckled at her best friend's dramatics. "And no, the closest thing to a nice restaurant we have here is Merle's Diner."

"Sounds shmancy."

"That's not a word."

"It should be. It means super fancy. Much better than regular fancy." Much like her life, Lizzy liked to infuse pizzazz into her words. It was just another thing that made the woman so loveable.

They chatted for a few more minutes before hanging up, Lizzy promising to take some time off soon to visit her. Maggie got ready for bed, brushing her teeth and hair before putting on a large nightshirt and slipping into bed.

After she closed the shop tomorrow, she would head up the mountain to her grandmother's cabin, find the recipe box, pick out the perfect cupcake to knock the socks off the blogger, and everything would work out perfectly.

Right, because her life had been perfect so far.

Slipping a hand out from beneath the covers, she reached over to the bedside table and knocked on the solid oak nightstand.

A little superstition never hurt anybody.

Chapter Three

The cold, May morning air burned Maggie's lungs as she ran, her sneakers crunching as they hit the dirt path. The sun was just starting to peek out over the eastern horizon. She quickened her pace, knowing she was only minutes away from Merle's Diner and a hot cup of coffee.

Mornings were not her friend. At the restaurant in LA, they only provided dinner, so she didn't need to be at work until noon in order to prep the desserts and breads. Gran's shop had always been open from nine in the morning to five in the evening. She wanted to keep that consistency for the loyal customers. It was just good business sense, or so Lizzy had told her.

When Gran died and left her the shop, she had considered just selling it. Even had an offer from an anonymous buyer. But her life in LA had been falling apart. She'd lost her mother to cancer three years ago, her job at the restaurant was good, but stagnant, and her love life…no, she wasn't going to think about that again. Miles had turned out to be a bastard of the highest degree. Uprooting everything and moving to Peak Town to take over Cupcakes Above the Clouds had seemed like the perfect opportunity for a fresh start.

So far, her bad luck seemed to have followed her across the country. The problems with her distributor and the decrease in business were starting to show in her accounting books. The economy was on the rise, but people were still counting their pennies. And people counting pennies did not spend them on luxuries like cupcakes.

That was why she needed this review with the blogger to go so well. Peak Town was only an hour away from some very popular ski resorts. A good review on the top viewed blog, Guilty Pleasures: A Cross Country Food Journey, would bring in the tourists. Tourists spent money, and money was necessary to stay in business, or so Lizzy kept telling her.

Coming to the end of the dirt path, Maggie slowed to a walk. Stepping from the trail to the concrete sidewalk, she headed for Merle's and a hot cup of coffee.

It might be spring, but springtime in the Rockies could mean sweaters or tank tops. This morning was the former. Her blood still pumped from her run, but the sweat on her body began to cool in the cold morning air. By the time she entered the small, cozy diner, her body temperature had gone from warm to freezing.

"Morning, Maggie. Cup of joe?" asked Ellen, Merle's wife of thirty years.

She smiled and nodded at the cheerful older woman. "You know it."

Ellen turned to the freshly brewed coffee pot and filled a cup with the black, steaming liquid as Maggie sat on a barstool at the front counter. The early morning crowd at Merle's usually consisted of a few old-timers sitting at a back table, enjoying coffee, eggs, bacon, and flapjacks, and one or two shop proprietors grabbing a morning coffee. As she looked around, she saw today was no different. Unfortunately, one of those shop proprietors happened to be Natalie Brake.

Ellen set the cup of coffee, along with a small bowl of creamers, in front of her. Reaching for the bin of sugars on the counter, Maggie doctored her coffee to her liking and tried to ignore Natalie standing at the other end of the counter. Maybe she would get lucky and the other woman wouldn't notice her.

"Maggie Evans, you look positively dreadful. Are you all right?"

Damn my luck! She gripped her cup tightly, reining in her temper. "I just came in from a run, Natalie. Just stopped in for a cup of coffee before I open the shop."

"Oh yes, your shop. I've been meaning to talk to you about that."

She sighed, preparing herself for another tirade. Natalie owned Rejuvenations Beauty Supply, the store next door to the cupcake shop. She sold makeup and anti-wrinkle creams along with fancy smelling lotions and bath products. Maggie had never set foot in the store. She hadn't needed to; she could smell all the pungent products from half a mile away.

The woman had never liked her. The summer Natalie and Colton started dating, the cheerleader had told her, in no uncertain terms, that Colton was hers and Maggie had better back off if she wanted to keep all her teeth. The cheerleader had never liked the fact her boyfriend was friends with a teenage girl, even though Maggie was four years his junior.

Ever since she'd come back to town, and took over Gran's shop, nothing had changed; it had been one complaint after another. And she had no idea why. Apparently, Natalie and Colton had broken up after only a year and a half.

Small towns were notorious for gossip. When she came back into town, Ellen had filled her in on all the juicy details she'd missed over the years. According to Merle's wife, Natalie had gone off to college at CSU. Colton decided to stay and work the family ranch. They tried the long distance thing, but after a semester they broke up. Some people suspected Natalie had been fooling around with other guys and Colton found out. If she had been cheating on him, she had to be the stupidest woman alive, in Maggie's opinion.

"What is it now, Natalie?" she finally asked.

"You see, the smell from your shop seems to be seeping through the wall and coming into mine."

"The smell from *my* shop?" Seriously?

"Yes, and it's terribly upsetting for my customers. They are trying to improve their body image, relax, and enhance their beauty. How can they do that when the smell of sickening, sugary, fatty cupcakes invade their nostrils?"

Wow, she had never heard her delicious desserts described with such disdain before. "Well, what do you suggest I do about it?"

Natalie laughed, the sound grating, like nails on a chalkboard. "I have no idea, hun. I'm just informing you of the issue. What you do to resolve it is your problem."

Yes, it was her problem. Just like the sign she had out front taking up too much of the sidewalk was her problem. And the music she played in the shop being too loud was her problem. It seemed every time Natalie saw her the woman had another one of "Maggie's problems" to discuss.

"I'll look into it." *Next millennium maybe.*

"You do that."

"Order's up, Natalie," Ellen said, handing over a brown paper sack.

She breathed out a sigh of relief. A to-go order meant the obnoxious woman was leaving. Maybe now she could enjoy her coffee in peace.

Then the diner door opened, and a cold wind blew in, bringing with it a sexy, smiling Colton Denning.

Hadn't she knocked on wood last night? What was with all this bad luck coming her way? She was sorely tempted to grab the saltshaker off the counter and throw the whole damn thing over her left shoulder.

"Colton!" Natalie's voice went sickly sweet.

The cowboy's smile faltered. "Natalie." He turned and his face brightened. "Hey, Magpie, get in a run this morning?" He tugged at her ponytail, disheveled by the exercise.

"I know! Doesn't she look a mess?" Natalie interjected. "You know, Maggie, I have some body spray at my shop that does absolute wonders for running. It keeps you from sweating like a…well, a pig. No offense, dear."

Her teeth clenched together as she bit back a rude remark. She gripped her coffee mug to keep from smacking the woman upside her Botox-enhanced face.

"I think you look great, Magpie, and runners are supposed to sweat. It's called exercise, Natalie. Not everyone goes to Dr. Lipo to get their figure."

Beneath salon bleached blonde hair, the surgically enhanced cheeks turned a brilliant shade of red and her mouth opened, but no words came out. Maggie pretended to take a sip of her coffee to hide her grin.

"Well, I was only offering to help, Maggie," the flustered woman said with a huff.

Yeah, help me off a cliff maybe.

Gripping her to-go bag tightly in her hand, Natalie muttered a goodbye to them both and headed out the diner door.

"Dr. *Lipo*? Really Colt, that was a low blow. Even for you."

"Hey, I was defending your honor. Give me some points here."

She shook her head, chuckling at the image of Natalie's red face.

"Hey, Colton. Whatcha need?" Ellen asked, her eyes full of laughter as well.

"Well, I'd ask for a date, but Merle would skin me alive," Colton joked with a wink. "The coffee pot broke down this morning. I need four to-go cups of your delicious black brew."

Ellen blushed, swatting him with a friendly hand then turning to get his order. Everyone was used to his antics. Stupid, sexy, cowboy flirted with every woman he saw, well, except maybe Natalie. It wasn't really a problem, it was just who he was. Didn't mean Maggie had to like it. She scowled.

"What?"

"Do you have some medical condition where you die if you don't flirt with every woman you see?"

He tapped the end of her nose with his finger. "Awe, come on, Magpie, don't be jealous. You know you're my favorite girl."

But that was the problem. She *was* jealous, because he did flirt with everyone, including her, making her no one special. She also was not a girl anymore. Not that

Colton ever seemed to notice.

Finishing the last sip of her coffee, Maggie rose from her stool, dropping a few bills on the counter for Ellen. "Whatever. I've got to go."

"Hold on. I'll walk you."

Great, just what her hormones didn't need, more time in close contact with Colton Denning.

She waited until Ellen had finished his order and he paid. They left the warm diner, a smack of cold, May morning air hitting her in the face as she exited.

"Brrrrr. When does it warm up around here?"

He laughed, the sound sending butterflies through her stomach. *Stupid stomach.*

"I forgot, you never spent any winters here before."

"If I ever had, I don't think I would have come back. It's freezing here! Isn't it supposed to be spring?"

"It's forty-five degrees out, Magpie."

She shrugged her shoulders. "Yeah, freezing."

Colton chuckled again, then wrapped a big, strong arm around her as they walked.

"There, is that better?"

She turned her face in slightly and inhaled the delicious scent of him. "You're a regular electric blanket, Colt," she said with a shiver that had nothing to do with the cold.

"Har, har. Okay, Miss Funny Pants, here we are."

He stopped them in front of her shop. She had just enough time to head up to her apartment above for a shower before icing the cooled cupcakes she'd baked before her run.

Colton removed his arm from her shoulder, and she immediately missed the contact. *Ugh.* She had to get ahold of herself. She had no time for men. Men just brought lies and trouble. Hadn't she just learned that lesson not too long ago?

"See ya 'round, Magpie."

"I told you, I'm too old for nicknames."

He chucked her chin before turning and heading down the sidewalk, calling over his shoulder, "Whatever you say, Grandma!"

"You are not funny, Colton Denning!" she shouted after him. But he just lifted a hand and waved.

Maggie watched his retreating form. And boy, what a great form it was.

A cold gust of wind shocked her, bringing her back to her senses. Shaking her head, she started up the outside stairs to her apartment and a nice hot shower. Remembering the feel of Colton's strong arm around her, the intoxicating smell of him, she began to sweat again.

Maybe she'd take a cold shower instead.

Chapter Four

"Are you sure you can handle closing by yourself?" Maggie asked Jamie, for the third time.

"Yes, I'm sure." A slim, youthful hand gave an exasperated wave. "Go. You don't want to drive that mountain road in the dark."

She had filled her employee in on her plans to drive out to her grandmother's cabin and search for the missing recipe box. As her only worker, Jamie knew all about the blogger, and how important it was to get a good review.

"I've got this, Maggie. You better hurry up. I heard there's going to be a big storm headed our way tonight," the teenager said, as she printed out the nightly report from the register. "Could drop about three to six inches on us."

"It's springtime!" she exclaimed in horror.

Her young employee chuckled. "Welcome to Colorado, boss."

Groaning, Maggie grabbed her purse and coat. She really needed that recipe box, and she preferred to get it before another snowstorm hit. Living her whole life, up until eight months ago, in Southern California, she never had to drive in anything worse than a light rain. The winter here had been brutal, and she opted for staying indoors during most of the snowfalls. She hated driving in snow.

For Pete's sake, there were leaves budding on the trees. It was not supposed to snow in May!

"Fine. I'm going. You have your key?"

"It's on my key ring. Now go. And watch out for wild animals. They're starting to wake up and wander about again."

Great. One more thing to add to the wonderful world of driving in the mountains. *Mountain lions, deer, and bears, oh my!*

"See you in the morning." She waved as she left the store.

It was a fairly warm afternoon, by Rocky Mountain standards. She headed around back to where her used, blue Subaru Forester was parked. After driving around Peak Town for a month, she had realized her cute, little, red Mini Coupe just wouldn't cut it on the mountain roads. Reluctantly, she'd gone to a dealership in Denver and traded it in for the car of Colorado. Everyone had a Subaru out here.

The drive up the mountainside to her grandmother's cabin—now hers, she guessed—took longer than she anticipated. There were still patches of snow and ice on the road from the previous winter storm. Or maybe it had always been there.

Snow probably doesn't even melt up here, she thought irritably.

The twists and turns eventually evened out to the straight road that led to the cabin. There were a number of them scattered about up on the mountain. Some were vacation rentals, others owned by Peak Town residents. Not many people came up here this time of year, but the cabin just down the road from Gran's had smoke coming out of its chimney, so she guessed someone else had braved these roads, too.

She pulled up onto the dirt driveway in front of the small, one bedroom vacation home. Turning off her car, she stepped out and inhaled the fresh mountain air. Crappy weather or not, there was something about the air up in the mountains that cleansed the soul. In LA, the only air one could get not choked with smog was from a trendy oxygen bar.

Shutting the car door, Maggie made her way up the front steps. There was no lock on the door. Gran's father had built this place back at the previous turn of the century. No one had locks out here back then. No one had them now either. The closest neighbor was about two miles away; close enough to get help if you needed, but far enough away for privacy. Bears were more of a worry than burglars, and bears didn't bother with locks.

The door squeaked open. She would have to put some oil on that rusty hinge. A musty smell hit her in the face as she stepped into the cabin. And air out the place as well. There was no telling how long it had been since someone had been here. She'd not visited up here since she came back to Peak Town, and who knew when Gran had last come up before her death. An eighty-nine year old woman did not make mountain getaways a top priority.

"Okay, down to business," she said aloud.

The place needed a thorough going over, but that would have to wait. Right now, she had to focus on her mission: Find the recipe box.

Best to start in the kitchen, the most logical place.

An hour later, she had searched the entire cabin top to bottom. It was small, so she figured there wouldn't be many places to hide a box. Once again, her luck sucked. No recipe box. Not in the kitchen, living room, bedroom…heck, it wasn't even in the bathroom.

Defeat hit her like a sucker punch to the gut and she flopped onto the old couch. She had been so sure the box had to be here. *Where the hell else could it be?*

Maybe she should just pack it in now, sell the shop, and go back to LA. Lizzy would give her job back in a heartbeat.

But Maggie didn't want to go back to LA. There was nothing there for her anymore.

No. I came out here to start over, and that's what I'm going to do!

Pumped up by her little pep talk, she rose from the couch and prepared to leave. That's when she noticed one of the stones in the fireplace mantel looked slightly off color to the rest. Curious, she walked to the fireplace and tapped. The stone shifted slightly under her fingers. Heartbeat racing, she grasped the large rock, and pulled.

It popped out with ease.

Maggie looked into the small, empty hole. Only it *wasn't* empty.

"Gran, you sneaky old genius."

Reaching in, she grabbed the object and pulled it out. A small, scratched, but well loved, wooden box. Her body lit with excitement as she opened the lid and peered inside. Multi-colored cards with familiar handwriting. Gran's recipe box.

"Hallelujah!"

Clutching the very thing she had been searching for tight to her chest like the Holy Grail, she jumped up and down in celebration. Now, all she had to do was get back home, pick a recipe, and everything would be golden.

Leaving the cabin, she headed to her car, noticing only now the sky had darkened during her search. The temperature had dropped as well, but Maggie was too happy she found her prize to care. She was on cloud nine. Her luck was finally turning around!

Her excitement was so great, she barely noticed the small flurries of snow beginning to fall.

****

Colton cursed, kicking his backup generator. It was just his luck to have the thing break during a storm. Dade had told him to buy a new one, noting the fact this generator was older than Colton. He should have listened. Then again, when did he ever listen to his big brother? He was wishing he had now. Not that he would ever tell Dade that.

This trip to his cabin out in the woods was for some much needed R and R. He had listened to the forecast and knew there was a storm coming. However, he wasn't prepared for how big the storm had gotten. Two hours ago there were just a few light flurries. An hour into those flurries, the main power in his cabin went out. Half an hour after that the backup generator had gone and those small flurries had turned into a white out.

Some R and R this turned out to be.

Wind howled in the dark night sky, kicking up snow, making visibility next to impossible. The snow was as deep as three feet in some places, more in the drifts. The temperature had dropped from thirty to three degrees below zero. He felt like an icicle, but he needed to get the generator up and working if he wanted to thaw out. Why the hell hadn't he listened to his brother?

Spewing out a list of nasty four letter words that would have his mother smacking him upside the head if she heard, he kicked the uncooperative generator once more. It did nothing. Relegating himself to the fact he would have to camp out in front of the fire tonight with a ton of blankets, he turned to go back inside. At least he had plenty of firewood.

As he trudged through the deep, cold snow something caught his eye. He was surprised he could see anything in all the swirling white flakes, but this was something red and stood out. He took a few more steps to get a better look. A coat. Did a hiker lose his jacket? It was possible. There were trails all over these mountains and things tended to get lost no matter how careful people were.

He took a few more steps toward the discarded clothing, intending to grab it and bring it back into town in case anyone was looking for it. Then he noticed the coat had a pair of blue jeans attached to it, a pair of jeans, shoes, and a yellow hat.

Shit!

That wasn't a lost jacket. That was a lost person.

Running as fast as he could in two-foot deep snow, he made it over to the mound and dropped to his knees beside the body face down in the snow. No sign of movement.

Please don't be dead, please don't be dead, he repeated to himself.

"Hey. Hey, buddy? Can you hear me?" No response.

Working on a horse ranch his entire life, he'd seen

a few people get thrown from a mount. He knew you weren't supposed to move an injured person, but there was no way an ambulance could make it up the mountain in this storm. Left outside, the guy would freeze to death in a matter of hours. Hoping that the man had just passed out and didn't have a neck injury, Colton gently put his gloved hands through the snow and under the body to roll it over.

"Don't be dead, don't be dead," he said, out loud this time.

"Holy shit!"

He wasn't dead. He wasn't even a *he*.

She wasn't a lost hiker either.

"Oh God, Maggie!"

What the hell was Maggie Evans doing up here? What reason did she have to come up the mountain? And in a snow storm!

Tapping her gently on the cheek, he tried to wake her. "Maggie, honey. Can you hear me?"

She didn't say a word, didn't move. *Shit*. He had to get her inside. Now.

Placing his arms under her legs and shoulders, he lifted her gently and started walking back toward his cabin. Her red coat was huge, but it didn't add much weight. She was a tiny thing, five foot three tops and couldn't weigh more than one fifteen.

The wind made the short trek back to the cabin difficult, but they made it. Once inside, he rushed her over to the couch directly in front of the fire. It was dying down, so he quickly added two more logs, very grateful he had restocked his woodpile before the storm hit.

Removing his jacket and gloves, he turned back.

Her dark hair looked like it had been braided, but the wind had pulled it out and whipped it every which way around her head. She was pale, though her pert little nose was red, as were her cheeks. The full lips, that always called him out on his bullshit, were a disturbingly pale blue.

"Maggie, wake up." He patted her cheek. Ice cold. "Open those pretty green eyes for me."

She had to be okay. She had to.

A soft moan escaped her lips, and he breathed a sigh of relief. She was alive. Now, he just needed to get her warm before hypothermia set in. He needed to wake her up, so he tapped her cheek again.

"Magpie, come on."

"C-c-c-cold," she managed between chattering teeth.

Her jeans were soaking wet. The coat seemed dry, but he bet some snow got inside as she was lying on the ground. Why had she been face down in the snow? Why was she up here at all?

She moaned again. Her body started to shiver.

"I know, I know. I'm going to get you warm, but I have to get these wet clothes off you, okay?"

She simply moaned again. He took that as an okay. Not that he was waiting for her permission. He had to get these wet clothes off to warm her up. With the power out and the only heat source coming from the fire, it was going to be a lot harder to get her body temperature up.

Carefully, he lifted her to a sitting position so he could unzip her jacket and remove it. As he took it off, he noticed a large bulge in the inner pocket. Glancing inside he saw a small wooden box. Ignoring it for now, he tossed the jacket aside. He was right. The snow had gotten under the material. The bottom half of her dark blue sweater was soaked. It came off as well, along with her wet, long john undershirt. Next came the boots and the soaking wet thermal socks. Then the jeans, which were tricky, wet denim was tough to get off, but he managed.

Now, she was left in nothing but a simple black bra and panty set. Colton tried to be a gentleman. He tried not to look, but he was only human, and he did have to see if she had any wounds.

Damn, Maggie was beautiful. He felt like an ass for noticing, but this was the girl he had played with as a child. Though, she definitely wasn't a child anymore. Not with that smoking hot body.

"Maggie, I'm going to check you for injuries. Did you fall? Does anything hurt?"

She was leaning against the back of the couch, a frown marring her face, but she still hadn't opened her eyes.

"Cold…hurts." She sounded like a pouting five year old. It was so cute it made him smile.

"I know, and I'll get you warm as soon as I make sure everything is okay."

Running his hands gently up and down her torso, legs, and arms, he tried to detach himself from the smooth feel of her skin. Cursing himself for being a bastard, he gently ran his hands through her hair, feeling her head for lumps. She didn't appear to have any injuries. That was good. He grabbed the heavy quilt off the back of the couch and wrapped it around her, rubbing her arms to get the circulation flowing.

"Cold," Maggie cried, eyes still shut.

The blanket was cold, but it would warm up soon through her body heat.

Except that she had no body heat.

Damn. He needed another strategy. If the power was working, he would cook her some hot soup or tea. But it wasn't, so that idea was out. Damn electric appliances. The fire would warm her eventually, but he needed to get her body temp up now, fast.

A grin spread across his face. There *was* another way. A way she would hate, and he would love.

"Maggie honey, open your eyes." He needed her to be fully aware for this.

She shook her head, so he repeated himself. Slowly, her eyes opened. Soft green moss. That was what he had always compared them to in his mind.

"There you are."

"Colton?" She sounded a little confused, her eyes still hazy.

"Yeah, it's me, Magpie."

"St-t-top with the ni-ni-nickname," she stuttered through her shivers.

He chuckled. There was his Maggie. "You have the beginning signs of hypothermia, and we need to get your body temperature up."

"Warm p-p-please."

"The thing is, the power is out in the cabin, so the only heat I have is the fire, and that's not enough to get you warm."

"Back up?" Her eyes closed again.

"On the fritz."

"Didn't D-D-Dade tell you to re-e-eplace that?"

She had to bring that up. "Sure, but I didn't listen."

Opening her eyes, she speared him with a glare.

"Never d-d-do."

He laughed. She had her feisty spirit back. That was a good sign. Mossy hues disappeared as her lids drooped once more, as if it took too much effort to keep them open. He had to get her warm.

"I know, and you can yell all you want later, but right now, I have to get you warm and there is only one way to do that."

"What?"

He bit back a grin at what he was about to suggest. "Shared body heat."

Her eyes flew open and narrowed on him. Another shiver racked her body. That did it. He wasn't waiting any longer. She was cold, and she needed to get warm. It didn't take long for hypothermia to set in, and if it did, it could kill her.

Standing, he pulled his sweater and T-shirt over his head. Those beautiful green eyes went from narrow to wide. He smiled as he noticed the way she stared at his chest. Running a horse ranch was laborious work. Mucking the stalls, moving hay bales, heck, even riding was an activity that used a lot of muscle. He was an active man, and it led to a strong physique.

He kept watching her as he flicked open the button on his jeans. Toeing off his boots, he dropped his pants and kicked them away, too. The shivering Maggie watched him the whole time. Her gaze moving down his chest to his stomach and his...whoa! If she stared there any harder, he was going to tent the boxer shorts. Then she'd never let him warm her up, die of hypothermia, and ruin his perfectly good R and R time.

Swinging her into his arms, blanket and all, he moved to the rug in front of the fire, set her down on the soft, thickly woven material, and gently tugged the blanket from under her so he could place it atop them. He laid down next to her and pulled her into his arms.

Jesus, she's freezing! Pressing her close to his chest, he rubbed her back, trying to transfer his heat to her.

"Mmmmmm, warm," she mumbled into his chest.

"Take all the warmth you need, sweetheart."

"Not your sweetheart," she murmured.

No, but damned if he wasn't feeling something, something strange that he had never felt around Maggie before. She'd been one of his best friends growing up. Every summer when she had visited her grandmother, she followed him and Dade around. They treated her like a kid sister mostly. Letting her tag along, protecting her from anyone who tried to give her a hard time. As the years went on, they became closer. Until that one summer she started pulling away from him. Then she had just stopped coming. He never knew why. Her grandmother kept him up to date on her life out in LA. Little tidbits Ms. B would share with him whenever he came into her shop to get cupcakes.

When Maggie had come back to town eight months ago, after her grandmother died, he'd been excited to see his old friend. But things were different between them. He wasn't an idiot. Over a decade had passed since they had seen each other, but he thought they could pick up where they left and continue the friendship. They were friendly, but it wasn't the same. The beautiful, grown woman who replaced his gangly childhood friend seemed closed off from him. She didn't open up and share like when they were kids. Something changed, and it wasn't just her body, but, damn, had that changed, too.

He may be her friend, but Colton was also a man. She'd been a cute kid, but Maggie had really grown into a stunning woman. On the small side, but with just enough curves to make a man's mind wander to places. Hot, sexy, places, where clothes were missing and bodies entwined.

Thoughts like that had been rattling around in his head for months, and he wasn't quite sure what to do with them. So, he teased her every chance he got. He may have grown into a man, but that didn't mean he was mature.

The two visions he had of Maggie Evans battled in his mind. The cute kid who'd followed him all around town to become one of his best friends, and closest confidants. And the smoking hot, sexy woman who had just moved into town, taken over her grandmother's business, and made it her own.

Having her in his arms, now mostly naked, the woman was winning. And it was killing him. He should get a freaking medal for the restraint he was pulling.

She moaned again and snuggled in closer, rubbing her body against his.

He needed a distraction, quick, or he was going to embarrass himself and freak her out. No matter how out of it the lady was, if she felt "little Colton" getting excited, she would knee him in the balls for sure. Particularly fond of his balls, he'd rather that not happen.

Trying to distract his mind from the luscious, partially naked body he was currently holding in his arms, and needing to keep her awake in case she'd hit her head and had a concussion, he decided to ask the question burning in his brain.

"What are you doing up here, Maggie?"

She rubbed her face on his chest, warming her cold nose on his pectoral. So far, the distraction thing was not working.

"I n-needed to get Gran's recipe box." She gasped, making a feeble attempt to sit up. "Gran's box...where—"

"Shhhh." He held her tight, rubbing his hand against her back in a soothing motion. "You mean that wooden thing in your coat pocket?"

"Thank goodness." A sigh escaped her and she calmed against him. "Came for...box."

That's right, Maggie's grandmother had owned the cabin next to his. When Mrs. B died, of course it would go to her granddaughter. But her cabin was over a mile away. Why had she walked so far in this weather?

His unspoken question was answered when she continued.

"Thought I could...beat the storm home." Her shoulders hitched as she took a deep breath. "They said...wasn't going to be bad."

Yeah, when were the weather forecasts ever right?

"Guess I was wrong." She shifted against him, seeking his warmth and driving him crazy. "Snow started coming down in sheets. Could barely see three feet...in front of my car."

"What happened next?" It was still difficult for her to talk, but he needed to know what happened. He needed to know she was okay.

"Must have run over something. I heard this big pop and then..."

"Then what, Maggie?"

"Boom, flat tire."

"Damn. Unlucky time for a flat," he muttered, rubbing the soft skin on her back. She was getting warmer. That was good. Her smooth flesh felt like heaven on his rough, calloused hands. That was bad. He had to stop thinking things like that.

"I know," she said on a yawn. "Luck is a bitch determined to mess with me."

"So, you got a flat, and…?"

She grumbled something about annoying cowboys who wouldn't let her sleep. He smiled at her crankiness, but there was no way he was letting her sleep until he knew whether or not she had a head injury. First aid 101, never let someone with a knocked noggin fall asleep.

"Couldn't change the tire in this storm. Saw the lights of a cabin and started walking toward it." She took another breath, pushing on with the story he insisted she tell. "Figured whoever was here could help. Forgot you owned…"

"Did you fall?" he asked quietly, when she didn't finish.

She pulled her head out of from his chest. Her eyes fluttered open, puzzled. He stared into those soft green eyes and felt his heart stutter. Damn but this woman was beautiful. If he hadn't chosen today to come up to the cabin, he might have lost her. Not that he ever really had her to begin with. Wasn't that the damnedest thing?

"When I found you, you were face down in the snow. Did you fall? Hit your head on something?"

He moved his hand up her now warm back in a gentle caress. She shivered as he cupped the back of her neck, stroking her cheek with his thumb. He shouldn't be touching her this way, but he couldn't stop himself. His mind flashed back to her pale, still form in the freezing snow.

"Took damn near ten years of my life off when I saw it was you lying there, Maggie. You looked dead."

She stared at him with confusion, as if wondering if he really meant the words he was saying. He meant them. How could she think he didn't?

"I didn't fall. I just kind of…got tired. The wind was blowing so hard. I thought, if I got down lower it wouldn't blow me around as much." A yawn escaped her no longer blue lips. "I started crawling, and I guess I just kind of collapsed out of exhaustion."

Her words were starting to slur together; her eyelids drooped. She was indeed exhausted.

Now that he knew there was no risk of concussion and her body temperature was back up where it should be, he could let her sleep.

Tucking the blanket firmly around them, he kissed her softly on the forehead. "Sweet dreams."

"Colton?" she murmured, nestling her head against his chest.

"Yeah?"

"Thank you."

"Anytime, sweetheart."

A sleepy frown pulled at her lips as she whisper softly, "Not your…sweetheart."

"Not yet," he replied.

But Maggie was already fast asleep.

Chapter Five

Maggie woke up feeling warm.

Warm.

She never thought she would feel that again. Snuggling deeper into the balminess, she enjoyed the sensation for another moment, before fully waking. Damn, it felt good not to be cold and wet. How did she get so warm?

She slowly lifted her heavy eyelids. Sunlight streamed into the room—a room that was not hers. A room that was...not familiar.

Where the hell am I?

Last night, she'd been at her grandmother's cabin. The storm hit. Her car got a flat. She tried to go back on foot...got lost...tired...cold...so cold. How did she end up in this cozy bed?

In nothing but her bra and panties!

Her heart accelerated as she pulled back the thick blankets to discover she *was* mostly naked. Her mind raced back to last night. Cold...snow...a voice. A voice she recognized, calling her name. She remembered a handsome face and deep blue eyes. There had been a voice calling her things, like sweetheart and...Magpie.

Oh shit.

It all came rushing back. This was Colton's cabin. He had saved her last night. Brought her inside, tried to get her warm, but his generator was down. By the feel of the heat pouring into the room, it was on now.

Her face heated with embarrassment as it all came back to her. Colton's strong hands removing her wet clothes, warning her about the dangers of hypothermia. His warm, strong, sexy, mostly naked body pressed against hers.

She groaned at the memory. Since she came back into town, she had tried to keep her distance from Colton Denning. Been pretty damn successful, too. Until last night.

Why hadn't she waited 'til after the storm to go get the recipe box? Why hadn't she listened to Jamie? How had she forgotten he owned the cabin next to Gran's, and what the hell was he doing up here anyway?

Now, she was going to have to suffer the humiliation of getting out of bed and facing the man. She sooooo did not want to do this. He wasn't going to let her live this down. He'd tease her mercilessly and—truth be told—she kind of deserved it. What kind of idiot drove a mountain pass in a snowstorm? She remembered him teasing her last night, calling her sweetheart. Everyone was the flirtatious cowboy's sweetheart. The man was too charming for his own good.

As much as he teased, she gave it right back, calling him out on it, because what else could she do? Jump him and say, *"Yes, Colt, I am your sweetheart. Make love to me now!"*

Yeah, that'd go over real well.

To him, she was and always would be Magpie, little tagalong, kid sister substitute.

Her crappy luck continued.

But he *had* saved her life. She supposed she would

have to thank him for that.

Grudgingly, she pushed back the covers, surrendering the warmth of the bed for the humiliation of facing Colton. Grabbing a plush, terry cloth robe she found hanging on a hook on the back of the door, she slipped it on, tightened the belt, and headed out to thank him and get the ribbing over with.

Tempting smells of coffee, bacon, and eggs led her down the hall into the small kitchen. He was there, whistling a silly tune as he shoveled scrambled eggs onto a plate. His back was to her, so she took advantage of his position to look her fill.

The years had been very kind to Colton Denning. Working on the family ranch his whole life had made him toned and fit. The man had a six-pack you could do laundry on.

Remembering her first glimpse of it last night caused her body temperature to rise and her nipples to peak under the borrowed robe. She pulled the material tighter around herself, thankful it was thick enough not to give her away. Just another thing he would tease her about, she was sure.

He was currently wearing a dark blue sweater and a pair of faded blue jeans that hugged his perfect, scrumptious ass. Oh, he was fine all right, and he knew it, too. That was the problem.

Maggie stepped fully into the kitchen. She was trying to think of what to say when his deep voice surprised her.

"I was beginning to wonder if you were ever going to wake up." He didn't turn around, just kept shoveling food onto the plates. "I didn't want the breakfast to get cold."

He turned then, gracing her with a smile that made many a woman in Peak Town swoon. Herself included. Not that she would ever admit that to anyone.

Colton picked up the plates and set them on the small table. Two cups of steaming coffee were already placed in front of two chairs. He sat in one and motioned her to the other. When she hesitated, his smile faltered.

"You okay, sweetheart? You're not still cold are you?"

The real worry in his voice went straight to her damn, stupid heart. She didn't need his concern; she did not want his concern.

Mentally putting her guards up, she marched over to the table, pulled out the chair across from him and sat. "I'm fine," she said, adding tersely, "and for the last time, I am *not* your sweetheart."

Sinfully sexy lips chuckled into his coffee mug before taking a deep sip of the hot, dark liquid. "Oh yeah, you're fine."

They ate in silence. The eggs were delicious, the bacon crispy, and the coffee hit the spot just right. After all the effort he put into making her such a delicious breakfast, she felt a little bad about her tiny temper tantrum.

"Thank you, Colt," she finally said, taking a sip of her coffee.

"For breakfast? No problem, Magpie."

Frowning, she set her mug on the table a little harder than necessary. "I'm not sure what I dislike more, 'Magpie' or 'sweetheart.' And yes for breakfast, but also…thanks for last night."

A devilish smile lit his eyes. She realized how he

might have interpreted her thanks, remembering that parts of last night included him and her almost naked, under blankets, skin to skin. Her nipples hardened even more.

Stupid body.

"I meant for getting me out of the snow and getting me warm."

His eyebrows bobbed suggestively. Well crap, she had just referenced their nudity once more. That wasn't how she meant it, dammit.

"Oh, never mind!"

Rising from the table, she threw down her napkin, turned, and headed out of the kitchen in a huff. She made it about three feet before Colton's hand grabbed her. He pulled her to a stop, forcing her to turn back to him.

"I'm sorry, Maggie." His eyes no longer held that teasing light. "I didn't mean to make you feel embarrassed. I was just teasing."

That was the problem, he was always just teasing.

"I want you to know that I was strictly business last night. I would never take advantage of anyone, especially someone who was injured."

Those mesmerizing blue eyes were sincere as he stared down at her. She knew he would never take advantage of anyone. He was a good man. An incredibly sexy, flirtatious, hound dog, but a good man nonetheless. He'd saved her last night and even cooked her breakfast this morning, and she was acting like a bitch just because he was being his ornery, playful self.

"I know and I'm sorry. I guess I'm still just stressed out. Almost freezing to death really messes with your nerves."

She meant it to come out as a joke, but he didn't laugh. His brows drew together in a scowl as he pulled her into his arms. She resisted at first, but when he didn't let go, she relaxed into his strong embrace and allowed him to comfort her.

"Damn, you scared the crap out of me. I thought you were dead."

She had scared herself, too. At first, she'd been so cold she felt like she was being sliced by thousands of tiny razors. Then the cold made her sleepy. She knew it was a bad sign, but she hadn't had the energy to care at the time. Once Colton brought her inside and started warming her up, the bitter cold had grabbed hold of her again. Mostly, she just remembered thinking she was never going to be warm again. How she was going to freeze to death and become the ice queen her ex had so frequently called her.

But she hadn't frozen. She hadn't died. All thanks to the man holding her.

"Thank you for saving me," she mumbled into his chest.

His arms tightened around her, but he didn't say anything. They stayed that way for a minute or two, until Maggie realized she was in *Colton's* arms, his strong arms, and then the relaxed embrace became uncomfortable and...heated. Quickly, she pulled away, keeping her head down as she resumed her seat at the table. Her coffee was almost gone, and she finished off the last sip.

"Another cup?" He held up the coffee pot.

Smiling, she nodded. A caffeine addict, she didn't even feel semi-normal until she had at least two cups. Blame it on the early hours of the bakery. Customers wanted fresh baked goods, and since she opened her doors at nine, that meant getting up three hours earlier to ensure freshness. As much as she hated early mornings, she loved baking, so it was a sacrifice she was willing to make. Plus, with enough coffee, the early hours didn't seem so bad.

Colton refilled her cup. She felt the need to fill the awkward silence, so she said the first thing that popped into her head. "So, what was wrong with the generator?"

Those tempting lips turned down with a frown. "Frayed wire. Luckily, I had a replacement in the shed."

"You know that thing has needed replacing for a while now."

He gave her a mock scowl and clutched at his chest. "Bite your tongue. Ol' Bessie has gotten me through more blizzards than I can count. No way am I giving up on her."

"Ol' Bessie?" She snorted. "You named your generator?"

He sent her a pointed stare. "This coming from the woman who named each one of her mixing bowls?"

He'd caught her talking to them one day in her shop. Talk about embarrassing.

"Touché." She tipped her mug to him.

With breakfast finished, she picked up her plate and mug and took them to the kitchen sink. She desperately wanted another cup of coffee, but just the fact she wanted to stay to enjoy more coffee, and more of Colton's presence, was a sign she had to leave. Plus, she had to get back to town and open the shop. It was already…she looked at the clock hanging on the wall. *Crap eight-thirty!*

She'd just have to open late today.

"Well, thanks for breakfast and…last night." She twisted the coffee mug in her hands. "I better go dig out my car, put the spare on, and head back into town."

Colton chuckled as he took another drink from his cup.

She knew that chuckle. It was never a good thing. "What?"

"Oh nothing," he said mildly. "You might want to take a peek out the window before you make any plans for today though."

She had a really bad feeling as she walked over to the kitchen window and drew back the white curtain.

Oh, hell.

The curtain wasn't white. It was sheer. The massive amount of snow piled high outside was white. There had to be at least three feet out there, and it was still coming down. Big, white, fluffy flakes fluttered to the ground in a beautiful dance that mocked her. There would be no going into town today. No opening her shop. No getting away from the tiny cabin that housed the one man who made her heart race and her body burn. Just her luck. Her crappy, stupid, horrible luck.

She sighed, dropping the drapery back down and returning to the sink. "Guess I'm not going anywhere for a while huh?"

"Nope," the irritating cowboy said around a smug smile. "We're stuck here for the duration, Magpie sweetheart."

She wished very much at this moment that she had the power of pyro-kinesis and could burn him with her glare.

"What? I thought I'd see if you liked it better when

I combine the two. I guess that's a no?"

Grabbing a dishrag off the counter, she lobbed it at his head. He laughed, ducking the cloth with ease.

He brought his dishes over to the kitchen sink. She plugged the drain and filled it with warm water, squirting a bit of the lemon-scented dish soap into the basin. White, frothy bubbles soon began to form, causing her to think of the snow again.

It's May, dammit. May!

She reached out a hand for the plates.

Instead of handing them over, Colton held them close to his chest. "You don't have to wash the dishes."

"Look," she huffed impatiently. "Gran would roll over in her grave if she knew I didn't reciprocate hospitality by helping out with the chores, so shut up and hand over the dirty dishes."

He smiled as he did as requested. "Ooooh, snippy this morning are we? Need more coffee, Magpie?"

"Yes, as a matter of fact I do. And I'm not snippy. I just had things to do today, and now it looks like I'll be stuck here all day with—" She almost bit her tongue cutting off the last part of her reply.

"With me?" he finished for her.

Maggie winced. She hadn't meant to be rude. As proven by the recent events, he wasn't really a bad guy at all. It wasn't his fault she'd always had an overwhelming attraction to him. An attraction she was absolutely, unequivocally never going to do anything about.

"I'm sorry, Colt. I didn't mean it like that. I just had some very important things to do today. I need to find a new distributor and go through Gran's recipes. The shop's supposed to open in half an hour, and I can't even call Jamie to tell her where I am because you can't get any reception up in these stupid mountains." She knew that because she had tried to call for a tow truck after her car got the flat last night. No bars. No service. No luck.

"I've got a sat phone you can use."

A satellite phone? Why did he have a satellite phone?

"Cell service is always iffy up here, so anytime Dade or I come up we bring the sat phone. Now that you live here, you gotta start thinking more like a mountain girl and less like a Hollywood glamour girl."

She snorted. "Yeah, I'm sure I look very glamorous this morning. My hair hasn't seen a brush since yesterday, and I haven't even showered yet."

"You always look beautiful, Maggie."

She froze. He sounded serious. Colton always gave compliments, especially to women. They were always kind and charming, but this—this had sounded sincere.

Risking a glance up, she noted his deep, clear blue eyes held no hint of his usual teasing in them. His face wasn't exactly frowning, but he wasn't smiling like he always did when he flirted. He looked…damn sexy.

"So, why do you need a new distributor?" he asked, breaking the tension of the moment.

"Oh, it's nothing." She scrubbed a plate with more force than necessary. Anything to distract her from that strange look he just had in his eyes.

"It's not nothing if you're planning on switching. I own a ranch, remember? When the people who help you run your business screw up, you gotta move on before they take you down. So, tell me, what did they do?"

She really didn't want to discuss her problems with him. Though they were so close once, now they were more like acquaintances that traded small talk when their paths crossed. That was the way she liked it, too.

Okay, she didn't really like it, but it was all she could handle. If they got close again and she had to witness another woman getting a part of Colton she so desperately wanted…she just couldn't handle that again.

"It's nothing, really. I'm handling it fine on my own."

"I'm sure you are, but why not unload some troubles on me? Vent a little. That's what friends are for, right?"

He just wouldn't let it go. Men, they thought they could fix everything.

"Right, because we're such good friends." She unplugged the sink and watched the dingy water drain. "I told you, it's fine. I don't need your help, and I don't need to vent. I'm not a child. I can handle my own problems."

His eyes narrowed. Jaw clenched.

"My mistake." He walked out of the small kitchen. Grabbing his coat off a hook by the door, he paused. "I need to go get more firewood."

Crap. She'd hurt him. "Colt, wait—"

"Stay here where it's warm. It's still snowing and you're not one-hundred percent yet." With that, he stormed out the door, shutting it loudly behind him.

Maggie felt terrible. It hadn't been her intention to hurt his feelings. She was just tired, stressed, and unbelievably sexually frustrated. And it wasn't his fault he was the source of it.

Guilt began to gnaw a hole in her stomach, turning the delicious breakfast she had just eaten to a lump of cement.

There was only one thing that could work that lump out. She would apologize again with her secret weapon.

Opening the cupboards, she rooted around until she found everything she needed. Colton had saved her life. He deserved her thanks. He was going to get it, too. Maggie style.

Chapter Six

Colton stepped back into the cabin half an hour later. His mood had not improved. Ever since Maggie came back into town something had been off with them. He wasn't stupid. It wasn't like he expected them to go back to being best friends like when they were kids. Years had passed. But he always thought they were still the kind of friends that confided their problems to each other.

Guess I was wrong.

The snow was still coming down hard outside. He dropped the firewood in the bin by the door. A tarp covered the pile outside from the elements, but the walk to the front door resulted in the logs receiving a decent dusting of snow. They would dry soon enough. Hopefully, the house would stay warm until then. The old heater only did so much in a snowstorm.

Shrugging off his coat, he noticed the cabin was indeed warm, and it smelled delicious. What was that enticing aroma? Following the smell into the kitchen, he stopped in shock. It looked like a war zone. Dirty bowls, spoons, and measuring cup were stacked precariously in the sink. Various food items and spices lined the counter tops. A fine white powder covered almost every surface, and in the middle of all the madness…Maggie.

Singing, very off tune, she stood in the middle of

the kitchen holding a large mixing bowl in one hand and stirring the contents with a wooden spoon in the other. She obviously found her clothes where he had set them out to dry, because she was dressed.

She hadn't noticed him yet, so he watched as she sang, stirred, and shimmied around the kitchen. It was the sweetest thing he had ever seen. Then she swiveled her hips in a little booty shaking motion. Scratch that, it was the hottest thing he had ever seen.

"What in the world have you done to my kitchen?"

The sexy woman screamed, nearly dropping the bowl in her hands. She spun toward him, her expression going from shock to anger in an instant.

"Jeez, Colt. Don't sneak up on me like that!"

He chuckled. "I didn't sneak. You just didn't hear me because you were too busy getting your groove on."

She blushed. "I was making you a peace offering, but now I'm thinking I might just eat it all myself."

Maggie was making him something?

"Oh come on, Magpie, don't be like that. You have a…beautiful singing voice."

She laughed. "Please, I'm tone deaf and I know it."

"Yeah, but with moves like those no one's going to pay attention to your voice." He waggled his eyebrows.

Round, apple cheeks tinged pink. She had an adorable blush. It turned her whole face slightly rosy. Made a man wonder if the same coloring came out during the throes of passion.

Walking over to the counter where she was cooking, he leaned against it. "So, what are you making me?"

Her eyes narrowed, but she gave in. "Lemon tart cookies."

"Really? Those are my favorite!"

She gave him a sheepish grin. "I know. I remember."

She did, huh? Well, that was a good sign. So was the cookie apology. It meant she still cared about him on some level. He wondered, for the first time, just how deep that caring went. He always knew Maggie had a little crush on him, but he had discounted it as puppy love. A schoolgirl-crush. He'd seen her as a friend, a kid.

But she wasn't a kid anymore, and the feelings he was beginning to have for her were much more than friendly.

"So, how long 'til they're done?"

She turned to the counter and began scooping out small spoonfuls of batter onto a cookie sheet left by his mother the last time she visited.

"I've got a batch in the oven now," she answered. "Should be done in about five minutes, but they'll need to cool."

"Sounds good. I'll just go hop in the shower real quick."

He started to go down the hall until a soft voice stopped him.

"Colt?"

"Yeah?" he said, turning back to face her.

"I…could I still use your sat phone real quick?"

"Oh, sure. Let me just grab it for you."

That wasn't what she was about to say, he was sure of it. He could always tell when Maggie was nervous as a kid. She would twist her hands together like she had just done in the kitchen. He walked back to the bedroom closet where he kept the phone.

The question was…what the hell did Maggie Evans have to be nervous about?

A few minutes later, the second batch of cookies in the oven and the first cooling on the counter, Maggie clutched the sat phone tight in her hands. She could hear the shower water rushing through the pipes and tried not to imagine what was happening in the bathroom right now. Colton washing himself, naked. The hot jets of water pounding on his bare skin. Sliding over his hard, toned chest and down his killer stomach, all the way down to…

Tried and failed.

Clearing the image of the naked, wet cowboy from her mind—okay trying her best to—she focused on the phone instead. She dialed Jamie's home number, hoping the girl was at home. It was sad to say, but in the eight months she lived in Peak Town, she hadn't really made any friends. Sure, people were friendly and nice, but running the cupcake shop took up so much time, she didn't really make an effort to go out and connect with people.

"Hello?" a soft voice said after the phone picked up.

"Mrs. Thompson? It's Maggie Evans. Is Jamie at home?"

"Yes, she is." Her employee's mother must have covered the phone because she heard a muffled yell. "Jamie, telephone! It's Maggie." Then the older woman was back. "Is everything all right? Did Jamie make a mistake at work?"

"Oh no, nothing like that. She's a fantastic employee and a very smart young lady. I heard about Harvard. You must be so proud."

"We are." A beaming smile could be heard in the woman's voice. "We always knew she was smart, but Harvard! I just don't see how we could be any prouder of her."

"I'm sure she'll give you a lot of opportunity in the future for that. You both did a great job with her."

"Thank you, Maggie. Oh, here she is."

The phone was handed off. Maggie heard the younger Thompson thank her mother before she came on the line. "Hey, boss, what's up?"

"I was wondering if you could do me a huge favor?"

"What'd ya need?"

Opening the oven door, she checked the cookies. Not quite done. A few more minutes, tops. "I need you to go put a sign on the front of the shop saying we're closed due to the weather. My car got a flat last night, and I'm stuck up here because of the snow."

"I told you about the storm."

Teenagers. They thought they knew everything. It didn't matter this teenager just happened to be right this time.

"I know. You were right, Ms. Harvard."

Youthful laughter filled the line. "Yeah, that's why I got in, my uncanny ability to follow the weatherman's advice. So, your car got a flat. You need me to call Pete and have him come up there?"

Pete Miller ran the local auto body shop and owned the only tow truck in town.

"No. I'm good. I've got a spare. I'll change it once the storm dies down."

"Changing tires isn't like baking cupcakes. Plus, it's a pain in the as—butt—in the snow. You sure you can handle it?"

She smiled at the way the young girl corrected her language. Jamie may be smart and mature, but she was still a teenager. Maggie used to swear up a storm in high school. She didn't blame her employee for the occasional slip.

"I'm fine. I'm…I'm not alone actually. I got lost in the storm last night trying to get back to my cabin and…well, I came across Colt."

That wasn't quite the way it had happened, but no one needed to know that.

"Colton Denning?" The girl's voice went high with shock.

"Is there another Colt in Peak Town?" she replied dryly.

"Nope. So, you and Colt, huh?"

Was that a suggestive tone from her underage employee?

"We're friends."

"Riiiiight."

Teenagers.

"He took me in last night, and we are just waiting out the storm together. No big deal."

"Stormy weather. Small, cozy, warm cabin. A man and a woman. Sounds like a plot to a romance novel." The girl laughed.

"No romance. Just two friends stuck together due to unforeseen circumstances."

"Unforeseen if you don't watch the weather channel."

"Jamie, you are the only person under the age of fifty I know who watches the weather channel."

"What? I like to be informed. And the morning

weatherman is super hot, too."

Maggie laughed.

"Speaking of hot. Have you seen Colt naked yet?"

"Jamie!"

A chuckle trilled over the phone line. "Oh come on, boss. Colton Denning is hot with a capital H!"

"Maybe," she grudgingly admitted. "But I already told you, it's not like that. We're friends."

"He flirts with you all the time."

She sighed. "He flirts with everyone."

"He teases you," the persistent teen pressed. "Like a schoolyard boy."

"Wonderful, he's immature. Such a fine quality in a man."

"You know what I mean. He likes you."

"As a friend." She refused to believe anything more. It would just hurt too much when she was proven wrong.

"Think what you want, but I think there's more to it than that."

"We were friends as kids. There's nothing more."

The young girl was silent for a beat. "Haven't you ever heard of friendship turning into love? Two people who have been friends forever suddenly see each other in a new light and BAM! Love."

Love? Who said anything about love? She wasn't sure Colton liked her, let alone loved her. The childhood crush she had on him might be considered love, puppy love maybe. Infatuation definitely. But did she love Colton now? She was afraid to examine her feelings for him. If she did fall in love him and he didn't love her, or worse, didn't even like her in a romantic way, what would she do? Better to just stay friends. Less pain that way.

"Go watch a Nickolas Sparks movie and get off my case. And put the sign up at the shop while you're at it."

Jamie laughed loudly into the phone. "Sure boss, no problem. You enjoy your time with your *friend*."

"Oh, go study for a test or something," she grumbled.

She could still hear the youthful laughter in her ear as she hung up the phone. Her employee was a sweet kid, but she'd gotten it totally wrong. Colton did not have romantic feelings for her. He flirted and teased her, but in a buddy-buddy way. The way he did to everyone. They were just two old friends stuck in the woods together.

Nothing more.

The ding of the stove timer reminded her about the cookies. Placing the phone on the counter, she grabbed an oven mitt and opened the door. Perfect. The sweet, lemony scent wafted out of the oven and wrapped itself around her. Grasping the tray firmly with her gloved hand, she pulled the cookies out.

"Mmmmmm, smells great, Magpie."

Startled, she spun, straightening from her bent position at the oven. Colton stood before her with nothing but a towel wrapped around his waist. Gleaming droplets of water still clung to his chest. His hair was a shade darker when wet and slicked back from his face. A drop of water started a trail down his neck, over his pectoral muscle, and down his sculpted abs. Mixing in with his happy trail and making its way down underneath the towel that was currently…tenting?

Holy shit! Colton was aroused?

Chapter Seven

If the woman stared any harder Colton was going to embarrass himself. He was to blame really. He had intentionally forgone clothing once he finished his shower. Coming into the kitchen with nothing but a towel wrapped around his hips was supposed to get a reaction from Maggie.

Boy had it.

There was definitely something there. Her gaze ate him up with barely contained greed, heat, and lust. Oh yeah, the sexy little cupcake maker felt more for him than friendship. He was sure of it.

He took a step forward, and the spell was broken. Face turning bright red, she turned back around to the counter and slammed the cookie tray down with more force than necessary.

Okay, so she might have thoughts other than friendship for him, but she didn't want to admit it. He could deal with that. When dealing with a skittish mare you had to be calm, gentle, and patient. He could be patient with this woman.

"I better go get dressed. Don't want cookie crumbs in unmentionable places."

His joke had the intended effect as she chuckled and some of the tension left her shoulders.

"Be right back."

He left and headed down the hall to the bedroom.

Dressing quickly in a pair of well-worn jeans and a black, long sleeve shirt, he tugged on socks before making his way back into the kitchen. The cookies were already cooling on the rack.

Maggie stood at the window, her back to him, watching the snow. "It never snowed in LA."

He stayed silent, letting her continue her thoughts out loud.

"Lizzy and I went to Big Bear once to try skiing. It was a disaster. We both fell about a hundred times. I swear I bruised my tailbone, and Lizzy almost broke her ankle, but the snow was so pretty and fluffy. It was really fun."

"Who's Lizzy?" he asked, pulling out a chair at the small table and sitting.

"My best friend."

She turned then, and he was blown away by how beautiful she was. The heart shaped face gave her such a youthful appearance. That adorable button nose and those full, pouty lips just begged to be kissed. Colton had to remind himself he was trying to take it slow with her. Not jump over the table and drag her down onto it so he could rip her clothes off and make love to her right there. That was not slow.

"We met sophomore year of high school."

The year after she stopped coming to Peak Town.

Did that have something to do with it? He could imagine a teenage girl not wanting to leave her best friend for months at a time.

"We clicked right away. Her parents are in 'the Biz,' but she saw how Hollywood could destroy families, and never wanted that for herself."

"Did it destroy her family?"

That cute little nose scrunched up as she crossed her arms over her middle. "Her parents are still together, but I don't think either one of them has ever been faithful. They also weren't around much for her. She spent a lot of time at my place. Mom worked, but she always came home at night." Maggie smiled with a faraway look. "Lizzy and I used to make dinner, and then Mom would come home and we'd play card games until bed. We used to play poker with M&Ms. Lizzy would always beat us. Mom used to laugh and say she lost on purpose so she wouldn't ruin her diet by eating all that chocolate."

Sadness crept into those emerald green eyes.

"You must miss her. Your mother," he clarified when she looked at him.

A few years ago, the news had spread around town that Maggie's mother lost her battle with cancer. Mrs. B had rushed out to California to spend time with her grieving granddaughter. Maggie's mother had never been married to Mrs. B's son, but Maggie was still Betty's flesh and blood. The old woman loved her and therefore felt her granddaughter's pain at the loss of her last living parent.

"Yes, I miss her. Everyday. I miss Lizzy, too, but at least I still get to talk to her."

Mossy hued eyes blinked back tears. Colton cursed himself, feeling like an ass for bringing up such a painful subject. He hadn't intended to make her cry.

"So, what does Lizzy do, since she's not in, what did you call it…?" he asked, trying to move the conversation in a different direction.

"'The Biz.' Hollywood lingo." Maggie grabbed the plate of cooled cookies from the counter and brought them to the table, taking the seat across from him. "Lizzy went to UCLA to study business management. I studied culinary arts at California Culinary School. We rented an apartment together instead of living in student housing. Then Lizzy got a job as an assistant shift manager at Le Central, a little French restaurant just off Hollywood and Vine. She worked her way up to manager and turned the place into a four star restaurant in under five years. She hired me on as pastry chef about three years ago."

Grabbing a cookie from the plate, he bit into it. Sugary, lemon flavor exploded in his mouth as the sweet treat melted over his tongue. Leaning back in his chair, he closed his eyes and moaned. "I can see why. God, Magpie, these cookies are almost better than sex."

"Really?"

He opened his eyes, taking in her shocked expression. "I said *almost*." He winked, and she blushed again. Damn, it was fun making her blush. "Must have been great living and working with your best friend."

"It was. People always say don't live with friends, but with Lizzy and I…we're more like sisters, so it was never a problem. She really helped me get through Mom's death and Gran's. And then that whole thing with Miles—" She cut herself off, but not soon enough.

"Who's Miles?"

"No one."

She said that far too quickly. *Must be an ex.* Thinking of Maggie with another man set his teeth on edge. Which was ridiculous. She was a twenty-eight year old woman, of course she'd have had a few relationships. Hell, Colton was thirty-two and there had been women in his life. A few relationships, a few just for fun. So, why did it rub him the wrong way to think of another man touching her?

"So, tell me what you've been up to the last few years?" she said, obviously switching the conversation.

Fair was fair. She'd shared with him. Not a problem. His life was pretty mundane. Satisfying, but mundane.

"My parents retired to Florida a few years back, so me and Dade took over at the ranch. When the economy took a nosedive, we needed to do something to bring in more money. Riding lessons and boarding alone wasn't paying the bills, so I took a couple of online classes in equine studies and breeding management."

"Wow."

"It's not that big a deal." It really wasn't, but he liked that it impressed her. Suddenly, he was finding he wanted her to think of him as more than just a hound dog cowboy. "I took a couple trips out to Kentucky and bought Thunder."

"Is he that brown Quarter Horse you guys have out in the pasture?"

He was surprised she noticed considering Maggie had only been out to the ranch a time or two since she got back, mostly to deliver cupcakes. That girl never had any fun. He would have to change that.

"Yeah. He's a retired racing stallion. I got him for a great price because he had behavioral issues. No one could get him to breed. I took one look at him and knew."

"Knew what?"

"That he just needed someone to be gentle with

him. Be patient." He held her gaze with his. "I'm a very patient man, Magpie."

She swallowed, her hands twisting together on top of the table.

Sensing her discomfort, he let his gaze drop, breaking the contact. "I brought him back home and worked with him. He was traumatized by all the years of racing. Crowds, noise, loud bells, and screaming." He shook his head. "People don't realize how much that can spook a horse. They need calm and space. Animals aren't meant to be raced around a track like cars." Grabbing another cookie, he shoved it into his mouth, chewed, and swallowed before continuing. "Anyway, it took about a year, but I finally got Thunder to trust me. Once he realized he could have his pick of pretty lady horses, well, he cheered right up. Now, in addition to lessons and boarding, the colts we sell from Thunder help. The ranch is doing great, that's why we had to hire a couple of hands to help out."

"I guess people will pay a lot for the pedigree of a racing horse's offspring."

"They sure do." He raised a cookie in a toast.

"You're going to ruin your lunch if you keep eating those."

"Oh come on, Magpie. Live dangerously." He waved a cookie in front of her nose.

She swatted at the treat, laughing.

"I think I'll stick to a nice, healthy salad thank you. I make cupcakes for a living. If I 'lived dangerously' with everything I bake, I'd be four hundred pounds."

"Just more of you to love."

Her green eyes narrowed, and she grabbed the plate just as he reached for another cookie.

"Hey!"

"No more until you've had a proper lunch, Romeo."

He placed a hand to his chest. "You wound me, sweetheart."

She rolled her eyes. "You made breakfast so I'll make lunch."

"As long as it's more than salad." Colton shuddered. He was a big man with a physically taxing job. Salad was not going to cut it.

"How about Philly cheesesteak sandwiches and a spinach side salad?" she asked, peering into the fridge.

"Do I have the ingredients for that?"

The pantry was always stocked with various canned food for emergencies, but he always made sure to do a grocery run before heading up to the cabin. You could only eat so many cans of beans before your stomach turned on you.

"I can improvise with what you have." Maggie started pulling things off shelves.

"Then it sounds awesome. I think I've got a deck of cards around here somewhere. Want to show me how good your poker skills are after lunch?"

She glanced at him over her shoulder. Her hair was down, free of that braid thing she usually wore. The dark strands fell like waves over her shoulder. He sucked in a breath, feeling like someone had just sucker punched him. Damn, the woman was beautiful.

"I don't have any M&Ms," he added. "But I think there's a bag of chocolate chips in the back of the pantry."

She smiled "Oh, you are so going to lose."

"Don't count on it, sweetheart." He winked. When

it came to Maggie, he didn't plan to lose a damn thing.

****

Lunch had been delicious. Even the salad had been good. After they cleaned the dishes, Colton found that deck of playing cards, and Maggie searched through the pantry until she came up with a half-full bag of chocolate chips. They kept it simple. Five-card stud.

The sneaky baker was up five games to two.

"I swear you're cheating."

"You're just mad 'cause I'm kicking your butt." Maggie gave him a deceptively innocent smile. "Two cards please."

She said the words a little too sweetly. He'd been trying like hell to figure out her tell. Everyone had a tell. His brother would always rub his fingers together when he was bluffing. Maggie twisted her hands when she was nervous, but he had no idea what she did when she was lying.

He drew two cards from the deck and handed them face down to her. She plucked them from his fingers and added them to her hand. He watched her very closely. Nothing.

Wait, there!

A slight move, but the thumb on her right hand ever so slightly touched the ring on her pointer finger. Her grandmother's ring. Colton knew that because he remembered seeing Mrs. B wear it every day when he was growing up, and then had given it to her granddaughter the first summer she came to visit. He'd never known Maggie to take it off since.

So, she touched her ring. Was that a good sign or bad? Great hand or lousy? Guess he'd find out soon enough. He looked at his own cards. A pair of jacks.

Not great. Time to play a little chicken.

"I bet ten." He tossed a handful of chocolate chips in the center.

Dark brown eyebrows rose. "Good hand, huh?"

"Maybe. Why don't you find out?"

She narrowed her gaze, staring at him, trying to call his bluff.

Good luck sweetheart. Everyone had a tell…everyone except him.

"I see your ten, and raise you fifteen." She slowly dropped each chip onto the pile.

Chocolate scent filled the air, reminding him of all the sweet things in the room he'd like to get his mouth on.

"So confident, Magpie. I call." He dropped another handful onto the table. "What cha' got?"

"You first, darling," she said with a curl of her lips.

"Oooo I like it, but maybe next time try not to make it sound like an insult."

"Stop calling me silly nicknames and maybe I will. Now, stop stalling and show me what you have."

There was no way he could let a set up like that get away. "I'd love to show you what I have, but maybe the kitchen isn't the best place for our first time."

Those pretty green eyes rolled upwards. "Your cards, Colton. Get your mind out of the gutter and on the game."

He laughed, flipping his cards face up on the table. "Pair of jacks."

Beaming, Maggie turned hers over. Three tens and two fives. "Full house! I win. Again." Scooping the chocolate chip pile into her hands, she dragged her winnings over to her already huge pile.

"Unbelievable." Guess the ring thing was a "good" tell.

"Not really. You are a lousy poker player, Colt."

Affronted, he sat back in his chair. "Am not."

"You have a very overt tell." She grabbed the fallen cards.

He crossed his arms over his chest. "No way."

Her shoulders lifted in a shrug as she shuffled.

No way. No way did he have a tell. He'd been clearing the table with his brother for years. He was a great poker player. Unless…Dade was lousy at poker.

"Okay fine. Then I won't tell you what it is, and I'll get all the chocolate chips to myself."

They sat in silence as she finished shuffling, then dealt five cards out to each of them. Colton picked up his cards, glancing at them. A two, pair of eights, a ten and a king. Awful. He glanced across the table. No expression, no ring touching.

"Three cards please." He passed the king, two and ten to her.

She put them in the discard pile and gave him three new cards from the top of the deck. Then she put down two of her own cards, replacing them with new ones. He waited, watched. She touched her ring.

"Okay, I give. What's *my* tell?"

Maggie glanced up from her cards and smiled. "You tilt your head slightly to the right when you bluff."

Really? A head tilt? How had she noticed that? No one had ever mentioned that before, and he played poker every week with his brother and their ranch hands. He won a lot, too. Never had anyone noticed his tell. Hell, he hadn't even noticed it.

Maggie had.

She noticed something about him that no one else had. He smiled. Another good sign.

Picking up his new cards, he glanced at them. A three, a seven and another two. Crap.

"Two," she said, tossing chips into the center of the table.

She was playing low ball, trying to get him to up the ante. Not with this hand.

"I fold."

"On two?" Her mouth dropped in astonishment.

He tossed his cards down on the table. "I may have a tell, Magpie, but so do you. Another full house?"

Open mouth closing, she grimaced. "No, I had a straight."

Colton laughed, drawing a smile out of her.

"Shoot. It took Lizzy years to figure out my tell." She rubbed her ring again. "Gran was the one who taught me how to play poker. Her ring always brings me luck. Well, in the game at least."

They played a few more hands, both trying unsuccessfully to hide their tells. After a few hands of fruitless betting and folding, they called it quits. Maggie suggested stew for dinner. They worked together chopping up the meat and vegetables and tossing everything in the small crockpot he kept at the cabin. It was strange how right it felt. How totally normal it was to stand beside this woman and make a meal. Like they had been doing it forever.

Colton shook his head. He was starting to sound like a freaking Hallmark card. He glanced out the living room window. It was still snowing outside, but it had tapered off to small, sparse flakes.

"We'll be able to get out of here tomorrow morning," he said. "You can ride into town with me."

"What about my car?"

She wandered over to the living room couch. Sitting, she curled up with a blanket and grabbed a book of crosswords puzzles from the coffee table. Who had left that here? Probably his mom on her last visit; his mother loved her word games.

"There's no way you'd get down this mountain on a spare. I'll give Pete a call when we get back into town and have him come get it. He can tow it back and fix the tire for you."

"I can make the call myself you know. I do know how the telephone works."

He turned to face her; her arms were crossed, a stern set to her jaw. Too cute. Time to tease the bear.

"Hey, I'm just trying to be helpful. I take you in, save your life, feed you, offer to call a tow, and what do I get—"

"Cookies."

He smiled. "Oh yeah. Those were great. Any left, Magpie?"

She smiled, just as he had intended her to. "No porker, you ate them all."

"Porker?"

She shrugged. "You make a nickname. I make a nickname. You don't like it?"

He gave her a playful wink. "I love it, sweetheart."

They spent the afternoon chatting about various things. The ranch, the stars she met in LA, nothing too serious. After the hearty dinner, he suggested a movie. There was no cable, but there was a stack of DVDs in the cabin. Maggie picked out a B rated monster flick, one of those so bad it was good. They laughed the entire way through, making jokes as the film went along. He couldn't remember the last time he had this much fun with a woman—with her clothes still on. By the time the movie finished, it was past ten. Maggie's mouth opened on a jaw-cracking yawn.

"I am beat."

"We should probably turn in so we can get an early start tomorrow."

She stood, tossing the blanket she had been snuggled up with back onto the couch. "Yeah, I need to open the shop tomorrow. I hope no one is upset about it being closed today."

"People here understand about weather emergencies, Magpie."

She snorted. "I guess they would."

Time for bed. The question was, who was going to sleep in it? The answer he wanted was both of them. But as he watched her hesitant green gaze glance back to the bedroom, the realization that there was only one bed dawning, her hands starting to twist, and he knew what he had to do.

"I'll take the couch."

Her mouth turned down. "That's silly. I'm smaller. I'll fit better. Plus, it's your bed."

"We can share it," he said with an overtly suggestive tone, only half-kidding.

She blushed. "Dream on, Colt."

"Seriously, take the bed. I'll be fine out here. It's where Dade always shoves me when we both come up anyway."

"Okay."

Then, shocking the hell out of him, she went up on

her tiptoes and leaned in. Her soft, sweet lips pressed against his cheek in a barely there kiss. It took everything in him not to turn his head and claim her mouth.

"Thanks, Colt."

With that, she turned and headed down the hall.

"Maggie."

She paused, glancing back at him.

He gave her his best wolf grin and whispered just loud enough for her to hear, "I will dream tonight. Of you."

Chapter Eight

"Rise and shine, Magpie. The snow has stopped. It's time to head out."

Maggie groaned, pulling the covers over her head. The room was warm, and the bed was comfy. Why did he have to go ruin it by reminding her of the freezing snow waiting just outside? Couldn't she just stay in bed all day?

"Come on, sweetheart. We got to move if you want to open your shop on time."

"I'm not your sweetheart, Colton Denning," she grumbled through the covers at the door.

She could hear him chuckle on the other side.

"I've got fresh coffee."

If only coffee would work this morning. "Give me ten minutes."

"You got five." The sound of his footsteps retreated.

Stupid man.

It was his fault she was so tired and grouchy this morning. All that teasing and flirting yesterday had wound her up tighter than a pair of skinny jeans. Then he had to go be all sweet and concerned. Offering to call a tow for her. Drive her into town.

Why couldn't he just be an asshole so she could hate him?

And then there was the proximity. Bad enough she

had seen him nearly naked yesterday morning, but last night, while watching the movie, Colton had been so close. Sure, the couch in the cabin was really small and more of a love seat. Awfully convenient excuse. With the heater running full steam and the fire roaring away, it had been toasty warm inside last night, but she'd still kept that throw blanket wrapped around her like armor against him. Still, she remembered the warm, firm press of his thigh against hers, and the strong, lean muscles of his arm casually laid across the back of the couch behind her.

Her hormones had been raging so much she'd almost accepted his offer of sharing the bed. Somehow, she'd found the sanity to decline. No good would come from giving in to her stupid childhood crush.

Deep down, in her heart of hearts, she feared it wasn't just a childhood crush. She was afraid it might be much more than hero worship or silly puppy love. If it was, and she gave into it—and he didn't feel the same—it would crush her worse than Miles had.

For her heart's sake, friendship was all she could offer. Probably all he wanted anyhow. The cowboy was smart, successful, and sexy as hell. He could have his pick of women. Why would he want a mousy little baker covered in more flour than foundation?

Realizing two of her allotted five minutes were already gone, Maggie begrudgingly tossed the covers back and rose. She wore a long, dark T-shirt that she'd found in the dresser. It smelled like Colton. Another reason she had tossed and turned last night. Smelling the man had invoked all kinds of fantasies that kept her hot and bothered, all night long.

Stripping off the shirt, she tossed it on the bed and

reach for her clothes she'd thrown onto the floor the night before. She dressed quickly, not bothering with makeup since she had none here. She had her hair braided without even realizing she'd done it. It was automatic. Pulling a hair tie out of the front pocket of her jeans she fastened the end tail.

Hesitating at the door, she glanced to the bed.

One beat.

Two.

Oh, why the hell not.

Rushing back, she grabbed the T-shirt, balled it up, and stuffed the material in the inner pocket of her jacket, next to Gran's recipe box. Hoping it wasn't too noticeable, she headed back to the bedroom door. Just as she grabbed the knob, it swung open.

"Jeez, I was coming right out. Impatient much?"

Full, sexy lips smiled, and her stomach dipped like the first drop of a roller coaster.

Stupid stomach.

He held out a travel mug of what she prayed was coffee.

"I was hoping to catch you naked."

At his wink, she gave him a playful shove and pointed to the mug. "That better be coffee."

He handed it over. "It is, and seriously, we need to get going. The weather report says there's another storm headed this way in about two hours."

It would take them an hour alone to get off the mountain.

"Just let me hit the bathroom, and I'm good to go."

In less than five minutes, they were in Colton's truck, headed down the mountain. The radio played static intermixed with bits of country when the signal was good. Maggie sat in the passenger seat drinking her coffee, glad he had suggested she ride with him. The road turned icy overnight, but he was handling it like a pro. She would have been white-knuckled, praying every second of the trip. Snow may be pretty, but the stuff was hazardous.

A little over an hour later, they arrived back in Peak Town. The streets were plowed, but the town had seen some of the snowstorm, too. Small drifts were piled next to where the streets and sidewalk had been cleared. The sun was out, melting the snow, but there were dark clouds on the horizon. Doomsday clouds, as she now thought of them.

It's springtime, dammit!

Colton pulled up in front of Cupcakes Above the Clouds and put his truck into park, leaving the engine to idle.

"You want me to call Pete about your car? It's really no trouble. I have to talk to him about a new timing belt for Dade's truck anyway."

She wanted to say no. She could handle it on her own. But, with having to find a new distributor, going through Gran's recipes, and prepping for the blogger, she was a little overwhelmed. Would it really hurt to let a friend help out?

"If it's not too much trouble. I'd really appreciate it. Tell Pete to call me when it's fixed."

He grinned. "You got it, Magpie."

Rolling her eyes, she opened the truck door and slid out. She paused before closing the door. "Would you like to come over for dinner tonight?"

What? Where the hell had that come from?

She had just blurted it out without thinking. By the

look on his face, Colton was as shocked as she was. "I—I was thinking I'd make you dinner." *I was?* "To thank you for—you know. Saving my life and everything."

There, that sounded reasonable and friendly. Not pathetically lustful at all. Just making dinner for a friend to thank him for his help.

Colton recovered from his shock and smiled like he had just won the lottery. "Sure, Magpie. I'd love to."

Again with the nicknames. Maybe this was a bad idea. Too late to take it back now. "Six thirty okay with you?"

"Perfect. See you then."

"Bye."

Slamming the truck door, she turned and ran up the stairs toward her apartment. Her face burned. What the hell had she just done? Only an hour ago she'd told herself not to get involved with the tempting, flirtatious cowboy. Hadn't she agreed that it was a potential mistake that could rip her heart out?

Yes, she had.

So, why did she feel like a giddy schoolgirl whose crush had just checked the yes box?

Chapter Nine

Still grinning from Maggie's unexpected invitation, Colton pulled his truck into the driveway of the ranch. He had lived here his whole life and couldn't imagine living anywhere else. Less than ten minutes outside of town, the property had over fifty acres that included a small creek and a few riding trails. Pure heaven.

Stepping out of the truck, he shut the door and headed toward the house. He could already smell the coffee, eggs, and bacon. The morning chores would be done and everyone was sitting down to breakfast. That was the way it worked on a ranch. Chores first, food second.

Inside, he hung his jacket up on the coat rack and made his way to the kitchen. Sure enough, everyone was sitting around the large, wooden table chowing down. Standing at the coffee pot refilling a cup, his brother glanced up when he entered the room.

"Hey, Colt. How was the cabin?"

"Great." Work on a ranch never ended, but he and Dade made sure to take a few days here and there to recharge their batteries while the other stayed behind to keep an eye on things. "Anything happen while I was gone?"

"Molly's nose is leaking snot like a drippy faucet. I think she had a cold," grumbled Juan Ortiz, their ranch foreman and right hand man of three years.

"I called Doc Billings. He said he'd come by later today."

Billings was the only vet in a fifty-mile radius. In horse and cow country, that made him a very busy man.

"We should move her to the empty paddock in back. If she's sick, we don't want the others catching it."

Dade nodded. "Already done. You eat yet?"

He shook his head. His brother motioned for him to sit, already fixing up a plate for him. Only two years older, Dade had always taken his role as big brother very seriously.

Juan and the other hands finished their meals and headed back out to tend to the horses.

"So, anything interesting happen this weekend?"

A plate piled high with eggs, bacon, and toast was set in front of him. He glanced up to see a knowing gleam in his brother's eyes. Though Dade had darker hair than him, their eyes were the same, clear blue. That blue was now staring a hole in Colton.

Shoveling a forkful of eggs into his mouth, he shook his head and stayed silent.

"I hear you dropped Maggie Evans off at her place this morning."

What the hell? "Who told you that?"

"Carl when he dropped off the feed delivery."

Nosy, small town busybodies. He wasn't all that surprised; nothing in Peak Town stayed secret for long. He *was* surprised at how fast it had gotten out, though. It had only been twenty minutes ago that he dropped her off.

"Yeah. So?"

The elder Denning crossed his arms, waiting. His

brother had that intimidating stare down to a tee. Too bad it didn't work on him.

"Spill it, Colt."

"Fine, but it's not really that big a deal."

He told his brother about finding Maggie passed out in the snow. Glossing over the methods he used to keep her warm, he gave a brief summary of their time together. Making food, playing cards, watching a movie. He explained about the flat, which was why she had been out in the storm in the first place.

"Which reminds me," he said, taking a sip of his coffee. "I need to call to Pete and have him go up to get her car."

"What the hell was she thinking going out in that storm?"

He shrugged, pushing his empty plate away. "She's not used to them. Thought she could make it back to her grandmother's cabin, I guess."

Dade huffed. "It's a good thing you found her."

He nodded in agreement. It still scared the shit out of him remembering how lifeless she had looked when he first found her. He never wanted to see her that way again.

Standing, he grabbed his plate and mug and took them to the sink. "I'm going over to her place tonight for dinner."

His brother was silent, but out of the corner of his eye he could see broad shoulders tense up.

"What?"

Dade rubbed a hand over his jaw, taking his time before speaking. His brother was never one to rush, analytical to the point of annoying. While Colton was always go-go-go, Dade took his time to examine things from every possible angle. They balanced each other out, which made for a great business partnership, just didn't always translate well to sibling harmony.

"You sure you know what you're doing?"

"What does that mean?"

"Maggie's a special girl."

He knew that. They'd been close friends as children, closer than her and his annoying older brother.

He gripped the counter behind him tightly. "What are you getting at, Dade?"

"Maggie's always had a crush on you. Some childhood hero worship thing. Don't start anything unless you're serious about it. She's not the kind of girl you screw around with."

Since when did he screw around with people? Sure, he was a bit of a flirt, but that was just being fun and friendly. Something his brother knew little about. He'd overheard more than one female accuse Dade of being cold and distant. His brother preferred the term "stoic." Colton called him a stick in the mud. Not to his face, of course.

"What's going on with me and Maggie is between us."

"I just don't want her hurt."

He knew his brother was just speaking out of concern. He saw Maggie as a little sister, always had. Until recently, Colton did, too. Now his feelings toward Maggie were…confusing.

"I'm not going to hurt her."

His big brother sighed. "You may not mean to, but if you go into this and you're not as serious as she is, things could get ugly."

The problem was, he had no idea how serious she

was...or he was for that matter. They hadn't talked about anything. For all he knew, this was just a sociable dinner from one friend to thank another.

Just because he wanted it to be more didn't mean it would be.

"It's just dinner. She's thanking me for helping her out this weekend. One friend to another."

Identical blue eyes studied him.

"But you want it to be more?"

Damn, his sibling could read him like a book. He remained silent. Letting Mr. Busybody come to his own conclusions. Truthfully, Colton had no idea what he wanted at the moment. He just knew he enjoyed being with Maggie and felt something for her, something more than the friendship they shared in their childhood. Was he feeling something serious? Something long term? He had no idea, but he at least wanted the chance to find out.

"Just be careful," Dade finally said. "There's no turning back once you head down this road. I don't want either of you hurt."

"Ya big ol' softie." He punched his brother in the shoulder.

Dade shoved him back. With the conversation over, for the moment, he grabbed his hat from the rack by the kitchen door and headed out to check on Molly.

Right now, he had work to do. There would be plenty of time to think about what he wanted from Maggie later.

Chapter Ten

Even with the late start, Maggie managed to open the shop on time. Sundays were big days for her. People liked to indulge their sweet tooth after church.

The bell above the door chimed. She glanced up to see Jamie coming in, a smile on her face, ponytail bouncing along with her steps.

"Morning boss. How was your slumber party date?"

"It was not a slumber party, nor a date."

The teenager moved behind the counter, stashing her purse in the cubby under the register.

"Whatever you say."

"Wipe that grin off your face. We have work to do."

Jamie rolled in her lips to smother her grin. It didn't work.

Sighing, Maggie went back to frosting a batch of Sinful Cinnamon cupcakes she had made first thing. Her employee started placing the three-dozen, already frosted cupcakes in the display. She always made sure to have a large variety, but with not opening yesterday and getting a late start today, the selection wouldn't be as vast as most Sundays.

"Did you make any Macadamia Nut Madnesses? You know Bonnie and Mort always stop by after church for one."

The sweet, older couple had been married for over sixty years and stopping by Cupcake Above the Clouds every Sunday since her Gran had opened the shop. They'd been the first people to offer their condolences on Gran's passing when Maggie arrived in town.

"Oh shoot. I was so frazzled this morning I forgot. Can you finish frosting these? They usually don't come in 'til ten. I can whip up a small batch before then."

Jamie nodded, grabbing the icing piper from her.

Maggie didn't want to disappoint the couple. They were so nice and loving. Watching them share a cupcake every Sunday, feeding it in little bites to each other, was one of the most romantic things she had ever seen. It didn't sound like much, but just the simple act of sharing food, sharing a life for so long, caused a yearning in her. She wanted that from life, just something so simple—someone to share with, someone to be there to split a cupcake.

As the product of illegitimacy, she didn't have much in the way of relationship role models. Her parents had been young, in their early twenties, and only dating for a few months when they conceived her. Her father hadn't even stuck around to see her, and her mother's family had all been gone before she was born.

She didn't even know she had any family besides her mother until they had gotten news her father died in a car accident. Never having known him, she hadn't known how to feel. The little girl who always dreamed of her daddy coming one day to pick her up and tell her he loved her, had been devastated. The girl who had never known what it was like to have a father had simply gotten on with her life.

Then word had come from her father's mother, a

request to know the child, a plea to spend time with her. At first, her mother was reluctant, but Maggie had been curious to know about the other side of her family. So, her mother had agreed to let her spend the summers in Peak Town. She had bonded with her grandmother, seen true love through Mort and Bonnie, and met Colton.

Maggie shook her head. She shouldn't think of long term and Colton Denning in the same sentence. Why had she invited him to dinner? Oh God, she was going insane.

Opening the pantry, she searched for the macadamia nuts. They were on a high shelf, so she grabbed the footstool, but still had to stand on her tiptoes to get the bag. Being short sucked sometimes.

Once she got them down, she headed to the electric chopper to grind the nuts into a fine powder for the batter mix. It was one of Gran's special recipes. She made it so much during her summers as a kid she had it memorized.

Dumping half the bag into the chopper, she closed the lid and hit the power button. Nothing.

She hit it again.

Still nothing.

Reaching back, she checked to make sure the appliance was plugged in. Yes. She hit the button again.

More nothing.

Frustration mounting, she wiggled the cord at the base. A small cracking sound and it popped off in her hand.

"What the hell?"

The cord had come clean off the base. Unplugging the device, she brought the broken end to her face and examined it closely. It *was* a clean break. Not frayed or worn out from natural wear and tear. No, more like someone had sliced clear through the cord and glued it back on, as there was some clear lacquer type material coating the end.

Who the hell would cut a cord and glue it back on?

"Jamie, could you come back here for a second?"

She didn't want to accuse her best employee, but the part-time worker was her only employee. There was no other explanation. She hadn't done it, and Jamie was the only other person who ever came back here.

The young girl came around back, the half-empty icing bag still in her hand. "What's up?"

"Did you…accidently cut through the chopper cord and then try to fix it?"

Jamie looked at her like she was crazy. Maybe she was.

"No. Why the heck would I do that?"

No idea. But if it wasn't her, then who the hell did it?

"Come look at this." She motioned her over.

The teenager set down the icing bag on the counter and peered closely. "What the hell?"

"That's what I said!"

Jamie took the cord from her hand, staring at it intently. "Uh, boss I hate to say this, but it looks like someone did this on purpose. It's a clean cut, intentional."

That's what she was afraid of.

"There's also something like"—short nails scraped the end of the cord—"glue? Someone cut the cord and tried to glue it back on? Why? Any idiot would know that wouldn't hold a current."

"Not everyone is a Harvard egghead," she joked, but the college-bound girl was right. Even she knew that cutting a wire then gluing it back together wouldn't work, and she had failed shop class. Twice. Whoever did this wanted her to know they messed with her equipment. "But who could have done it? No one is back here except for you and me. And *why* would they do it?"

"The delivery people are back here when they unload. Any of them got beef with you?"

The delivery people!

She had been fighting with her distributor lately. It was their mistakes, but perhaps they didn't see it that way. Could they have gotten so mad one of them decided to mess with her?

"Maggie?" Big brown eyes held unease.

"Don't worry about it. I'm sure it was just a mistake. Maybe one of the delivery guys was unloading something and accidently cut through the cord. Then worried I'd complain to his boss and tried to fix it."

That sounded plausible. Farfetched, but plausible.

"Yeah, that sounds about right. No one likes getting in trouble with the boss," the young girl joked, but her eyes said she wasn't buying it.

Neither was Maggie.

"I'll just use the hand chopper for now. Go finish with the frosting and open the doors. People should start arriving soon."

Jamie turned and headed back toward the front. Maggie bent and grabbed the manual chopper from a lower cabinet. This was going to suck. The manual chopper was killer on her hands. She transferred the nuts and worked the hand crank, grunting at the force she had to exert to crush those hard nuts into powder.

Forty minutes later, she had just finished frosting the macadamia cupcakes when Mort and Bonnie came in. The day was busy, as usual for a Sunday. She smiled and made small talk with her customers, but in the back of her mind, she couldn't get the image of that cut cord to go away. Was it really an accident? Had someone sliced the cord somehow and then tried to cover it up? Or had it been done deliberately? Who would do that, and why?

The only thing she could think of was her distributor, Pansy's. But it didn't make sense for it to be them. Why would they do it? Because she was a complaining customer? None of this made any sense.

Between the unanswered questions and steady run of customers, the day passed quickly. It wasn't until she closed up the shop and headed through the back to the indoor stairs to her apartment that she remembered Colton was coming over for dinner.

"Crap!"

Rushing, she headed to her kitchen, opened the fridge, and sighed in relief. There was a package of steaks left in there for Friday's and Saturday's dinners. Well, now they would both be Sunday dinner. Whipping up a quick marinade, she placed the steaks back in the fridge. She had some carrots she could steam with a little butter and dill.

Opening the cabinet, she spied her rice cooker. Some wild rice would top off the meal nicely. Getting it down, she went to plug it in, but paused, glancing at the cord. Perfectly fine, no cuts. She shook her head; she was being paranoid. *Great.* She plugged the cooker in.

When the water in the rice cooker was ready, she

poured in the rice and set it. The oven was preheating and the carrots were peeled and ready to be steamed. Now, for a quick hop in the shower.

She washed, using her lavender soap. There was no time to blow dry her hair so she kept it pinned up and out of the water. Five minutes later, she applied a little bit of eye shadow and mascara, then glanced at her makeup. This was not primping. Simply getting ready like she would for any normal dinner with a friend.

Another glance at her makeup, and she grabbed a tube of Sinfully Sweet red lipstick and applied it to her lips.

Okay, she was primping.

Before she could get too angry with herself for gussying up for her not-a-date dinner date, "We Are Family" blared from her cell. She smiled, picking up her phone. "Hey, Lizzy, what's up?"

"I fired his ass, and now I'm screwed."

Maggie laughed at her friend as she wandered over to her closet. What to wear, what to wear? "I'm assuming you're talking about your pastry chef?"

"*Ex*-pastry chef, and yes. He ran out of rum for the pudding flambé so he used Everclear. Everclear!"

She winced. "Oh no."

"I thought he was going to burn the restaurant down! The idiot. Who substitutes Everclear for rum? Can you believe it?"

She stared at the open closet. How could she have nothing to wear?

"Maggie? Are you listening to me?"

"What? Oh yeah, sorry. He's a dunce. You were right to fire him."

There has to be something in here besides jeans

and T-shirts.

"What are you doing?"

"Oh, nothing. Just…getting dressed."

"Maggie." Her best friend drew out her name in a no nonsense tone. Lizzy always could call her out on her bullshit.

"Okay, fine. Colton is coming over for dinner tonight, and I have nothing to wear."

"Wait, back that train up. Colton the cowboy is coming over for dinner?"

She flopped down on the bed and proceeded to relay everything about the weekend in the mountains. Her friend gasped and oooh'd through the story, making it far more dramatic in her Hollywood-raised mind than it actually had been.

"So, you invited him over for dinner to thank him?"

"Yes. Just to thank him. One friend thanking another. Nothing more."

"Mmmm hmmmm." Lizzy made the agreement sound far too sardonic.

"Really. I just want to thank him."

"Yeah and spank him," her friend replied with humor.

"Ugh, what am I doing?"

"You're having fun, and it's about time. Miles was a total D-bag, sweetie. Not all men are like that. It's been over a year. Time for you to start dating again."

"I am not dating Colton." But her best friend was right about her ex, Miles, being a D-bag. With a capital D.

"But you want to?"

She couldn't lie to Lizzy. "Maybe."

"Then put on those black capris that make your ass look fantastic and the green silk top that brings out your eyes. He won't stand a chance."

She laughed, but found herself going to her closet to grab that exact outfit.

"And call me tomorrow morning with the details. Or tomorrow afternoon if it goes *really* well."

She smiled, almost able to see her best friend winking and elbowing her. "Goodbye, Lizzy."

"Goodbye. Oh, and Maggie?"

"Yeah?"

A wicked giggle came over the line. "Save a horse, ride a cowboy!"

Chapter Eleven

There was a knock on her door at exactly six-thirty. *Gotta love a guy who shows up on time.*

No, she did not. She really needed to stop thinking of the L word and Colton in the same sentence.

A quick peek in the oven to check the steaks, and she hurried to the door, pausing to glance in the oval mirror on the wall. She had left her hair down; running a hand through it, she fluffed the wavy strands. It had a permanent kink because she'd kept it braided while working. Nothing ruined a delicious cupcake like finding a long, strange hair in it.

Maggie cursed herself for primping again. *This is not a date*, she reminded herself. No matter what Jamie, Lizzy, or anyone else thought.

It is not a date. It is not a date. It is not a—

She opened the front door, and there stood Colton dressed in dark, pressed jeans and a deep cobalt sweater that made his eyes impossibly bluer, and with a V-neck just deep enough to show a few manly strands of chest hair. His sandy-blond hair was long enough to just start the curl she knew it had when he grew it out. He had a sexy grin on his face and a bouquet of beautiful yellow daisies in his hand.

Crap, this might be a date.

He extended the flowers. "For you."

"Thank you, Colt. They're beautiful." She took the

bouquet, inhaling the soothing scent. "Yellow daisies are my favorite."

"I know. I remember."

She gazed up. He remembered? Once as children, they had been playing by the creek at his family's ranch. The bank had been dotted with dozens of yellow daisies. She'd mentioned they looked happy, like the sun. Colton helped her pick every flower, telling her she should put them in her room so when the sky was cloudy she would always have the sun with her. Ever since then, daises had been her favorite.

"May I come in?"

Maggie realized she was staring stupidly, lost in thought.

"Oh yes, of course. Come in." She stepped back to let him pass. "Dinner should be ready soon. I'll just go put these in water. Make yourself at home. Would you like a glass of wine?" she called, going to the kitchen. She was babbling, she knew, but he'd shown up with flowers. This was supposed to be a friendly dinner. Friends didn't bring each other flowers, did they? Lizzy had certainly never bought her any.

"Sounds great," his voice sounded from the living room.

She grabbed a light green vase from a shelf and filled it with water. Placing the flowers within, she inhaled their fragrance once again. He brought her yellow daisies; she couldn't keep the smile off her face.

Placing the vase in the center of the table, Maggie grabbed the open bottle of red wine off the counter where she'd left it to breath. Taking two glasses down from the rack above the toaster, she filled them each. Wine and flowers. This was inching closer and closer to a more-than-friends dinner.

Her apartment was small, but perfect for one person. Gran had moved in after her husband died. Long before Maggie was ever born. Its location above the shop was an added convenience. Wine glasses in hand, Maggie came around the partial wall between the kitchen and living room to see Colton inspecting the place.

"You haven't changed it much."

No, she hadn't. A few pieces of art. A picture of her mother, one of Lizzy, a new flat screen TV. The rest was just as Gran left it.

"It always felt like home. Didn't seem right to change it." She handed him a glass.

"Thanks."

He took a sip, and she watched in fascination at the way his Adam's apple bobbed when he swallowed the red liquid. *Oh damn*. She was in trouble.

"Is this the famous Lizzy?" he asked, pointing to a picture of her and Lizzy, arms around each other, big grins on their faces.

"Yeah. That was our trip to Catalina Island a year ago."

She stared at the picture. Lizzy had flawless, porcelain skin, smoky gray eyes, and strawberry blonde hair that women paid hundreds for the same look in Hollywood. As with everything on the woman, it was natural. She couldn't help but compare her own mousy brown hair and dull green eyes to her best friend's features. If she didn't love Lizzy so much, she'd hate her.

"She's beautiful, isn't she?"

"She's okay, but she can't hold a candle to you,

Magpie."

Wine glass inches from her mouth, she froze. She wasn't ugly, she knew that, but men were always flocking to Lizzy. Her best friend was beautiful, inside and out. Whenever she compared herself, Maggie always felt lacking.

"What, you don't think you're beautiful?" he asked.

She shook her head, unable to form words.

Setting his glass down on the coffee table, Colton took a step, eliminating the few feet between them. Placing a hand under her chin, he brought her face up. Her heart started beating a fast tempo in her chest. Bright blue eyes stared into hers, reminding her of a soft summer sky. Sunshine and blue skies, daisies and Colton's eyes. Sounded like a cheesy country song.

"You *are* beautiful, Maggie."

Her heart beat so fast she was afraid she was having a heart attack. She gripped her wine glass so hard she was sure it'd break.

Colton's hand stroked her jaw, then his fingers moved back to tangle in her hair.

She should stop him. This was only supposed to be a friendly thank you dinner.

When he gripped the back of her neck in a gentle hold, pulling her toward him, she knew she should really stop him, but she didn't. He was going to kiss her, and she was going to let him. She leaned toward him, closing her eyes. They were a hairsbreadth apart; she could feel his warm breath on her lips. Almost there—

The timer on the oven buzzed.

Maggie pulled back, snapping her eyes open with

shocked realization of what had almost happened.

Saved by the buzzer.

"Th-that's dinner. I better get it before it burns."

"Sure." He smiled, yet looked disappointed.

Join the club, buddy.

Spinning on her heels, she hurried toward her tiny kitchen. She had been *that* close to finally knowing if Colton Denning tasted as good as he looked. Now, the moment was gone, and Maggie mentally kicked herself for getting caught up in it. She did not want to start something with this man.

Did she?

"Can I help at all?"

"No thanks." She pulled the steaks from the oven. "It's all ready. I just have to plate."

"Smells delicious."

He smelled delicious. *Dammit.* She was so mixed up right now.

Transferring the steaks to the waiting plates, she added the rice and carrots. As she came back to the table, she saw that Colton had grabbed her wine glass from where she'd set it on the counter and placed it at her seat. Sexy and sweet. He just didn't play fair.

"Wow. It looks fantastic," he said as she set a plate in front of him.

"Thanks. It's nothing really. Just a mesquite lime marinade, some wild rice, and butter dill carrots." She set her own plate down and took her seat.

Picking up his fork and knife, he cut a piece of the steak and placed it in his mouth. A deep groan rumbled from his chest as he closed his eyes and chewed. "Oh my God, Magpie. This is amazing!"

She felt heat rise on her cheeks, ridiculously

pleased by his compliment. "It's nothing really."

"Smart, sexy, makes killer cupcakes, and she can cook? How the hell hasn't some guy snatched you up already?"

It was a throwaway question. An innocent remark meant to be taken hypothetically, but it struck a chord. She tended to be drawn to losers. Steve the moocher, Marv the mama's boy, Jess the "can't we be friends with benefits" boozer, and a mess of first dates who thought dinner was a free pass to panty town. Not even if she ordered the lobster, losers. Then her last relationship had been a mess of lies and betrayals. Her luck in men ran like her current luck in life. Poorly.

"Sorry, did I hit a nerve?" he asked when she didn't respond.

"No, it's fine."

He sat back in his chair. "Bad breakup?"

"I thought you weren't supposed to talk about exes on a first date."

"Is this a date, Magpie?"

Crap, why had she said that? It *wasn't* a date. Isn't that what she told Jamie and Lizzy? They disagreed, but still. Just because she wanted it to be a date didn't mean Colton thought it was a date.

But, he brought her flowers.

"No—I didn't—I mean, it's not—"

"Because I want it to be," he said, interrupting her stammering. "I want it to be a date. Don't you?"

Did she?

Yes.

No.

Ahhhh!

She was going insane. Could she handle letting

herself fall for Colton again and risk her heart breaking into a million pieces when he found someone new? He may call her beautiful and amazing now, but she knew who she was—a plain Jane, ordinary woman. How could a woman like her keep Colton's interest when he was so…so…well, just look at the man. Way out of her league, and always had been.

"Why did you leave?" he asked softly.

"What?"

"Why did you leave after that summer and never come back?"

She glanced up. His dinner was half-eaten. She'd hardly touched hers. Those sexy lips turned down. His usual happy demeanor was gone. The teasing, flirtatious cowboy was nowhere to be seen, and in his place was a confused—and if she wasn't mistaken—hurt, man.

"You barely spoke to me that last summer, and then you never came back until your grandmother died. You didn't call, didn't write. Did I do something to upset you?"

"Colt, no. Of course not." His prissy girlfriend had.

"Then why did you leave without saying goodbye or staying in touch? I thought we were friends."

Guilt swam in her belly. The delicious food she had cooked looked as appetizing as cow dung. She stared across the table at the man who was once her childhood friend. Those clear blue eyes held so much pain. His brow drew down, causing harsh lines to cross his handsome face. Had she actually hurt him by leaving and never saying goodbye? Remorse formed a solid lump in her throat, making it hard to swallow.

"I didn't think you'd care," she shrugged.

"That's bullshit." Anger replaced the pained expression on his face. "We were friends…best friends."

"I was the annoying little kid who followed you around everywhere like a puppy."

"Did I ever give you the impression I found you annoying?"

"Well, no, but people thought…"

"Thought what?"

She twisted her hands together as his voice rose. She hated seeing him so upset. Hated that she was the cause of it. "Some people said I was just an annoying little kid globbing on to you, and you were too nice to tell me to get lost."

His jaw clenched. "*Who* said that?"

"Natalie," she mumbled.

"Who?"

"Natalie," she answered louder, getting angry herself. This was supposed to be a nice evening, and he was ruining it with almost kisses, date talk, and memories of the past. "Your perfect, cheerleader girlfriend, Natalie Brake."

"Natalie? She told you I wanted you to get lost?" His brows rose incredulously. "And you believed her?"

"Well, no, not really. But she didn't like me hanging out with you and…jeez, Colt, it's ancient history. Can't you just drop it?"

"No," he said, a little louder than necessary. "Natalie is a bitch. Everyone knows that, even Natalie."

"Then why did you go out with her?"

"I don't know. We're all idiots about dating at some point in our lives right?"

Yup, she had been a big idiot a year ago.

Colton stood, coming around the table. He placed a hand on the back of her chair, the other in front of her and leaned forward, boxing her in. His face was inches from hers. His warm breath whispered across her lips. It was slightly intimidating.

And completely tempting.

"Look, Maggie, you were my friend, one of my *best* friends. When you left and never contacted me I—I thought I'd done something to hurt you."

He had. He started dating someone else.

"I felt guilty, then I felt angry that you never explained what I did."

"You didn't do anything," she said softly.

"I know that now."

"So…we're still friends?"

He stared at her with such intensity she found she couldn't look away. That sky blue gaze captured her, refusing to let her hide. And what a deliciously, sexy gaze it was.

"What I feel for you now feels like more than friendship, Maggie."

Oh.

"You came back into town, and I thought we could be friends again, pick up where we left off. But after the other night, after spending time with you. I don't think I can do just friendship."

Oh my.

"So, I'll ask again." He leaned in closer until their noses were almost touching. "Do you want this to be a date?"

The air left her lungs. She couldn't breathe with him so close. Couldn't think. Could only utter the one word she kept locked inside ever since the day she came back to Peak Town and saw Colton Denning again. "Yes."

"Good. Then it *is* a date." A smile curled his lips. "Now, let's talk about something more pleasant and finish our dinner."

He leaned closer, gently brushing his lips over hers in the barest of kisses. Her entire body tingled from that one point of contact. His lips were soft, yet firm, delicious and addicting. She knew this one small kiss was just the beginning. Now that she had a taste of Colton Denning, she would need more. It was a terrifying thought, but as he pulled away from that too brief kiss, her body screamed, *Yeehaw!*

Chapter Twelve

Breaking contact, reluctantly, Colton retook his seat. Though Maggie had agreed this was a date, she still twisted her hands together. He needed to take things slow. Just a small kiss. Because he found he couldn't be that close to Maggie and not kiss her. He'd kept it light and brief, but it was still a sucker punch to the gut. Imagining what it would feel like to *really* kiss her...oh man, he couldn't wait. But he would, because she was nervous and still unsure. When he truly kissed her, he wanted her to be as sure and hungry for it as he.

Discovering what Natalie said to her all those years ago made him furious. He knew his ex-girlfriend hadn't liked him hanging around Maggie when they were younger, but he just chalked it up to teenage jealousy. He had no idea his ex actually threatened the poor girl. But it was in the past now—like his relationship with Natalie. This was the present. He wanted to focus on that and his new relationship with the strong, sexy, amazing woman in front of him.

"So, tell me more about your gran's recipe box, and why you needed it so badly. You never really got around to explaining that yesterday."

"What?"

Big green eyes gave him a startled look. Her fingers reached up to her lips; the lips he had just kissed. Then she scowled and dropped her hand. It might not be very enlightened of him, but he liked the fact he could make her forget everything with just a simple kiss.

"Well, the truth is, business has dropped a bit since I took over. Looking at Gran's books, it seems to have been steadily declining for a few years."

He shook his head. "I understand. The boarding and breeding has been going well, but our trail riding has suffered since the economy took a turn. It's coming back around, but people tend to cut out the extracurricular activities when they have to count pennies."

"Same goes for their sweet tooth." She nodded. "I've been trying to branch out with my marketing more. I figure a good online presence is a necessity these days, especially for grabbing the tourist crowd."

He agreed. Over half of their trail riding business came from online referrals. His parents had been lost dealing with a website for the ranch and the online advertising. Luckily, his cousin, Joe, was a computer nerd and had been programming since the age of ten. Colton and Dade knew the basics of computers and web use, but programming was out of their reaches. Joe lived in Denver now, working in the DTC as a freelance web designer. They hired him a few years ago to handle all their online needs, and so far, things were working out great.

"There's this blogger—Guilty Pleasures: A Cross Country Food Journey is her site. She travels all over the United States reviewing unique restaurants and eateries. I saw she was planning a trip to Aspen and contacted her. I convinced her to come up here to review my shop. She really liked the 'handed down through the generations' story, so she agreed. She's coming in less than two weeks, and the recipe I planned I can't make anymore because my distributor is an ass."

Maggie had rushed through the speech, but he locked on to that last bit. "What's going on with your distributor?"

"I've been having problems with my deliveries for a few months now. First, they were delivered at the wrong time, then the wrong product came, and now orders are being cancelled. It's a giant mess, and they keep telling me it's my fault."

"That's not very professional."

"That's what I said!"

She took a healthy sip of her wine. Noticing the glass was almost empty, he grabbed the bottle and refilled it, then after a moment of thought, refilled his as well.

"So, you needed your grandmother's recipe box for new ideas?"

"Yes. Since I can't do the recipe I wanted, I figure I can work the 'passed down through generations' angle and make one of Gran's recipes. She did make some killer cupcakes."

Grabbing her now full glass, she smiled. The woman had a beautiful smile. He hadn't seen enough of it since she came back to town.

Time to change that.

He raised his wine. "I'll toast to that."

They clinked glasses, pausing the conversation to drink to her grandmother.

"I hope you're looking for a new distributor. You shouldn't put up with poor service like that."

"Oh I am. Especially after..." she tapered off, not

finishing her thought.

"After what?"

Pushing the last few carrots around on her plate, Maggie averted her gaze. "It's nothing."

Bullshit—she was twisting her hands again. "Magpie?"

Dropping her fork, she glanced up, her brows drawn down, mouth tight. "Look. If we're calling this a date—"

"It *is* a date," he insisted.

"Fine, since this is a date…"

He grinned. "Thank you."

"You have to stop with the nickname."

"You don't like it?"

She shifted in her seat. "It's not that. It just, it makes me feel like a kid."

He roamed his gaze over her body, eating up every sexy, womanly inch of her. "Trust me, sweetheart, you are all woman. But I'll try not to call you Magpie anymore."

"Thank you."

"For now."

She rolled her eyes, but the grin stayed on her face.

Happy that he put it there, he took another bite of dinner. "Now tell me, *Maggie*, what else did your distributor do?" Her hands started to twist together again, and he tensed.

"Well, I can't be sure. I mean, it's only speculation, but I think one of the delivery people might have tried to sabotage my shop."

His fork fell to his plate with a clatter. "What?"

"I'm not one-hundred percent sure, but today I went to use my electric chopper and the cord had been cut and glued back on. Jamie didn't know anything about it, and I sure as heck didn't do it."

He rubbed a hand along his jaw in thought. "No one else goes back there?"

She shook her head. "No. Just me, Jamie, and the delivery people."

"And you don't think Jamie accidently did it and lied because she doesn't want to get in trouble?"

"No." Her head shook emphatically. "She's a great kid. If she made a mistake, she'd fess up to it. Plus…" She hesitated.

He didn't like where this was going. "What?"

"The cord was cut clean. Not ripped or frayed as if by accident. It was a smooth slice like someone cut it with a knife. Purposefully."

That wasn't good. Not good at all. So much for light dinner date conversation. The thought of someone deliberately trying to harm Maggie's shop made his gut burn.

"Why would your delivery person want to sabotage you?"

She shrugged, pushing her plate back. The dinner portion of the night was clearly over.

"I don't know. Maybe I complained one too many times and they want to get back at me? Maybe it was just someone having a bad day, they needed to vent their frustration on someone, and my shop was a handy target. Or maybe it really was an accident and they didn't want to get in trouble with their supervisor, so they attempted to fix it."

He doubted that. By the look on her face and the nervous way she had started to fidget with her hands again, he bet she doubted it, too.

"It doesn't matter anyway. I'm getting a new distributor tomorrow. I'll find the perfect recipe from Gran, wow the blogger, and then people will come flocking to the shop."

There's my girl. Maggie's can-do attitude had always impressed him.

"Wow, I'm just full of fun first date chatter, aren't I. You must be counting the minutes 'til you can escape."

"Actually," he began at her self-deprecating laugh. "I'm having a great time, but what do you say we take our wine into the living room and watch a movie?"

She smiled, and his breath left his lungs. Damn, she was beautiful. A sight to behold. Her entire face lit up when she smiled.

"Sounds great, let me just get these dishes." She stood and started to grab for the plates.

Reaching out, he placed his hands over hers. "I got them. You go pick out a movie."

"Oh no, I—"

"Sweetheart, you know my momma would skin me alive if I didn't take care of the dishes after a beautiful woman cooked me one of the finest meals I've had in years."

Her lips pressed together, trying to hide a smile. "Flattery still won't get you free cupcakes, Colt."

Still holding onto her hand, he stood. "Then maybe this will."

Pulling her to him, he captured her lips with his own. She tasted like rich red wine and heaven. Her lips were soft and so damn sweet. The hand he clutched tightened in his grasp while the other fisted in his shirt, dragging him closer.

Yes.

Placing his free hand on her lower back, he pressed her tighter against him. She gasped, and he took the opportunity of her open mouth. Plunging his tongue inside, he tasted her, fully tasted her. *Damn*, and she tasted good.

Her tongue came out to meet his. She wasn't shy or hesitant, not his Magpie. She met his kiss with full gusto, rubbing that sweet little body of hers against his while their tongues simulated what their bodies wanted to do. If they didn't stop soon, he would forget his mother's lesson about doing the dishes, and he'd be doing Maggie instead.

As much as he wanted that, it was too soon. He needed to take things slow with her. Do this thing right. She deserved that.

Reluctantly, Colton pulled away. Her lips clung to his, and he kissed them softly once, twice, before pulling back.

They were both breathing heavily. Maggie's eyes were closed, cheeks pink and warm. Her lips were parted, and her tongue peeked out to lick her bottom lip, as if savoring the taste of him still clinging to her. He groaned at the sexy little move.

Sometimes being a gentleman sucked.

"Okay, that will get you a free cupcake."

He laughed, kissing the end of her nose. "Go pick a movie, and let me take care of these dishes. We can discuss cupcakes later."

Her eyes opened. She grinned, turned, and walked into the living room. He waited until she was out of sight before reaching down to adjust himself.

Hot damn, the woman can kiss.

Had he ever been this hard just from a kiss? He didn't think so.

Grabbing the plates off the table, he decided to forgo her small dishwasher. He needed to give himself a minute. Turning on the tap he set the water to cold, but with the taste of Maggie still on his lips, he didn't think it was going to help much.

Chapter Thirteen

Her luck was finally turning around.

Maggie smiled as her feet pounded the dirt road. It was Wednesday, and she had already accomplished so much this week. She found a new distributor who not only promised to alert her to any and all changes on her orders, but also quoted her a price ten percent cheaper than she had been paying with Pansy's. She'd also been going through Gran's recipes and narrowed her choices down to a few scrumptious cupcakes sure to impress the blogger.

Best of all, Colton had called and asked if he could take her to dinner Friday night.

Their friendly dinner-turned-into-a-date had been three days ago, ended by watching another silly horror movie and cuddling on her couch. He'd then given her another toe-curling, body-melting kiss at her door before leaving. He also stopped by the shop Tuesday morning to pick up a cupcake order and steal a few more kisses.

Friday couldn't come fast enough.

The sun was just rising and the sky bright blue with not a cloud in sight. Even the weather had taken a turn for the better. She could hardly see her breath anymore as she jogged toward Merle's for her morning cup of coffee.

"Morning, Ellen," she said cheerfully as she

stepped into the warm diner.

"Hey, Maggie. How was your run?"

Ellen pulled a mug down from a high shelf and began filling it.

"Great. I'm glad the snow seems to be over for the season. The days just keep getting warmer."

Slightly wrinkled cheeks chuckled as the older woman set the steaming mug of coffee in front of her. Maggie sat at the counter, wrapping her hands around the warm cup of liquid heaven.

"Don't let the good weather fool you. Happens every year. Just when you think it's safe to put away the hats and gloves, bam! Two feet of snow in June."

Her mouth dropped open in horror. "No."

"Yup. Every June. Like clockwork."

Lifting the mug to her lips, she inhaled the strong brew. *Oh well.* Things were going so well at the moment not even the impending threat of snow could bring her down. Yup. Life was good.

"Well, look who it is," a snide, high-pitched voice said from behind her.

Crap, spoke too soon. Taking a fortifying sip from her coffee, Maggie turned in her seat to face a very peeved Natalie Brake.

"Hello, Natalie. How are you?"

"Cut the crap, Evans. Just what do you think you're doing?"

She glanced at her mug then back up. "Um, having coffee. What does it look like?"

The prissy woman waved an angry hand through the air. "No, I mean just what do you think you're doing with Colton?"

Uh oh. She knew this was going to get around town

sooner rather than later. Peak Town was worse than TMZ when it came to gossip.

"What's going on between Colton and me is our business. Not yours or anyone else's." She glanced around the restaurant. Sure enough, they had everyone's attention.

"He's just paying attention to you because you're new in town. A novelty."

She snorted. "I've been coming to Peak Town since I was eight. Just because I live here permanently now does not make me 'new in town.' And Colton and I have known each other for years. I'm not a novelty."

"No, you're a pathetic little clinger who always had puppy dog eyes for him. He's only paying attention to you because he feels bad that your mom and grandmother died, leaving you with no one."

Behind her, Ellen sucked in a sharp breath. Maggie agreed—that comment had been a little below the belt. Even for Natalie.

"You're just a charity case. Stop playing the sympathy card and leave Colton alone." She pointed a long skinny finger in her face.

Maggie rose from her seat. Natalie had threatened her once, but she was no longer that shy fourteen-year-old girl. She was a strong, successful woman who owned her own business. This pathetic woman would not intimidate her now.

"Shove it, Natalie. I'm not playing anything. You're just pissed because you had a great guy and ruined it by spreading your legs for some drunken frat boy. You treated Colton like crap and lost him. That's not my fault. It's yours. So stop making me the bad guy and go look in a mirror."

The thin, hard face turned bright red. Anger seethed out of every pore. She looked like one of those cartoon characters. All she needed was the steam coming out of her ears. If Maggie weren't so angry, she might find it funny.

"Oh, and I'd get that finger out of my face unless you want to lose it."

The perfectly manicured hand lowered at Maggie's dark tone. Someone at a back table coughed, breaking the tension. The angry woman looked around, only just realizing they had an audience. With Natalie, appearances were everything.

With an obvious dig for some form of composure, she backed up a step. "Yes, well, all I'm saying is don't get too happy in la la land. Colton Denning is a love 'em and leave 'em type of guy. He'll get tired of you in a week or two. You'll see."

With that, the snobby, silicone-enhanced harpy turned and headed out the door. The entire diner remained silent. Nothing like a morning show to start the day.

"Sorry about that, Ellen." Maggie turned back to her coffee. It didn't smell so wonderful anymore.

"You have nothing to be sorry about." The older woman glared at the door. "That girl has always been a witch with a capital B. What she did to that sweet boy still eats at me. Who would cheat on a boy as nice and handsome as Colton Denning?"

Got her. She had always thought Natalie a world-class idiot. If Maggie had Colton, she would never hurt him.

Wait, I do have Colton.

But, for how long?

One thing the witch with a B had said struck a chord. The man *did* flirt a lot, and she knew he had a bit of a reputation with the ladies. He didn't date much in town; he preferred tourists. Because they were temporary? A guaranteed fling? Where did that leave her? How soon before he got bored with her and moved on? She lived in LA for most of her life, but that did not make her some exciting Hollywood starlet. She was as boring as apple pie. How long before the flirtatious cowboy got tired of her?

"I see what you're doing," Ellen said, giving her a stern look. "Stop it. Don't you think a minute on anything that idiot girl said. She's just trying to rattle you because of her own jealousy. Fool treated the poor man like dirt and still wants to claim him as her own."

She could understand Natalie's jealousy. What woman wouldn't want to claim him?

"You just focus on you and Colton. Don't let others come creeping in trying to ruin what you two have."

"It was just one dinner."

The kind, round face broke out in a smile. "It's the beginning. Beginnings are always fun. Tricky, but fun. Enjoy it, and to hell with what everyone else tells you. As you said, it's not their business." She'd voiced the last part louder. A few heads turned; most started mumbling as if they were focused on their own issues instead of spying on hers.

She downed the rest of her coffee and tossed a couple of bucks on the countertop.

"Thanks. I better go open the shop."

"Anytime, sweetie," she called as Maggie left the diner.

Ellen was right. It was nobody's business. Only two people needed to know what she and Colton were doing. Everyone else could go take a flying leap.

Despite her self-assurance, worry still crept in. Because honestly, one of those two people had no idea what the hell she was doing.

****

A slamming metal sound woke her, like something hit the dumpster outside. A wild animal rooting around in the garbage? Didn't bears wake up from hibernation about this time?

Oh God, bears!

She did not want to deal with a bear. Maybe it was just a raccoon. A cute, cuddly, rabies-infested raccoon. She'd take a rabies shot over a bear mauling any day.

Maggie tried to open her eyes, but it felt like they were glued shut. *So tired.*

Everything felt kind of hazy. Was she even awake? Maybe she was dreaming about the raccoon bear. Good, she didn't feel like waking up anyway. Except...*holy smokes*, what was that smell? It smelled like the time she was five and hid decorated Easter *eggs* all over the house then forgot about them for a month. How was she to know they were supposed to be hard-boiled?

Something pricked in the back of her mind. Rotten eggs were bad right? She was a baker. You couldn't make cupcakes with rotten eggs. She needed to get up. It was important. She had no idea why, she just knew she had to get up.

Struggling, she finally managed to open her eyes. And oh, she felt sick. Like she was going to hurl sick.

Grabbing her cell from the bedside table, Maggie tried to focus on the screen, but her vision was blurry for some reason.

"Call Colton." Her attempt at a yell was a weak croak into the phone. She prayed the voice app actually worked this time.

"Calling Colton Denning," the robotic voice responded. When the sound of ringing came over the line, she sent up a silent thanks.

"Hey, sweetheart. I was just thinking about you."

The deep timber of his voice made her lips tilt in a smile and her head go fuzzy. Wait, that wasn't why her mind was cloudy. Something was wrong. Something woke her.

"Colton?" she gasped out.

"What's wrong?" His tone changed from sensual to concerned in an instant.

"I don't know. I think…a bear outside in my dumpster."

"A bear?"

The nausea was getting worse, and her head started to spin. "Yeah…something's wrong. I don't feel…" She tapered off, unable to form the right words anymore.

"Hang on, sweetheart. I'm coming."

Maggie heard Colton shout at his brother to call the sheriff.

"Just…a…animal. Probably…raccoon…rabies."

"Maggie!" he shouted through the phone.

Ouch. That hurt her ears.

"Stay on the line. Dade's calling the sheriff. Don't go outside. Stay in your apartment, but open a window."

A window? Why did he want her to open a window? Couldn't raccoons climb brick?

"Maggie!" he shouted again, but his voice was drowned out by the sudden alarm blaring from her ceiling.

Now that *really* hurt her ears.

"Maggie, answer me. What's going on?"

She tried to respond, but the phone dropped from her hands. Blackness enveloped her as she fell toward her bed.

Chapter Fourteen

"Maggie!" Colton swore, but the line had gone dead. "Shit, shit, *shit!*"

He tossed the phone on the passenger seat and slammed his hand on the steering wheel of his truck. He could hear sirens in the distance. Peak Town only had one fire truck, and Dade had been dialing the sheriff before he made it out the front door of the ranch. He knew where those sirens were headed.

He pressed his foot harder on the gas pedal. He lived ten minutes from Maggie, but he was going to make it there in five.

She hadn't sounded right. Fear had been in her voice, and it slurred as if she was stoned. Maggie didn't do drugs. Hell, the woman barely drank. Even the other night at dinner, she stopped after just two glasses of wine.

His heart was in his throat as he turned down the main road and saw flashing lights in front of her place. The sheriff, fire department, and Peak Town's only ambulance were all parked right at her shop.

Oh God, no!

Slamming on the brakes, he shoved the gear into park, not even bothering to turn off his truck before jumping out and racing toward the chaos.

"Maggie!" he screamed as he scanned the group of professionals and rubberneckers conglomerated around the shop.

Heads turned toward him and someone waved.

Maggie.

Colton swore in relief. She sat in the back of the ambulance, an oxygen mask covering her face; an EMT checked her vitals. She looked annoyed, but, thankfully, okay. She had either not been asleep or had dressed because she was wearing jeans, a long sleeved shirt and a pair of old sneakers.

He rushed to her side, running his hand over her hair, face, arms, checking to make sure she was all right.

The paramedic huffed in irritation. "Sir, I need to check her. Please step back."

She waved the young man off. "I'm fine. I feel much better now. Thank you."

"What happened?" he asked, gripping her hand tightly in his, refusing to let go.

The man sighed with annoyance, but continued with his examination.

"Gas leak," Sheriff Jake Ryder answered, walking up to them.

"A gas leak?"

"Oven hose was ripped clean from the wall." The sheriff pulled a note pad and pen from his breast pocket. His dark brown eyes focused on Maggie. "Did you do any moving today? Shift the appliances around? Maybe move the oven to clean behind it?"

Her eyes went wide with shock, and she removed the mask from her face. "No. I keep a clean shop, and we don't do any heavy cleaning for another month."

Ryder nodded, writing in his notebook. "You said you heard a noise. That was what woke you?"

"Yeah, it sounded like something banging against the dumpster. I thought it was a raccoon or bear or something."

And she had called him. Colton hated this happened, but the fact she sensed danger and called him, soothed some of his raging emotions.

The sheriff nodded again. "The window just above the dumpster was open. Do you normally keep it unlocked?"

Her brow furrowed. "Well, yeah. It's like eight feet off the ground and two feet wide. A bear couldn't fit through that, and no way a raccoon could jump that high."

"No," Ryder agreed, absently rubbing the back of his neck. It sent his long, dark braid over his shoulder, and he flicked the hair back again. "But a raccoon could climb up the drain pipe and stretch over to the window. It's highly unlikely, but not impossible. If the window was left open, even a crack, a hungry animal could get a whiff of your sweet cupcakes and think it was perfect for a midnight snack. Once inside, it could have scrambled behind the oven and pulled the hose out accidently."

Colton shook his head, lips turning down in a frown. That was quite the stretch the sheriff was reaching for.

"But, I never open that window. Yes, it might be unlocked, but not opened."

"Maybe Jamie opened it."

Maggie made a sound of disbelief. "Please, she's shorter than me."

"Could it have been sabotage?" he asked, joining in on the conversation.

Ryder looked at him. "Why do you ask that?"

Mossy green eyes gave him a stern warning, but he ignored it.

"Maggie's been having some issues lately."

"Colton!" she admonished. "It's nothing. Just some problems with my distributor, but I got a new one now and everything's fine."

Obviously, things were not fine. He didn't care if she didn't want her troubles getting out. Her life had been in danger. If she didn't tell the sheriff everything, he would.

"What problems?" Ryder asked, pen to paper.

Maggie growled, sending him a death glare. Didn't bother him. She could be pissed at him for making a big deal about this all she wanted. When it came to her safety, it *was* a big deal.

"Nothing. They just screwed up one too many orders, and I got tired of it. I complained. They didn't care. I switched distributors. End of story."

"What about the chopper?" he prompted.

She glared at him harder.

The sheriff glanced up from his notes. "What chopper?"

"My electric chopper had a cut cord. It looked like someone sliced through it then glued it back on so I wouldn't notice. And before you ask, no it wasn't Jamie."

He nodded, but kept writing. Colton had every faith Ryder would look into everything Maggie told him.

"It was probably just an accident. One of the delivery guys was moving something and cut through the cord then tried to fix it so he wouldn't get in trouble. They most likely knew I was complaining lately and didn't want to give me any more fodder."

"Or," Ryder said, pausing in his writing. "They were angry that you were making them look bad and decided to get back at you."

That's what *he* had been thinking. People did stupid things when they got angry. Especially when their jobs were in jeopardy. He was glad to see the sheriff on the same page as him.

"That's absurd. Besides, I switched my distributor, so they had no reason to want to mess with me. Not that they were." She motioned to the high window above the dumpster. "Anyway, no one could fit through that window."

"If they were small enough they could," the sheriff mused, staring at the rectangular opening.

"Great. I'm being sabotaged by a gang of angry children because I won't give them free cupcakes."

Colton dipped his head to hide a smile. Her sarcastic humor always got to him, and the fact she still had her spunk took some of the worry off his chest. She coughed again, the sound tearing into his chest like a knife.

"Ma'am you really need to put the mask back on," the EMT said, interrupting their conversation.

"Oh, I'm fine. My head barely hurts and the nausea is gone."

"Do as he says, Magpie."

"You are not the boss of me, Colton Denning," she grumbled, but put the mask back on. "And I thought we agreed to retire the nickname," her mask muffled voice added.

He smiled, placing a soft kiss on her forehead.

"You're right, sweetheart. I'm sorry."

She rolled her eyes, but through the clear plastic he could see the hint of a smile at the corner of her lips.

One of the firefighters rushed over to Ryder and spoke softly with him. The sheriff nodded, turning back to them as the man left.

"They've shut off the gas and are fixing the hose. You should leave all the doors and windows in the shop open tonight to air the place out. Same goes for your upstairs apartment. The gas got up there, too, which is why your alarm went off."

"Why didn't the alarm in the shop go off?" Colton asked, since she still had the mask on.

"They're checking that now. Could be a dead battery or a faulty detector. Have you checked the batteries recently?" The sheriff directed the question at Maggie. She nodded. "Okay. I'll post a watch tonight, make sure no one messes with your place while we air it out, but you should go get some rest. And not at your apartment. It's not safe."

"You can stay with me." The words left his mouth without a thought.

It wasn't like she had many options. The nearest hotel was over ten miles away. They had only been on one date. It was early in their relationship, dating, whatever they were doing, but they had been friends for a long time. He would never leave a friend out in the cold.

And there was no way he was letting Maggie out of his sight tonight. Not after what had happened. The woman kept scaring the life out of him.

She glanced up, eyes wide, hands twisting.

"Dade took the master bedroom so his old room is

a guest room now. You can bunk in there as long as you need."

Relief filled her eyes. Relief...at his offer or at not having to sharing his bed?

She wanted to. He could tell by the way she arched into him when they kissed, rubbing the sweet little body of hers all over him. Making him crazy.

Yeah, she wanted him, but she was also nervous. Of going too fast? He'd be a liar if he didn't admit to the same thing. Whatever this thing with Maggie, it was special. *She* was special. He didn't want to screw it up, and if that meant taking it slow, he was fine with that. He'd just have to get used to cold showers for a little while.

"Thanks, Colt." She turned to the EMT. "Can I take this off now?"

"How do you feel?" He placed a stethoscope on her back, listening to her breathing.

"Just peachy, you?"

The man didn't appreciate her humor. Colton thought she was a riot.

"You're fine," the EMT said, taking the mask off her. "Just be sure to drink lots of water and get plenty of fresh air the next few days."

With that, the guy packed his stuff up. Colton led her out and away from the ambulance as the young man closed the doors and drove off.

"I'm going to need the name and number of your distributor, and I'm going to talk to Jamie Thompson tomorrow. Just to confirm everything. I don't want to miss anything." Ryder handed over his pen and paper.

She wrote down her old distributor information and handed it back.

"You might want to think about keeping the shop closed tomorrow. Don't want any lingering gas making people sick," the sheriff suggested.

She shook her head. "I already had to close Saturday due to the weather. I can't afford another day."

Stubborn woman. How could she ignore the fact she almost died, again? He wrapped an arm around her waist, pulling her close. "How about a half-day? Give it the morning to finish airing out then open in the afternoon. That's when most people come in anyway right? The after school crowd."

She sighed. "I guess I could do that. It's already after midnight, and I could really use the morning to sleep in."

"It's settled then." Leaning down, he brushed his lips softly over hers. "You need to grab anything before we go?"

"Do you have something I can sleep in?"

His mind whirled with tantalizing possibilities. "I'm sure I can rustle something up." He waggled his eyebrows, and she laughed as he intended her to.

Ryder cleared his throat, reminding them he was still standing two feet away. "I'll set a few of my guys up here for the night. Tell them not to leave until you return tomorrow."

"Thanks, Sheriff."

Ryder nodded and put his notepad away. "You think of anything else, just give me a call. I'll let you know if I find anything more." He inclined his head to Colton. "Take care."

He returned the other man's nod. Maggie trembled slightly in his arms. He may not have any idea what they were doing, but he knew one thing for sure. He cared about this woman, and if anyone was trying to hurt her, they'd have to go through him first.

****

No one noticed her, just another curious townsperson peering around the emergency personnel to see what was happening. The rumors were already starting to circulate.

"An animal broke into the bakery."

"I heard it was a bear."

"My mom said she heard an alarm go off. Was it a fire?"

"No. I think it was a gas leak. Faulty machinery or something."

Or me.

She had almost broken her neck crawling through that window. Twisted an ankle when she fell back out onto the dumpster. Good thing it had been there or she would have snapped the damn thing in half.

But it had all been worth it.

When a fireman carried a pale, unconscious, Maggie Evans out in his arms, she almost squealed with glee. Then the EMT had brought the bitch around, and her joy withered. It wasn't as if she wanted Maggie dead, not really. She just wanted the woman gone.

Dead is a kind of gone.

Maggie was a resilient, stupid bitch. After months of messing with her business, she couldn't believe the woman was still determined to stay where she wasn't wanted. Screwing with her orders had just been the beginning, a subtle warning to close up shop and go back where she came from.

Perhaps too subtle.

Cutting the chopper cord had been more direct. It was just pure luck the bakery door had been left open that day. Easy to sneak inside, cut the cord, glue it back, and sneak out while Maggie had been busy up front with customers. But even that act hadn't caused the cupcake maker to rethink her decision to stay in Peak Town.

Time to be more aggressive.

If hurting her business wasn't going to get Maggie to leave then maybe attacking her directly would.

Tonight was only the start.

If the little bitch didn't take the hint and leave soon, she'd have to up the ante. Maggie Evans needed to leave, and she would make that happen.

Any way necessary.

Chapter Fifteen

The ten-minute drive out to the Denning ranch felt like an hour. It probably just seemed that way because she was tired, her head hurt, and she was starting to feel a little silly for calling Colton. Any sane person would have called the cops or animal control. What did she do? Called the man she'd gone on one date with.

Can you say clingy?

Sure, they were friends. Had been friend. Were still friends? Oh crap, she had no idea what was going on. Her business was either suffering from some major coincidental problems, or someone was intentionally messing with her. And here she was, getting all panicky over what to call this thing with Colton.

How had she let Lizzy talk her into this? She should've kept the dinner friendly and not agreed with that whole stupid "I want it to be a date" thing he brought up. She had given into her inner wants, and now, she had no clue what was going on.

Great job self.

The truck pulled up to the ranch. The porch light was on in welcome as well as a few house lights, but everything else was dark. It was darker out here than in town. No streetlights. Just a thousand twinkling stars, lighting up the night sky like sparkling diamonds across black velvet. Colton had called Dade just before they left and given his brother the brief details.

Including the fact she was coming home with him.

Putting the truck in park, Colton turned the keys, shutting off the ignition. He reached for the door handle, but before he could exit the truck, she reached out and placed a hand on his shoulder.

"Colt, I'm sorry."

He turned back with a puzzled expression. "For what?"

She brought her hand back to her lap, twisting her fingers together. "For dragging you out of bed in the middle of the night. For having to crash with you, again. For bringing you into my problems when we've only had one date. I really can take care of myself, I swear."

He was silent for a moment. She ducked her head, sure he was going to tell her she was too much trouble, too dependent, that the first date was the last.

"Don't be an idiot, Maggie."

Her head snapped up. "Excuse me?"

"First of all, I wasn't in bed yet. Second, it's never a problem to lend a hand to someone in need. Third, it doesn't matter if we've had one date or a hundred dates. We're friends first and forever. I'm *always* here for you, no matter what."

A hundred dates? That sounded promising.

"And lastly," he added, his brows drawing together. "You are the most capable person I know. You always have been. Even as a kid, you had to do everything yourself. Which is why Clementine knocked you over when you tried to mount her from the wrong side."

She remembered that. Her first time riding alone. She'd wanted to get on the horse herself. Only her pride had been hurt. Maggie smiled.

Hands came up, cradling her face. Colton stroked her cheeks with his thumbs. She shivered, and it had nothing to do with the cool night air. Those hypnotic blue eyes stared so deeply into her own, it felt as though he was looking into her soul.

"The only thing you have to apologize for is scaring another ten years off my life. This is the second time in a week you've nearly stopped my heart." His voice dropped to a husky timber. "Quit doing that."

Then his lips were on hers, soft, but demanding. He kissed her like she was oxygen and he was a dying man. His tongue pressed along the seam of her lips, and she opened willingly. She brought her hands up to rest on his broad, strong shoulders. Man, did he taste good. Like coffee and sex. Pure Colton.

Maggie made a little moan of delight when his hands started to move down, roaming over her neck and shoulders. One found its way to her waist, pulling her closer in the small confine of the truck. The other moved down to cover her right breast. She gasped as his rough hand stroked and squeezed, sending a thousand tingling shock waves racing though her entire body.

The hand at her waist moved down to her thigh, and in a move she only thought happened in the movies, he pulled her to him, lifting her leg over until she was straddling his lap. The steering wheel dug into her back, but she didn't care.

With both hands free now, he ran his palm under her shirt. The rough feel of skin on skin felt glorious. Shivers ran up and down her spine. Sensation started to tingle at the sweet spot between her legs. Had anything ever felt as good as this man's hands on her body? She didn't think so.

Colton's hands paused when they met her bare breasts. One of the female officers at the scene had been kind enough to grab her a pair of jeans and shirt to put on over the tank and underwear she'd slept in, but hadn't grabbed her a bra.

He growled in the back of his throat as he squeezed and said in a raspy voice, "Shit, Maggie. You may have the most perfect breasts in the whole damn world."

She laughed. "You haven't even seen them yet."

"Don't need to."

He ran his thumbs over her nipples, causing her breath to catch.

"Yup, perfect."

She moaned as he tweaked and rolled the hard little buds between his fingers. She could feel the thick length of him beneath her, and moving her hips, she ground down onto him. He swore, meeting her thrusts with an excited fever. They were lined up perfectly.

If only they were naked in a bed, instead of fully clothed in a small, cramped truck cab.

"Colt? Maggie? Is that you guys?"

Her back was to the house, but she recognized Dade's voice calling from the front door. Heat flooded her face. They were both fully clothed, but it was pretty obvious what they were doing. She had never been one for exhibition. Had Dade seen?

"He can't see us, sweetheart. The headlights are on," Colton said, answering her unasked question.

Sure enough, she turned her head to see Dade standing on the porch, squinting into the bright beam of light emitted by the truck's headlights. She scrambled off Colton's lap, in a hurry to get back over to her side of the truck. Unfortunately, in her haste, her knee hit a spot that only seconds ago she had been quite enjoying. He sucked in a sharp breath, hands going to his crotch.

"Oh shoot, Colt. I'm so sorry." She reached for him, but his palm snaked out, grabbing her wrist, stopping her from checking the damage.

"I'm fine, but trust me, your hand anywhere near that area is not going to help at the moment." He shifted in his seat, adjusting his jeans. "Don't worry. You can kiss the boo boo later."

She shook her head, but couldn't keep the smile from tilting her lips "In your dreams."

He leaned over, grazing her ear with his lips, his breath a warm, soft promise. "And yours."

Damn the man for being right.

"Come on, let's not keep my brother waiting or he'll know what's going on."

With that, he shut off the headlights, opened the door, and exited the truck. Maggie followed, walking up the front steps to where Dade waited on the porch. Taller, with hair a few shades darker than Colton, the older Denning brother stood calmly in his usual stoic manner. They both had those amazing blue eyes and enough facial similarity to depict them as siblings, even if their personalities were polar opposites.

"You okay, Maggie?" Those clear blue eyes, so like Colton's, filled with genuine concern.

"I'm fine."

Colton slung his arm around her. "Nothing can get our Magpie down."

She shoved an elbow in his ribs.

"Ow." Removing his arm, he rubbed the offended

spot. "What was that for?"

"I'm going to start calling you Colt the Dolt. See how you like it."

He laughed off her irritation. "Sorry, sweetheart. I forgot I was supposed to stop using that name."

Tipping down, he brushed his lips against hers in a barely there kiss. When he brought his head back up, she noticed Dade staring at his brother with a strange expression. She wouldn't call it a happy one. Did he disapprove of her dating Colton?

The look was gone in a flash, replaced by relief when his gaze met hers again.

"I'm glad you're okay. Gas leaks can be deadly. You did the right thing calling Colt. I got the guest room all ready for you. Unless you want something to eat before bed?"

"No, thank you. I'm about ten seconds away from falling asleep right here on the porch." She shivered as a gust of cold night air wrapped around her. Okay, maybe she wasn't quite that tired.

Dade motioned for her to follow, then turned and headed inside. Colton placed a gentle hand on her back, bringing up the rear.

The Denning house looked pretty much the same as she remembered from her childhood. A few new pictures, a new fifty-inch flat screen, new appliances, but the feeling of home, the comfort, that was the same.

Often during her summer visits, she spent long hours at the ranch with the brothers. Mrs. Denning had fawned over her. Having no daughter of her own, their mother had doted on her at every visit. She'd always been so kind, and Maggie felt a pang of guilt for the way she'd treated the entire Denning family by never coming back.

The mistakes of a stupid teenage girl with a broken heart.

"Here you go." Dade stopped in front of his old room. "There are fresh sheets on the bed and extra blankets in the closet if you get cold. Do you remember where the bathroom is?"

She nodded. "Down the hall to the right."

"Bingo. Sleep tight, Maggie."

"Thanks, Dade, and thanks for letting me crash here tonight. I'll try not to be too big a bother."

The older Denning brother reached out, pulling her into a hug. It surprised her because he was not overt with his emotions. Not like his brother. Where Colton was outgoing and flirtatious, Dade was stoic and enjoyed his personal space.

"You're welcome here as long as you want, Maggie. Always were. Heck, I think Mom would have traded us for you in a heartbeat."

She laughed, pulling out of his embrace. "That's not true. She loves you two to pieces and you know it."

The brothers shared a grin.

"Well, I better sack out. Night." He waved as he turned and headed down the hall to the master suite, now his room.

"I'll go grab you something to wear for bed," Colton said. "If you need, there's a fresh toothbrush under the sink. We keep a couple around in case any of the hands need to crash for the night."

"Thanks, but I brushed before bed. I might use it in the morning though."

He crossed the hall to his room. Maggie stayed firmly where she was—after that make out session in his truck, she didn't think she could keep her clothes on if she followed him into his room. And she needed to keep her clothes on. This thing with Colton was going from zero to a hundred in no time flat. She needed time to process.

"Here you go Magpi—Maggie."

"Nice catch." She took the dark blue T-shirt from him.

"Do you really hate the nickname?"

No. In fact, it kind of felt special to have him call her something no one else did. At least, that's what she always thought as a kid. Something he did that made her special to him. After he started dating Natalie, the name had annoyed her as she no longer felt special. But now, now that they had started something, it was starting to feel special again.

"Fine, you can call me Magpie." She threw her hands up in pretend exasperation.

He chuckled, pulling her in close. "I don't really care what you let me call you. As long as I can call you mine."

He captured her lips in a hot, but too short, kiss.

"Good night. Magpie."

As he turned away, she pressed a hand to her tingling lips, still feeling him there. The night may have started out terrifying, but after having Colt's hand's on her body, his lips pressed against hers, it was turning out to be a very good night indeed.

Chapter Sixteen

Maggie woke up from a great dream. A very naughty dream involving a certain sexy cowboy and a private villa on a warm beach. No snow, no worries, just her, Colton, and a very large bed.

She rolled over in her current bed, snuggling into the thick, warm covers. Another morning waking up in a Denning owned bedroom. She wondered what it would be like to wake up with one particular Denning in bed with her.

The shirt Colton had given her to sleep in smelled like him. Pulling the collar up to her nose, she inhaled the rich, musky, scent. That smell was better than coffee, one whiff and her whole body was awake.

Awake and horny.

A glance at the bedside clock showed large, red numbers. Nine-twenty-seven.

When was the last time she slept this late on a weekday? Not since spring break her senior year of college. Those Long Island Ice Teas could do a number on a person. Lizzy had encouraged her to order the fourth one. Maggie was still planning her payback for that.

The house was quiet. She assumed Colton and Dade were already up. Ranch work wasn't like running a bakery. You couldn't close up shop just because you had some appliance problems. Animals needed to be fed, and they didn't care how late you stayed up last night.

A pang of guilt hit her. Here she was sleeping in, while the guys had just as little sleep as her, and they still woke up at the butt crack of dawn.

She'd just have to make amends…Maggie style.

Throwing back the covers, she hopped out of bed. Tossing on her clothes from last night, she made a quick pit stop in the bathroom, using one of the toothbrushes that Colton had offered last night, and then headed to the kitchen. She was sure she could rustle up some ingredients to make some yummy thank you treat for the brothers.

When she stepped into the kitchen, the strong aroma of coffee hit her nostrils. The shirt she wore to bed with Colton's scent woke her body, but her mind still needed a caffeine buzz.

"Oh good, you're up, Ms. Evans."

Standing in front of the stove was a tall, lanky, young man with a dark complexion and shaggy dark hair. He flipped a pancake from the griddle to a waiting plate.

"I just finished your breakfast. Colto—Mr. Denning said you would be hungry when you woke up. I was going to keep this warm for you until you were awake, but it looks like my timing is perfect."

"Thank you…?"

"Tony, Ms. Evans"

Right. Antonio Ortiz. The ranch Forman's nephew. She had met him a time or two when he came in to pick up an order of cupcakes for the ranch. He was young, seventeen or eighteen, she guessed. Town rumor had it the young man had been sent up here from Mexico by his mother. He had a work visa and was trying to get citizenship, like his uncle had. She hoped he did. From the little she knew, he seemed to be a good kid.

"Tony, now I remember. You can call me Maggie."

He smiled. He was a handsome young man. The ladies would be fighting over him in a few years, if they weren't already.

"I made you scrambled eggs, bacon, and pancakes. I hope everything is okay."

He set a plate of steaming food in front of her. She inhaled. Her stomach growled loudly when the delicious aromas hit her nose. "It smells wonderful. Thank you." Picking up her fork, she scooped a bite of the fluffy, yellow eggs into her mouth. Flavors exploded on her tongue, and she couldn't hold back a moan of delight.

"These eggs are fantastic! What did you do to them?"

The young man blushed. Shrugging with humility, he answered, "Nothing special. I add a bit of milk to keep them fluffy and a few fresh herbs and spices."

She took a bite of the pancakes next. The warm butter and sweet syrup complimented the soft cake that seemed to dissolve in her mouth. The kid had a serious gift.

"Tony, where did you learn to cook like this?"

A sad smile crossed his face. "*Mi madre.* My mother," he clarified.

Maggie set down her fork. "It must be hard for you to be so far away from her."

"Yes." He nodded. "But she wanted me to have a better life. I hope one day to make enough to be able to bring her here, to live with me."

He'd never do that on a ranch hand's salary.

He brought her a cup of coffee along with the sugar and creamer. As she doctored her drink she pondered. "Have you ever thought of going to school for the culinary arts? You have a gift for cooking. With a little training, you could be on your way to becoming a world class chef."

Judging by the shocked expression on his face, the idea must have never crossed his mind.

"I could help you find a school, go through the admissions process. After this meal, I am completely ready to write you a letter of recommendation." She smiled, but Tony didn't.

"I am here to help my uncle. Learn how to work a horse ranch."

"You'll never make enough money to bring your mother here on a ranch hand's salary, Tony." She shook her head. "Do you want to be a ranch hand? Is that your dream?"

He stared at his hands, refusing to meet her eyes. "It's good work."

Taking a sip of her coffee—*good Lord, the kid even made great coffee*—she nodded. "Yes, it is good work, but you have a talent. The great thing about this country is that the people who live here are free to pursue their dreams. You're working toward becoming a citizen, right?"

He nodded.

"Perfect. As a citizen, you have the right to become whatever you desire. This, Tony," she said, pointing to the almost empty plate of food in front of her. "Is a gift. You have a raw talent. The people I went to culinary school with would kill to be able to cook like you.

Think about it. If you're interested, I'd love to help you achieve your potential."

His gaze turned distant. A tiny smile turned up the corner of his lips. "I'll keep it in mind. Thank you, Ms. Ev—Maggie."

"Thank *you* for the delicious breakfast."

He blushed again before ducking his head and heading out the kitchen door.

Maggie finished off her eggs and bacon. The kid really did have a gift. Maybe she could use him at the bakery when Jamie went off to school.

Rinsing her plate off in the sink, she placed the dishes in the dishwasher and peered out the kitchen window. Ranch hands milled about, working on various chores. She didn't see Dade or Colton, but they were out there somewhere, she was sure. If they kept the same timetable as their parents had, then lunch would be at eleven thirty. That gave her a little under two hours to make some tasty treats.

Digging through the pantry and cupboards, she gathered ingredients. This raiding of Colton's kitchen to make him sweets was starting to become a habit.

****

Something smelled delicious.

Again.

Colton made his way into the kitchen and saw Maggie singing, swaying, and cooking.

Again.

She was so sexy when she shook and moved like that. He wanted to grab her in his arms and feel every inch of that amazing body against his.

Again and again and again.

"This is starting to become a habit, Magpie."

She screeched, wielding the spatula in her hand like a weapon as she spun to face him.

"Dammit, Colt. Stop sneaking up on me."

He chuckled, making his way to her side to give her a soft peck on the lips. The peck turned into something more as her lips parted, inviting him in.

He was never one to turn down a lady.

Their soft, slow kiss grew heated. He slid his hands into her loose, brown hair. The silky strands clung to his fingers. Her free hand came up to clutch his shoulder, and she rose on tiptoes to get a better reach. He obliged her by moving his hands down to her deliciously tight ass and lifting her into him. Colton feasted his mouth on hers, swallowed her muffled sound of surprise.

This was a much better fit.

Unfortunately, the guys would be coming in soon, and he didn't want to embarrass her.

Giving her luscious backside one final squeeze, he returned her to her feet. He gentled the kiss, making one final pass against her addictive lips before he lifted his head to look down at her. "Sleep well?"

Her expression was dazed, and he was pretty damn proud of himself for making it that way.

"Huh?" She shook her head, clearing the lust-induced haze. "Oh, yes. I did. Thank you."

He chuckled softly. "What's all this?" he asked, indicating the pot boiling on the stove.

"Lunch, and if you don't let me go, it's going to burn."

"Spoilsport." He bopped the tip of her cute button nose with his finger. "You didn't have to make lunch. We usually just make sandwiches or something."

Maggie turned back to the stove, lifting a lid and stirring. "I know I didn't have to. I wanted to. It's almost ready, so you better call everyone in."

He sniffed the air. "Chili?"

"Yup."

She replaced the lid and bent to open the oven. His pants tightened at the sight of her luscious rear poised high in the air like an offering.

Keep it together, man. Don't jump her like a stud in heat.

She straightened with a tray of steaming hot bread in her oven mitt and placed it on the counter. "And cornbread. I also made some cinnamon sugar oatmeal cookies."

"Ouch!"

She'd wacked his hand lightly with the soup ladle as he reach out for the cookie plate. "For *after* lunch."

Grabbing her up in a tight embrace, he kissed the stern look right off her face. "You are amazing." Damn, she was beautiful when she blushed.

She smacked him lightly on the shoulder, pulling away. "You better call everyone in before the cornbread gets cold. I'll also need someone to give me a ride back into town after lunch. I need to get baking as soon as possible. Can't open if I don't have cupcakes to sell."

The next words out of his mouth would have to be phrased very carefully. "Are you sure that's a smart idea?"

Body tense, she narrowed her gaze. So much for careful.

"Are you calling me stupid?"

"No. Don't put words in my mouth."

She crossed her arms in a defensive gesture. "Then

what are you saying?"

"Just that you've been having a lot of problems with the bakery lately, and with what happened last night, it might be a good idea to close down for a day or two until things get figured out."

Her arms uncrossed as she took a step toward him. Glaring up, she tried to give off an air of intimidation, but it was hard to be intimidated by someone half your weight and almost a foot shorter.

"I already closed once in the last week. I can't afford to do it again. I need to keep my business running, Colton. Money is tight, and I have to stay open no matter what. The blogger is coming in a week and a half, and I still have to prep for that. A few messed up orders and a freak gas leak aren't going to stop me."

The scant few inches that separated them closed as he took a step toward her. Two could play at this game.

"It wasn't a freak gas leak. It was intentional."

She waved a hand in the air. "It was an animal."

"How did an animal open the window?"

"Raccoons are very clever. They can get the lids off trashcans. I'm sure they can open up a window latch."

But her hands were twisting again. She didn't believe her theory any more than he did. She was nervous and scared, but determined to go on with her daily life. He respected her tenacity, even if it worried the hell out of him.

"What about the cut cord? Was that an animal?" No way. That had been a human. An accident or malicious, it had been done by someone with opposable thumbs. Add everything together and it looked less like coincidence and more like sabotage. Why couldn't she see that?

"Fine, someone might be out to get me. Or the shop, whatever," she admitted with a reluctant sigh. "But if I close up, they win. I don't know why someone would want to mess with me, but if they are, it's obvious they want to shut me down."

Made sense. All the incidents had been harmful to her bakery in nature. Orders changed or cancelled. Equipment damaged. It all pointed to someone who wanted to hurt her business, but who and why? When he found out, he was going to pound the bastard into the ground. No one messed with his Maggie. *No one.*

"I'm not going to let that happen. Gran started Cupcakes Above the Clouds forty-three years ago. I'm not going to let it die on my watch."

That pride, that spunk, that can-do attitude was classic Maggie. She was so strong. He admired it, even as he feared it. Feared because she might be putting herself in danger just to prove a point. She wasn't going to let anyone push her around, but what if whoever was behind this got tired of messing with her shop and started messing with her?

He was worried about her, for her. He was starting to realize his feelings for her went much deeper than he first thought. Something he would have to deal with at a later date. Right now, he had to focus on Maggie and her safety.

"Okay." Colton pulled her into his arms once again. She resisted for only a second before melting into him. "I'll take you into town after lunch, but promise me you'll be careful, and if anything else happens, *anything at all,* you call me right away. Got it?"

Lifting her head, she placed a soft kiss on his lips. Sweet, and over too soon.

"I promise."

He returned her kiss, deepening it and lingering longer. When he lifted his head, her cheeks were flushed and her heartbeat pulsed wildly against his chest.

"Still on for dinner tomorrow night?"

She smiled shyly and nodded.

"Great. I better go call the guys in for lunch. Then I'll take you into town." He turned, heading for the door. Her voice stopped him before he got there.

"Colt?"

Glancing over his shoulder, he saw her standing in his kitchen, his home. She looked so sweet there, so beautiful, so…right.

"Yeah?"

"Thank you. You seem to be saving my butt a lot lately"

He smiled. "And what a lovely thing it is to save."

With a wink, he headed out the door, leaving Maggie standing in his home. An image of it being her home, too, teased the corners of his mind. A strange warmth spread throughout his body and his smile widened at the thought.

Chapter Seventeen

Back in town by twelve-fifteen, Maggie had the doors of her shop open by one. A dozen carrot vanilla frosted cupcakes were shelved. She liked to have at least three-dozen before opening, but she already lost the entire morning clientele. She could keep baking and keep an eye on the front. It wasn't what she liked to do, but desperate times and all.

If someone was messing with her, she was going to bake them some laxative cupcakes and shove them down their throat.

She couldn't afford all these hiccups and closures. Plus, all this worry over a possible saboteur was only adding to her stress level. There was enough on her plate with the blogger and whatever was going on with her and Colton. She didn't need a crazy, cupcake-hating vandal added into the mix.

The bell above the door chimed. Filling the last cup with batter, she popped the cupcake tray into her recently fixed oven.

"Be right there!" she called to the front.

"No hurry."

She recognized that deep, calm voice. Taking a quick moment to wash the batter off her hands, she made her way to the front. Sure enough, there stood Sheriff Jake Ryder.

A handsome man with long, dark hair in a braid

down his back, brown eyes, caramel skin, and chiseled, high, Native American cheekbones, he was around the same age as Colton, but had arrived in Peak Town after she stopped coming. She had only known him for the past eight months. What she did know of him, she liked.

"Hey, Sheriff. I just put a dozen Vanilla Lemon cupcakes in the oven. Should be ready in about fifteen minutes or so."

He smiled, making his handsome face even more attractive. Still, as good looking as Ryder was, he didn't make her heart race like Colton did. Just thinking about the sexy cowboy made her breasts ache and her palms sweaty.

Damn. She had it bad.

"You sure know how to tempt a man, Maggie, but unfortunately, this isn't a social visit."

Her stomach twisted into knots. "You found something?"

He nodded. Just as he had promised, two uniformed officers had been waiting for her when she arrived home. With nothing to report, she'd thanked them both and told them to stop by later for a few cupcakes. On the house. The hungry light that filled their eyes at the mention of free sweets made her feel better about them having to sit in the cold all night watching her place.

"And?" she prompted when the sheriff said nothing.

Ryder took off his hat and placed it on the counter as he took a seat on the high stool in front of her.

"It looks like someone pulled out your hose. Intentionally."

The knots got tighter.

"I need to know if you have any enemies. Anyone who would want to harm you or cause harm to your business."

She shook her head. She just couldn't believe someone was actually out to get her. What the hell had she ever done to anyone?

"I can't think of anyone, Sheriff. I really can't think of anyone who hates me this much."

"How about someone who hates you just a little?" he asked, pulling out his notebook and pen.

"The thing is, Ryder," she began. "I'm so busy with the shop, I don't really have time to socialize enough to make anyone mad. Except…"

"Except who?" he asked when she trailed off.

"Well, Natalie Brake has never cared for me very much, but I highly doubt she's behind this." The woman was too wrapped up in herself to spend this much time messing with her.

"Why does she dislike you?"

No way was she airing out her cat fighting with Ryder. Even if he was the sheriff. "Does it really matter?"

He paused in his writing to glance up. "Maybe, maybe not, but I've found that every detail, no matter how insignificant it seems, is important to breaking a case."

Great, she was a "case" now. Wasn't her luck supposed to be turning around? Maybe it was on a roller coaster of hills and valleys.

"Fine. She owns the store next to mine and constantly complains."

"About what?"

She shrugged. What *didn't* the woman complain about? "The smells, the sounds. She says I'm disrupting her clientele."

His pen scribbled on the paper. "Anything else?"

This was the part she'd rather keep to herself. It seemed so juvenile, but he did say he needed to know everything.

"She never liked the fact Colton and I were friends. She, um, dated him in high school and kind of told me to get lost."

He paused again, catching her gaze with his dark brown one. A smile curled the corner of his mouth. "I take it she's not happy you two are dating?"

"Jeez. It's been less than a week." She threw her hands up in exasperation. "We've had *one* date. One. And not even in public. You'd think people in this town would have better things to talk about."

He chuckled. "Small town. Not much else going on."

A heavy sigh escaped her. "Yeah, she's not happy about it. But I seriously doubt Natalie Brake would waste her time trying to sabotage my business. She'd probably chip a nail breaking in and then try to sue me for damages to her perfect manicure." She was only half-joking about that.

"I still have to check every lead. Is Jamie working today? I need to talk to her, too."

Maggie glanced at the clock. Just after two. "She'll be in after school gets out. Should be another twenty minutes or so."

Grabbing his hat and placing it on his head, he rose, notebook and pen still in hand. "I'll come back in a half an hour then. I'm going to go next door and have a chat with Natalie."

Fan-freaking-tastic.

Just what she did not need. Another reason to piss off the bitchy blonde.

Hey, Natalie, I know you think I stole your man and I'm running your clients away with my sugary smells, but here's a cop to accuse you of sabotaging me. Hey, why are you trying to strangle me?

Yeah, that was going to go over real well.

"Don't worry, Maggie. We'll get to the bottom of this."

She nodded, but didn't feel as positive as he sounded. "I'll have some of those Vanilla Lemon cupcakes iced with buttercream frosting by the time you get back."

He smiled wide, revealing perfectly straight, white teeth. He really was handsome. Too bad it had absolutely no effect on her. A calm, gentle sheriff was probably a safer bet than the outlandish, sexy-as-hell cowboy who made her blood boil.

"My stomach is already growling," he said, opening the front door. "Colton sure is one lucky man."

"One date!" she shouted after him, but he was already gone.

Good grief, she and Colton hadn't even discussed their relationship yet, and the whole town was ready to marry them off. Good thing she was smart enough to know things were always temporary with men. They could promise you the world, but eventually, they always left you. Her mother had learned that, and so had she.

Didn't mean she couldn't enjoy the time she and Colton had.

She smiled, thinking of their dinner date tomorrow night. Time with Colton…yes, she was going to enjoy every single second while it lasted.

****

Dark.

Cold.

But, it didn't matter.

She sat in her car, across the street from that bitch's shop. The lights were off, the doors locked, but the apartment above the store was lit up. Maggie was in there now. Making dinner? Alone, or with Colton?

She had seen the way he rushed to the woman's side last night. Little slut clung to him like he was her goddamn hero. Colton was too good for Maggie Evans. The rumor around town had them pegged as an item. The rumor mill in Peak Town had been wrong before, but this time, it seemed to be spot on.

Damn it all to hell!

It wasn't fair. Maggie was ruining everything, and now that stupid sheriff was going around asking questions.

She should stop, wait until the heat died down. She would.

After one more warning.

Reaching out, she touched the heavy rock in the seat beside her. Large, bigger than her fist, and heavier than the hand weights she worked out with every morning. She'd found it in the creek bed. Anyone could have taken it. There was no way to trace it back to her. She watched the crime shows on TV. Peak Town may be small, but that Sheriff Ryder was a smart one. If she left any evidence behind, he'd find it.

Grabbing the red permanent marker she bought in

Aspen during her last trip—paid with cash at an out of town store—she scrawled out a message on the large rock.

There, that ought to get through to the bitch.

There was no room in this town for Maggie Evans. She needed to leave, the sooner the better. If she didn't leave, well, then things would get a little more personal.

The lights in the apartment turned off. *Perfect.*

Smiling, she grabbed the rock. Time to deliver a message to the cupcake maker.

Chapter Eighteen

Shattering glass.

Amazing how one could go from a deep slumber to wide-awake in an instant.

Maggie leapt out of bed. Her heart pounded a furious beat in her chest as her entire body vibrated with the awareness something was wrong.

From outside, a car door slammed and tires peeled.

Racing to the window, she pulled back the curtains to see a pair of red taillights racing off into the night. Someone was running off in a hurry.

She snagged her cell phone off the bedside table. Throwing on her robe, she rushed down the inner staircase that connected her apartment to the bakery below, entered the back of the shop, and flipped on the lights. Nothing appeared to be disturbed. Everything was as she left it a few hours ago.

Making her way to the front, she sucked in a sharp breath as the cool night breeze slapped her in the face. Shards of broken glass littered the entryway floor like a macabre crystal carpet. The once clear pane with the pretty Cupcakes Above the Clouds writing was now just a huge, gaping hole.

And there, sitting on the floor in front of her, among the ruins of her formerly beautiful front window was a large rock with blood red words scribbled onto it.

LEAVE BITCH

****

The sheriff arrived two minutes after she called. Two nights, two visits from the police. Her luck had taken another nosedive.

Two crime scene techs, the only two Peak Town had, were collecting the pieces of glass, the rock, and anything else they thought was important.

She had given her statement to Ryder. He moved her case up from suspected sabotage to known assault and suggested she close up shop until they discovered who was behind all this. But she wouldn't do that. Couldn't do that. If someone was after her, and it looked more and more likely that was the case, then closing up her shop would be exactly what they wanted. They would win.

She refused to let them win, whoever they were.

Ryder called her stubborn under his breath and promised to have extra patrols swing by her place for the next few days. He also gave her the number of his contractor buddy who could properly fix up her window in a day or two. She thanked him, placing the card on the counter. She'd call first thing in the morning. The blogger was coming next week, and she would not let this asshole, whoever he was, mess up her plans.

The sheriff and his crew finished up by eleven. They helped tape a large piece of cardboard over her window before leaving. Not the safest of fixes, but it would keep most of the natural elements out. No one thought the vandal would come back tonight anyhow. They had done their damage and left their message.

Not that she was going to listen to it. No one told her what to do, not anymore.

She thought about calling Colton, but there was

really nothing for him to do. Best just to try to get some sleep and tell him tomorrow at dinner.

Sleep, however, was fitful, but she managed to get a few solid hours before she woke in the morning to open.

Once Maggie had her cupcakes made, she picked up the phone and called Ryder's contractor friend. He seemed nice and competent, and promised to come in before five to check out the window. Without seeing it, he couldn't give her an accurate quote, but did give her an estimated price and timetable that she found agreeable and fair.

She knew she should be scared that someone was targeting her, but all it did was make her angry. Maggie fueled that anger into her work, whipping up a few more cupcakes from the recipes in Gran's box. They were delicious. After her third one, she realized she was anger eating.

Better stop if I want to enjoy my dinner with Colton tonight. Or fit into any of her pants.

"Wow, what the heck happened here?"

The bell over the door chimed as Jamie walked in, eyes wide, surveying the cardboard covered window.

"We had an incident last night. Someone threw a rock through the window."

The young girl's mouth dropped. "No way! I bet it was Tommy Zimmerman. He's such a jerk. Always pulling stupid stunts because he thinks it makes him cool. News flash idiot, prison orange doesn't look cool on anyone."

"I don't think it was teenagers."

"Why?"

She didn't want to scare her only employee away,

but since the attack happened to the shop, the teenager had a right to know if her workplace was becoming a danger.

Maggie sighed, pulling out a Chocolate Lava cupcake, Jamie's favorite, and placing it in front of the girl.

"That bad huh?" Berry Cherry pink lips grimaced before biting into the gooey, chocolate treat.

She nodded. "Yeah. Someone left a message on the rock thrown through the window. 'Leave Bitch.'"

"Whoa, harsh."

"Sheriff Ryder thinks the attack last night and the sabotage to the oven are connected. It's also possible the problems I had with our old distributor were part of the attack." She felt terrible for blaming Pansy's for a problem that might have been caused by someone who was out to get her.

"Someone's attacking the shop?"

"Looks that way."

Jamie licked a drop of frosting off her finger. "Why?"

She shrugged. "I have no idea. To shut me down I assume, but it's not going to work."

"Dam—I mean darn right it won't work. We aren't scared of a jerk who throws rocks through windows."

A smile curved her lips. She really liked Jamie. She was happy for her young employee's success, but sad to see her go.

"You don't have to come to work if you don't feel safe. You can take some time off until we catch this person. I can give you vacation pay if you need—"

"Forget that! If you're working, I'm working. That blogger lady is coming next week, and we're gonna blow her taste buds off! Right?"

She laughed at the youthful enthusiasm. "Right."

"Then let's get to work."

The afternoon flew by. The contractor, Eric Grimes, came in just after four. He surveyed, took measurements, and gave her a quote she found to be very reasonable. Luckily, he had the glass she needed in stock, so it would only take a day to install. She would have to call a sign shop to get replacement lettering for the window, more money she couldn't afford to spend. This vandal guy was really starting to piss her off.

Business was busier than usual. It seemed people heard about the incident and were curious. Since loitering was illegal in Peak Town, everyone bought a cupcake so they would have an excuse to linger, ask questions, and speculate.

By five o'clock, she was out of cupcakes and energy.

"One good thing about small town scandals," she muttered to herself. "It makes for excellent sales days."

At least something good was coming out of this whole mess. A few more days like this and she could afford all the damage this jerk was doing to her shop.

Suck on that saboteur!

Jamie helped her close up, shouting a "can't hold us down" solidarity cheer as she left for the night.

Maggie needed a hot shower to rejuvenate. Colton would be by in an hour to pick her up.

She had just stepped out of the steamy hot water, when a knock sounded on her front door. Quickly drying off, she threw on her thick, terry cloth robe and headed to the door. She knew she wouldn't have time to blow dry her long hair before the date, so she had pinned it up. A few loose strands stuck to her damp neck and face. Brushing one off of her cheek, she peered through the peephole of her front door.

Colton.

He was early...and looking very unhappy. *What the heck?*

"Open the damn door, Maggie!"

Change that to angry.

Flipping the lock, she opened the door a crack. "You're early. I'm not ready yet." He pushed his way in, forcing her to take a step back. "Hey!"

The door slammed behind him. "Why the hell didn't you call me?"

What was he talking about?

"You promised you'd call if anything happened."

Oh, that.

"I had to hear from Stacey about how your window got smashed by some asshole with a rock. What the hell, Maggie?"

Stacey? Why would he be talking to the local florist? She glanced down. His hands were clenched into tight fists. Well, one was a fist, the other was clutching a beautiful bouquet of yellow daises.

He'd brought her flowers, again. *How sweet.* And she'd neglected to call him. Now she felt like dirt.

"I was going to tell you about it tonight. I called the sheriff. Everything was taken care of. There was no need to call you."

His jaw clenched, nostrils flared. "No need? No *need!*"

Oops, maybe that was the wrong thing to say.

He crowded her, backing her into the wall. "How about the need to let me know you're safe? How about the need to tell me someone's trying to hurt you? How about the need to know the woman I care about is in danger?"

"I'm fine, Colton. I can take care of myself. I'm not a child."

"Oh, believe me, I'm well aware of that fact."

His eyes narrowed, tracking down her body with unleashed lust. Suddenly, her robe was very, very hot. Her bare nipples pebbled under the thick cloth. Heat gathered in her core.

He leaned in, his mouth inches from her. She could feel his hot breath on her ear. Her entire body tingled with anticipation. Why wouldn't he touch her? She wanted his touch more than her next breath.

"You promised, Maggie." His voice was a soft, broken whisper. "You *promised* you'd call me if anything happened."

"I-I'm sorry. I didn't want to upset you."

He pulled back to stare at her with those deep blue eyes, so blue the sky itself should be envious.

"The only thing that upsets me is you don't seem to realize *how much* I care about you."

Then his lips were on hers, kissing, tasting, bruising. He consumed her. His body pressed against hers, forcing her back. Pressed between the hard wall and Colton's hard body was hot, wonderful, perfect.

His hands reached up. Flowers gone. Where, she had no idea, and at the moment, didn't care. His large palms glided up her waist to her breasts. They cupped her, squeezing gently. Her breath caught in the back of her throat.

"Please tell me you're naked under there."

She couldn't tell him. Couldn't even breathe at the

moment. Instead, she nodded.

He growled. Actually growled.

"Bedroom." The word came out deep, dark, and full of sensual promise.

Maggie pushed gently at his chest, and he backed up. The lust in his eyes dampened. He thought he'd pushed her too far? She corrected his misconception, grabbing his hand and practically dragging him with her down the hallway.

His eyes lit with fire again when she opened the door to her bedroom. "Are you sure?"

Still ever the gentleman.

She answered his question with a scorching kiss.

He made a sound of protest when she stepped back, reaching for her, but stopped when she grabbed for the robe's belt.

He watched with fascination as the covering drop to the floor. "Sweet Jesus. You are beautiful."

The cool air kissed her heated skin, sending shivers over her body. She'd never been this bold with her previous lovers. They'd always taken the lead, and she had been happy to follow. Sex had been enjoyable, nothing mind blowing like in the romance novels Lizzy tried to get her to read, but pleasant.

Maggie had a feeling sex with Colton would blow her mind and then some. The way he ate her body up with his eyes, the burning fire in his gaze. It made her bold in a way she had never been before. He wanted her—badly—and that made her feel sexy and powerful.

"I think you have too many clothes on, cowboy. Take them off. Now."

A sexy grin curved his lips. "I love it when you get bossy."

Those beautiful, large hands started unbuttoning his collared blue shirt. Tanned, toned skin was revealed as he shrugged the open material off his shoulders.

"Now the pants," she indicated with a nod.

"No. Not yet." He fell to his knees. "First, I need a taste."

That was all the warning she got before his mouth closed over her sex.

Oh God!

The air rushed out of her lungs. She slammed her hands down on Colton's shoulders as her knees buckled. A laugh rumbled out of his lips, causing interesting things to happen down there.

Grabbing her thighs, he spread her wider to make room for himself. His tongue made one long, luscious glide against her. Her body began to pulse. She was so close, and he had barely done anything yet. His teeth closed over that small, sensitive bundle of nerves, nipping slightly.

"*Colt,*" she exclaimed as pleasure shot through her.

"Easy, sweetheart. We have all night."

She would never survive.

His tongue circled around her as one hand skated up the inside of her thigh. Her breathing hitched then stopped altogether as he stroked. He teased her, brushing, barely touching. Not entering her, not filling her like she needed.

"Colton," she demanded now.

He answered by pushing one long, thick finger inside her.

Yes. So good, but not enough.

"More." The single word rasped out with the little breath she still possessed in her lungs.

She could feel his smile against her. Another finger joined the first, and she bucked against him, the pleasure overwhelming her senses.

"Damn, you feel so good."

His dark rumble felt as if it came from within her.

"And so sweet. Never tasted anything so sweet."

Her heart raced; she was pretty sure he was killing her. What a way to go.

That talented tongue curled around her again. A third finger joined the other two. His lips closed over her and he sucked, using just the right amount of pressure.

Her world exploded.

She knew she screamed. She didn't care. Her entire body was on fire. The aftershocks went pulsing through her as he kept up the rhythm. Wonderful, magical, and still not enough.

"More." Her voice sounded hoarse from her scream, but he heard it.

Placing one last soft kiss on her, he rose. "Hell yeah more."

Colton walked her backwards until her legs hit the bed. She went tumbling down, hitting the soft, downy comforter. His hands, those amazing talented hands, went to his jeans. The zipper made a rasping sound as he tugged it down. He shucked them and boxers off at the same time. His shoes had been removed at some point. She didn't really care when.

Her eyes widened at the glorious sight of Colton Denning naked. The man was a god. It wasn't fair for him to look so sexy standing there with his rock hard chest, six-pack you could wash laundry on, and...*oh my*. That was much bigger than his fingers.

Oh yeah, *that* was what she needed.

Only then did she notice he had something in his hand. A mint? No, a condom. Thank God he had one, because the only protection she had expired over a year ago. She hadn't bought any recently because she hadn't needed to. Tomorrow, she was going down to the drug store to buy every single one they had.

Tossing the empty packet on the floor, he quickly donned the rubber and came down on top of her.

Yes.

She needed this, needed him.

"Maggie."

She glanced up to his face at the hesitancy in his voice.

"Are you sure? There's no going back after this."

She knew what he meant. A date, a few kisses, they could go back to friends after that. This? This would change their relationship forever. There was no going back to just friends. Could she handle that if things went south?

The real question was, no matter how things ended up, could she deny herself Colton when she'd wanted him for so long?

"I'm sure. I need you, Colton, now."

He kissed her and pushed inside, moving slowly, letting her body adjust to his size. He wasn't a small man, anywhere, but he fit.

They fit.

And groaned in unison as he seated himself fully inside her.

"Damn, you feel amazing."

Her sentiments exactly.

He started to move then. Long, deep thrusts that

she matched, pushing against him until he filled her so deep she couldn't tell where he ended and she began. Her body hummed and vibrated. His thrusts quickened, and she could feel another orgasm building.

"Colton!" She was close, so close.

His hand slipped between them and once again found her. He circled her nub while moving deep inside her.

"Oh God, Colton!"

She arched, pressing into him as her world exploded for a second time. He gave three more hard thrusts before tensing. A loud curse sprang from his lips, and she could feel him pulse inside her with his own release.

"Maggie," he whispered softly, stroking her hair.

She wrapped her arms around him. "If that was dinner," she said with a breathless laugh. "I can't wait for dessert."

Chapter Nineteen

Waking up in her own bed was nice.

Waking up with Colton in her bed even nicer.

Maggie snuggled back against him, loving the feel of his warm, hard body pressed against hers.

His arms tightened around her. Lips grazed her brow. "Easy, sweetheart. That sexy little body of yours is damn tempting, but I only brought the two condoms with me. So, unless you have some protection around here?"

Shoot. She didn't. She wasn't worried about disease. After she had discovered what a rat Miles was, she had gotten the barrage of testing done. They had always used protection, but you could never be too careful. And she hadn't been with anyone since getting the all clear on her tests.

"I'm clean, but I always use a rubber. That's not the only issue here," his deep voice purred in her ear.

No it wasn't.

An image suddenly appeared in her mind of a little girl with her dark hair and Colton's clear blue eyes. A lump formed in her throat, and she had to blink back tears.

Where the hell did that come from?

One night of sex—granted, *amazing* sex—and she was already imagining their kids? *Crap.* She *was* in deep.

"I'm clean, too, but I'm not on...I don't take..." She couldn't even say it. Not with the image of her and Colton's love child fresh in her mind.

He kissed her neck at the tender spot where her shoulder connected. A shiver racked her body. How had he managed to zero in on her most sensitive area?

"Then we'll find others ways to enjoy the morning."

His voice was a deep, sexy rumble in his chest as one hand played with her breasts, tweaking her nipple to a stiff point.

"Colt!"

"I'm right here, Magpie."

She shivered. He had never said her nickname like that before. Like pure sex.

One hand continued to worship her breasts as the other slowly, very slowly, made its way down her body. Fingers teasing, touching, tormenting.

"Let's see how ready you are."

She was way past ready. Had been since she woke up.

His fingers found her and dipped slightly inside. "Mmmmm." His lips grazed the shell of her ear.

The tip of his tongue snaked out, tasting her. Driving her wild.

"So ready for me, sweetheart."

Yes she was. By the hardness pressed against her backside, he was ready for her, too. *Dammit.* Why had he only brought two condoms!

His fingers thrust inside her, twisting. A moan escaped from her lips. *Oh God.* How did he do that?

His thumb found her sweet spot and began those soft, amazing circles from last night. She cried out, arching into his touch. She wasn't going to last much longer.

"*Please.*" She was begging, for what she had no idea, but he seemed to.

His fingers pumped faster, his thumb increased pressure, and his mouth went back to that spot on her neck, sucking, biting…it was all too much.

With a keening cry, she arched back as her inner muscles clamped tightly around his fingers. Moments later, her body went limp, intense pleasure draining all the energy out of her.

"Beautiful," he murmured softly.

His fingers slipped out, but he continued to pet her, stroking her down from an amazing orgasm.

He was still rock hard against her back.

"Turnabout is fair play," she said, looking over her shoulder with a wicked smile. Shifting, Maggie pushed him back to the mattress.

A smile on his face, he said nothing. Just put his hand behind his head. "Have your wicked way with me, Magpie. I'm all yours."

"Thank you. I think I will."

Her gaze ate him up. The man was truly too sexy for his own good. She leaned over, trailing her lips down his chest, pausing to lick and gently bite his nipples. He sucked in a breath, and she felt his harness twitch against her thigh. Moving lower, she circled his belly button with the tip of her tongue.

This time, the breath was a harsh gasp. "You're killing me here."

She chuckled. "Fair is fair."

Maggie glided her hand over his thighs, almost touching him, but not quite. Moving lower, over his hip, down his thigh, and back up to...*hello!* He was big and hard and looked good enough to eat. So, that's exactly what she did.

Parting her lips, she ran her tongue over the tip of him. He let out a harsh curse, using a colorful request she fully intended to fulfill, but later. Now, she wanted to taste. With a loud groan, his hand tangled in her hair, pulling, but not hurting. She was pushing him past his control, and she loved it.

Keeping one hand at the base of his shaft, she opened her mouth, wide, taking him in deep. Sucking in her cheeks, she reveled in the pure masculinity of Colton, twisting as her mouth devoured.

So. Damn. Good.

"Maggie. Damn, sweetheart...I'm gonna..."

She knew what he was going to do. Felt it in the tightening of his body, the thrusts of his hips against her.

"Maggie!"

He tried to pull away, but she didn't let him. She wanted him, all of him.

He let out a long, loud groan, and she reveled in the fact she made this strong man lose his control.

"Hell yeah. Damn, Maggie, that was amazing. You are amazing."

His hand untangled from her hair, stroking her cheek. She rose, unable to keep the satisfied smile from curling her lips. "Now, that's what I call a good morning."

He laughed. "Yeah, but I think I'll stop by the pharmacy today so we can make it an even better night."

Just what she had been thinking earlier.

After they took a shower together—to conserve water of course—they sat in her small kitchen drinking coffee and eating scrambled eggs with toast. It was nice, comfortable.

She sat there admiring the cowboy's very fine backside, clad only in a pair of jeans, as he refilled his coffee cup. Her stomach was full, her mind alert—thanks to the caffeine fix—and her body was deliciously sated.

"So, what did the sheriff have to say yesterday?"

So much for the afterglow.

"He thinks all the incidents might be connected. Including the problems with my old distributor."

Colton nodded his agreement.

"He suggested I close up shop until he discovered who's behind all this."

"Not a bad idea."

She glared. "Yes, a very bad idea if I want to keep my business running."

"What about keeping your life running?" he asked, though it sounded more like an accusation than a question.

"The person is attacking the shop, Colt, not me."

His hand tightened around his coffee mug. "Whoever is doing this has escalated. Fast. Who's to say they don't stop going after your bakery and start going after *you*."

She hadn't thought about that.

"Screwing with your orders and cutting power cords is one thing, but the gas leak? The rock through the window? Those things could have hurt you, Maggie, and this guy doesn't seem to care."

When he put it that way…

"I think you should follow the sheriff's advice. Close up. Maybe come and stay with me for a little bit. Until this all gets cleared up."

Stay with Colton? The idea had appeal. Still…

"I can't, Colt. You know that. I have a very important week coming up. The blogger will be here, and I need that good review to get the tourist crowd this summer."

He slammed the mug down on the counter. "Dammit, Maggie. This is more important than a stupid shop. This is your life."

Stupid shop? Oh, he did not just say that!

"Yes, it is *my* life. So I think *I'll* be the one to make decisions about it. And it's not a stupid shop, it's who I am. My legacy. Passed down from Gran."

He rubbed a hand across the back of his neck. She knew he was just trying to protect her, but that didn't excuse his acting like an ass.

At least he tried to look contrite as he answered, "That wasn't what I meant. I know how important the shop is to you. I'm just worried. I don't want to see you get hurt."

"I can take care of myself. Just because we had sex doesn't mean you get to dictate to me now."

His eyes turned hard. Maybe she went a bit too far with that last comment.

Jaw clenched, he stalked toward her. A hand went to the back of her chair; the other slammed on the table, caging her in. He was pissed, but she wasn't afraid. Colton would never hurt her. She knew that to the core of her being.

"What we have, Maggie, is a relationship. Yes, we had sex, and we'll have it again. But what we are…is

177

two people who care about each other and want what's best. I want you happy, satisfied, *and safe*. I don't want some crazy asshole hurting you because he wants to destroy your business."

His mouth was inches away. Was it strange that she really wanted to kiss him right now?

It must not have been, because before the thought left her brain, his head dipped and his lips were on hers in a hard, punishing, delicious kiss.

"Do whatever the hell you want, but know this. I care about you, and I'm not going to stop. Yes, you can take care of yourself, but sometimes it's nice to let someone else care for you, too."

With that, he stood and headed toward the door. He tugged on his shirt and boots. "I hope you'll call if anything happens, but I won't expect it this time."

Then he was gone, and Maggie felt like rotten, week old cupcake batter.

****

"What crawled up your butt and died?" Dade asked.

Colton threw another bale of hay down from the truck. Usually, he'd have one of the hands unload, but he was in a piss-poor mood and needed to let off some steam with a little physical work.

His brother shook his head. "Messed up things with Maggie already?"

"Leave it alone, Dade."

"What did you do?"

His brother could never leave it alone. Not when it came to him.

"*I* didn't do anything. She, on the other hand, is acting like an idiot."

He tossed the last bale down and sat on the end of the lowered tailgate. His brother handed him a bottle of water. Unscrewing the cap, he downed half in one gulp.

"Does this have anything to do with that rock being thrown through her shop window last night?"

He glanced at his brother in surprise. Dade shrugged.

"Small town, people talk."

Yeah, he knew. Wasn't that the way he'd found out, too? It still burned his ass she hadn't called.

"Yeah." Removing his hat, he wiped the sweat from his brow. The weather was finally starting to warm up again. "Ryder thinks she's got someone after her. Someone trying to close her down or something." He'd called the sheriff after he left Maggie's. Ryder couldn't reveal details, police protocol, but he told Colton as much as he could.

"Maybe she should close down," his brother said. "Just until this guy is caught."

Seemed everyone was in agreement. Everyone except Maggie.

"She won't. She's worried about losing business. Plus, there's this fancy blogger coming into town. She won't close down."

"But, she could get hurt."

That's what I said. "She doesn't care. She says the guy is after her shop, not her."

Dade grunted. Yeah, he agreed; the woman was being stubborn to the point of stupid.

"Let me guess, you told her you agreed with Ryder and now she's pissed at you?"

"Something like that."

His brother hopped up on the tailgate with him.

The truck bounced at the added weight. "So, what are you going to do?"

He glanced up. Colton had never really done serious relationships, not since Natalie made a fool out of him. He liked women, and they liked him, but he always made sure they knew the score before he started anything. He wasn't long-term material. When things got too heavy, he bowed out.

But with Maggie…it was different. The heavy stuff wasn't putting him off this time. He could see a future with her, and it looked damn good.

"I'm gonna go to her place tonight and make sure that bastard doesn't lay a hand on her."

Identical blue eyes studied him a moment, then a smile broke across his brother's face. "Damn, never thought I'd see the day you fell."

"What are you talking about?"

Dade laughed. "You got it bad, little brother. She's way too good for you, but I wish you all the best."

He shoved his sibling. "Go shovel some manure or something."

Dade walked away, chuckling to himself. As annoying as the big guy could sometimes be, his brother was right. Maggie was too good for him, and he did have it bad for her. So bad that an idea came to mind. A compromise that would make them both happy.

Very, *very* happy.

Chapter Twenty

"These cupcakes are amazing Maggie!"

"No, Eric, you're amazing. I can't believe you fixed my window so quickly."

The big man finished off the last cupcake on the plate she had set in front of him. "It was a simple job. Helped that I already had the glass you needed."

And the luck roller coaster started uphill again.

"It should be fine, but if you have any problems just give me a call."

"Thanks. I really appreciate it." She handed him a check for the amount they had agreed upon.

Stuffing the paper in his pocket, he grinned. "It's what I do."

"Don't forget to bring the kids by next weekend. I'll be sure to make some Volcano Chocolate Chippers for them."

They'd talked while Eric installed her new window. He told her about his wife and their twin, five-year-old boys with a fondness for chocolate and bouncing off the walls.

"Will do." He grabbed his bag and headed out the door, waving a hand over his shoulder "Take care."

The bell chimed as he left. It was an hour after closing. Eric had graciously waited until she was closed to do the installation so as not to disrupt her customers. In thanks, she made him half a dozen Chocolate Mint cupcakes. Which he gleefully accepted, ate two, and took the other four with him. It was evident from which parent the boys inherited their love of chocolate.

Locking the door and flipping off the lights, Maggie breathed a sigh of relief. She might have a crazy vandal attacking her shop, but at least some things were going right. The window was fixed, she felt prepared for the blogger, and Colton—

Damn.

Okay, not everything was going right.

Thinking of the way he had walked out that morning made guilt rise in her throat once again. She had not meant to make him angry by implying all they had was sex, but how was she supposed to know he wanted more? Yeah, he said he wanted to go on a few dates, but in her experience, men like Colton—flirty, outgoing men—tended to want to just have fun, keep things casual. Just because she felt something more didn't mean he did.

Still, she didn't have to be so rude to him. *Shoot.* She should probably call and apologize. If he would even take her call. He'd been pretty pissed when he left.

With a final check through of the shop, Maggie headed to the back door and up the inside stairs to her apartment. Always kept it on silent while she worked, her phone vibrated in her pocket.

Her breath caught as she fished it out. Was it—

Hope came crashing to a halt when she noted the name of the person wasn't the caller she had wished.

"Hey, Lizzy," she said, answering the phone.

"Wow, did I do something wrong? That was the most disheartened reception you've ever given me."

Maggie winced. "No, I'm sorry. I was just hoping

it was someone else."

"Oh, how you wound me!" Lizzy affected a dramatic tone. "First you abandon me, and now you've replaced me. How will I ever go on?"

She laughed at her friend's melodramatic antics. "You could never be replaced, you know that."

"But you don't deny abandoning me I see."

"I—"

"I'm only joking, you know that." Her friend cut off the protests. "So, who were you hoping to hear from?"

"It's no one really," she hedged.

"It's your cowboy, Colton. Isn't it?"

She stayed silent.

"Ah ha! I knew it!"

"I didn't say it was him," she objected.

"You didn't say it wasn't. Trust me, Maggie, after years of kicking your butt at poker, I can tell when you're bluffing."

"I beat you a time or two."

She could picture her friend's eyes roll.

"Only when I let you."

Maggie was at the top of the stairs now. Using her key, she let herself into her apartment. The sun had just started to set, so she flipped on the lights. Her small apartment seemed larger without Colton in it. How weird was that? The man had only spent the night once, and she was already used to having him in her home.

Pathetic.

"Maggie? Did you hear me?"

"Sorry what?" She shook her head, focusing on the phone call.

"I asked how things were going."

"How much time do you have?"

Silence, then, "That bad?"

"It's a bottle of wine type conversation."

She heard some scuffling over the line, a clink of glass, then a soft pop.

"Okay I'm ready."

Laughing, she asked, "Lizzy, please tell me you are not sitting on your couch with a freshly opened bottle of wine?"

"Okay, I won't tell you."

"At least get a glass."

"Pssshaw! Glasses are for asses with classes."

Typical Lizzy response. Damn, she missed her best friend.

"Now, spill it, sister. Before I die from curiosipation."

"That's not a word."

"It should be."

Pouring her own wine—in a glass, like a sane person—Maggie then sat on her loveseat and dove into the events of the past few days. The gas leak, the rock, the fight with Colton. Lizzy listened without interruption until she was finished. "So, that's how it's going. You?"

"Oh no, we are still on you, my dear."

Uh oh. Lizzy's angry voice.

"So, what you are telling me is some crazy whack-job is after you and you don't even think to call your best friend?"

Why was everybody so obsessed with her calling for personal updates lately?

"What could you have done? You're over a thousand miles away."

A sound of frustration came through the phone. "I care about you, Maggie. You're my best friend. I need to know when someone is messing with you so I can fly out there and kick their butt!"

"Love you, too, Lizzy." Laughter shook her shoulders. "Anyway, everyone keeps telling me to close up shop until this guy is caught."

"They must not know you very well." She chuckled. "Still, and you know I hate to agree with the majority, but I have to agree with Colton on this one."

"I didn't say it was just Colton."

"No, but he's the one whose opinion you care about."

"I never said that."

"You slept with him, Maggie. You would never sleep with someone unless you cared about them and what they think."

Embarrassment heated her cheeks. "I never said I slept with him."

"You said he came over for dinner and then you had a fight the next morning. I read between the lines." A pause, then, "So, how was it?"

She sighed, downing the rest of her wine. "Amazing."

"Yee haw! Are you seeing him again?"

She hoped so. He said they had a relationship. Mentioned they would have sex again.

"I don't know. He seemed pretty angry when he left."

"He'll get over it. Men just get their boxers in a bunch when a woman doesn't run to them with every little problem. Hurts their frail, little egos. If he really cares, he will realize he's being stupid and come back."

But who was really being stupid here…Colton or her?

She could take care of herself. The saboteur hadn't attacked her yet. Not directly anyway. On the other hand, if the situation were reversed, she'd be angry if Colton was having problems and didn't confide in her. Maybe they were *both* being stupid.

"You should also stop being stupid and cut the guy a little slack."

Leave it to Lizzy to speak what was on Maggie's mind.

"Then when you've made up, saddle that horse and ride him all night long." There was a snort followed by uncontrolled laughter.

"How deep are you into that bottle?"

"Hmmmm, too deep to drive, not deep enough to invite my new sexy neighbor over to help me *fix my plumbing.*"

She laughed at her zany friend. "Put the bottle down, Lizzy."

"Oh, you're no fun."

"And you're not serious about the neighbor."

Her best friend chuckled along with her. "No, but it's fun to think about. He's a bit player on the new crime drama."

Then she really wasn't serious. Lizzy never dated anyone in the industry. It was one of her rules. The tall, beautiful woman hardly dated at all, in fact.

"Put the bottle down and back away slowly. Drink some water, go to bed, and dream of Johnny Depp."

"Oh, Johnny." A soft sigh sounded over the phone. "The only man I'd ever break my rule for. Fine." Her voice took on her managerial tone. "I'll be responsible and go to bed unfulfilled. But you have to call your cowboy, work things out, and get fully filled. Then call me in the morning with all the dirty details."

"Lizzy!" She doubled over with laughter.

"Love you, Maggie."

"Love you, too."

Hanging up, she smiled. Her friend always knew how to make her feel better. She really did miss her. Maybe she could convince Lizzy to come out for a few weeks in the summer. They could paint the town crazy.

Heading to her kitchen, Maggie decided to have one more glass of wine before following instructions and calling Colton. She needed a bit more liquid courage to help her grovel. And she would grovel, because he had been right. She did promise to call him and hadn't.

Before she could grab the bottle of wine off the counter, a knock sounded at her front door.

Who could that be?

It couldn't be a delivery. All her orders arrived in the morning at the shop, never to her apartment.

Reversing direction, she went back to the door and glanced through her peephole…at a pair of piercing, blue eyes.

She should have downed the whole wine bottle while she'd had the chance.

****

"Colton."

Judging by the shocked look on her face, Maggie was surprised to see him. That burned his ass. Did she really think so little of him? Had she just expected him to walk away after one little fight, leaving her all alone when she had a crazy vandal after her?

187

Not likely.

"What are you doing here?"

Without responding, he grabbed the back of her neck, pulling her to him for a deep, thorough kiss. She melted into him immediately. She may not have expected him, but she was obviously glad to see him. That was good. It soothed his ragged nerves a little.

Her hands fisted in his shirt, and her lips opened at the gentle probe of his tongue. Exploring the depths of her mouth, he groaned. It'd just been meant to be a simple hello kiss. He should have realized with this woman, nothing was ever simple.

Pulling back, before he took her there in the open doorway, he stared down at her. Face flushed, eyes closed, lips swollen from his kiss. Beautiful.

"Hi."

Her eyes opened with hazy lust. "Um, hi."

"May I come in?"

The haze cleared as she realized they were standing in her open doorway, pressed close together where anyone could see. A blush rose, making her already pink skin turn rosy.

"Oh, yes, of course." She stepped back, allowing him to enter before closing the door behind him. "I was, uh, just about to make some dinner. Are you hungry?"

He turned to her and gave his best bad boy grin. "Starved."

"Casserole okay?" she asked, deftly ignoring his innuendo. "I have one in the freezer. I made it a while back. I was just going to pop it in the oven."

"Sounds great." He tossed his duffle bag on the couch.

Her gaze darted to it then back to him. "What's

that?"

Colton didn't look at the bag, instead joining her in the kitchen. "We'll talk about it in a minute. First, I want to apologize."

"Apologize?"

He stopped right in front of her. "Yeah, for this morning."

The tight lines around her mouth and eyes loosened as she shook her head. "You have nothing to apologize for."

Wasn't expecting that.

"Yes, I do." Reaching out, he cupped her cheek. "I know I acted like an ass. I realize how important your shop is to you. I know how hard you work, and if anyone can take care of herself, Magpie, it's you. I was just worried and upset. I care about you, and it would kill me if anything happened to you."

Her eyes had widened as he rambled through the speech he had been practicing all afternoon.

"Colton…"

He pushed on. "I already had to see you half-frozen and then sick from gas poisoning. There's only so much a guy can take in a span of barely two weeks."

She shook her head. Strands of soft, brown hair, which had escaped her braid, fluttered about her face. His fingers itched with the need to brush those strands away and take her lips once more, but he stopped himself.

"No, I'm the one who should apologize. You were just trying to look out for me, and I did promise to call you if anything happened. I'm sorry."

An apology from Maggie Evans? Now, there was something that didn't happen every day. He should probably mark this momentous occasion in his calendar or something.

Placing an arm around her waist, he pulled her closer, instead. Nose skimming her cheek, he pressed a soft kiss to the shell of her ear and whispered, "So, now that we've apologized to each other, wanna kiss and make up?"

She leaned back with a knowing grin. "The casserole should take an hour to cook."

"An hour huh?" He ground his hips into her, letting her feel how hard he already was for her. "That's enough time for an appetizer I think."

Pulling from his grasp, she started twisting her hands. "I didn't think you were coming over tonight. I—I didn't have time to go to the pharmacy…"

He thought about teasing her, but she looked so disappointed, he couldn't. Turning from her, he went back to the living room where he had left his bag.

"Colt?"

Unzipping the duffle, he pulled out a one hundred-count black box and waved it in the air. "I stopped by the drug store today."

Her smile turned wicked. "Then why are we still standing out here?"

Chapter Twenty-One

An hour and fifteen minutes later, they were sitting at her kitchen table eating. The casserole was delicious. It had just started to burn when they saved it from the oven. Even the slight char on top didn't detract from the mouthwatering taste. Good thing he had such a physically demanding job; if he didn't, Maggie's delectable cooking and cupcakes would make him gain a hundred pounds. Colton helped himself to a third helping of the tuna casserole.

"So, what else is in the bag?" she asked, drawing his attention away from her enticing dinner. "Don't tell me you actually bought every box of condoms the drug store had?"

"I was tempted, believe me, but no. I just bought the one box."

"Yeah, a *one hundred-count* box. I think we're stocked up for a while, Colt."

He let his gaze roam over her. After their appetizer, she had tossed his T-shirt on over her naked body. It was sexy as hell seeing her in his clothing. His blood heated, thinking of the cloth touching her naked skin. Who knew he could be envious of a T-shirt? He wanted nothing more than to rip the shirt off and take her right there on the kitchen table.

But they had both worked a long day, and after the calisthenics in the bedroom, needed to build up their strength by refueling. And she thought the one box was going to last them...*silly woman.*

"I wouldn't be too sure about that, Magpie." He scooped up another delicious mouthful of casserole. "I doubt we'll make them last the week."

She swallowed, hard. He knew his eyes were filled with raw lust and didn't care. He wanted her. Now, later, always.

"The bag is my stuff."

Her brows drew down. "Come again?"

Shoveling another forkful of dinner into his mouth, he chewed and swallowed. He had to do this the right way. If Maggie thought he was pushing her, she'd toss his butt out the door. Of course, if she did that, he'd just camp out on her doorstep. Her bed would be a much more comfortable option. The fact she would be sharing it with him made it all the better.

"I was thinking, this jerkoff is doing most of his work at night after you close up, right?"

Her eyes narrowed as if she tried to figure out where he was going. "Yes, that seems to be the case."

"Well, if you're not going to temporarily close— and I'm not saying you should," he rushed, before she could cut him off. "Then this guy is just going to keep attacking you. The daytime is safe enough. Your shop's open. Lots of people around, but at night...you're all alone, and it scares the hell outta me."

Her hands twisted together. Worry lines bracketed her mouth and eyes. It was obvious she hadn't thought about that.

Reaching across the table, he grasped her hands in his own, giving a reassuring squeeze. "I have to be at the ranch during the day, but at night, for now, until this bastard is caught, can I please stay here with you? I won't get much sleep if I'm at home worrying about you." Trying to ease her tension, he let his voice drop to a husky timber, gaze trailing over her body with unveiled hunger. "Plus, we'd get through that box much faster if we were sharing the same bed every night."

She laughed when he waggled his eyebrows. "I should have known you'd use this as an excuse to keep me in bed."

"What can I say, sweetheart? I'm a lover not a fighter."

Her smile dimmed. She was thinking about it, but something else worried her. Something other than the attacker was on her mind.

"Maggie?"

She pulled her hands out of his, placing them in her lap under the table. "It's a sweet offer Colt, but this…whatever we have going on—"

"A relationship." *Damn*. Why couldn't she admit that?

"Relationship." She nodded.

That's better.

"It's still very new."

"We've known each other since we were kids."

She glared. "Yes, but we've only been sleeping together for a few days."

The fire left her. That beautiful green gaze darted down to her lap. Where he would bet her hands were twisting in a nervous motion.

"I don't want to start depending on you too much."

"It's not bad to let people help you, Magpie. You aren't weak if you need someone."

Her gaze snapped up to clash with his. The fire was

193

back. The mossy green had sharpened to a deep emerald.

"And what happens when the people you need, the people you care about leave you? If you depend on people, they just let you down."

What? Where the hell is this coming from?

"Maggie, wha—"

"People leave, Colton. Especially men," she mumbled, cutting him off, anger coloring her cheeks. "When my mom got pregnant, my dad took off. When she needed him most, he just left her."

"Well, your dad was an ass." Was she comparing him to her father? Better not be. "I'm not going to abandon you just because you think you're getting dependent on me." As if Maggie Evans could ever be dependent on anyone.

"I *won't* depend on anyone."

See.

That stubborn little chin tilted high in the air, but he could see the fear in her eyes behind all her bravado.

"You can't rely on people. They just leave you or use you. My dad left before I was born. Mom and Gran both died. Every guy I dated in LA just wanted something from me, and then Miles—" She cut herself off, her face going red with embarrassment.

Miles. She had mentioned that name once before. An ex, he was now sure of it. He already hated the guy and didn't even know him.

"Who's Miles?

She shook her head, waving a hand in the air. "No one. It's not important."

"Oh no. I'm not moving from this spot until we clear a few things up." He held up a hand and started counting off on his fingers. "First, don't insult me by comparing me to that deadbeat dad of yours. Second, if *I* promise something, I *always* follow through with it. And third, people die, Maggie. It's a way of life, and no one gets to choose when it happens, but I don't plan on it happening to me for a long, long time."

The worry lines on her forehead started to soften. He wished he could stop there, but they needed to get things out into the open. Their relationship could never move forward if she didn't start opening up and letting him in.

"And again, who the hell is Miles, and where is he so I can kick his ass?" The last part was supposed to be a joke, but it came out a little more serious than he intended. He kind of did want to kick the guy's ass. If only for the fact he had Maggie and let her get away. What kind of idiot would do that?

A thought occurred to him—if Miles still had her, then Colton wouldn't right now. Maybe he should thank the guy instead.

Then he'd kick his ass.

"Miles is my ex." She crossed her arms over her chest.

"Okay. So, what happened?"

"We broke up. It's what happens to thousands of couples every day. Not a big deal."

But it was if she counted Miles in the group of people who left her. Colton would not be in that group. No matter what she thought.

"It *is* a big deal. When Sheriff Ryder asked if there was anyone who might have a grudge against you, why didn't you give him Miles' name?"

"Miles lives in LA. Why the hell would he fly

thousands of miles to sabotage my bakery?"

"Losing a woman like you would do crazy things to a man. Perhaps he thought if he messed with your business you'd close up shop and go running back home to him."

She laughed, sharp and bitter. "He didn't *lose* me. We broke up."

"Maybe he got lonely once you left and realized how stupid he was for breaking up with you."

Her hard gaze pinned him. Now, it was her turn to hold up a hand and count off. "A, I broke up with him. B, the break up was months before I left town, and C, he wasn't lonely because he had his other two girlfriends and *wife* to keep him company."

Whoa. Busy guy.

It did seem highly unlikely he would follow Maggie all the way to Colorado. But people have been known to go nuts when someone dumps them.

"I still think you should tell Ryder about him."

"Fine," she shouted, throwing her hand up. "I'll call him first thing tomorrow, but it's pointless. When I broke up with Miles, he didn't care. He had plenty of other women to run to. There is no reason for him to chase after me."

Okay, now he really did want to slug the guy. What an idiot. He hated cheaters, always had. It was why, even when she had begged, he never gave Natalie a second chance. The selfish woman knew what she had been doing and how it would hurt him. Yet, she hadn't cared. She only thought of herself. Miles sounded just as vain. A man like that didn't deserve Maggie.

"I still want to stay here until whoever is doing this to you is caught."

Her frustration was palpable. Rising from her chair, she grabbed their dinner plates and took them to the sink, slamming the plates down with such force he was afraid she'd broken them.

"Whatever. I'm sure I can't stop you anyway. You'd probably just camp out on my front stoop if I said no."

Damn right.

"But, you listen to me, Colton Denning." She brandished the dish sponge as if it was a sword. "I'm not some helpless little girl who needs you to defend me. I am a grown woman. More than capable of taking care of myself, no matter what is happening in my life or who's trying to ruin it." She started to turn back to the sink, but then snapped back around to add, "And the toilet seat stays down!"

A grin tugged his lips. He'd won. She might not be particularly happy about it, but she agreed to let him stay. Not that he would have let her kick him out. While she was right about being able to take care of herself, there was no way he was leaving her alone at night unprotected. There was safety in numbers, no matter who you were or how capable.

He walked over to where she stood. "Thank you, Magpie."

Placing his hands on her tense shoulders, he kissed her forehead. Since she had his shirt on, his chest was bare. It rubbed up against her own as he pulled her to him. Her nipples harden beneath the thin cotton. His jeans tightened as the scent of her invaded his nostrils. It had only been an hour, but he wanted her again.

"I promise not to make my staying here too hard on you," he said, rubbing a particular hard part of his anatomy against her.

A sigh rushed out of her on a shaky breath. "Well, they do say that the harder things are, the more they're worth it."

Cheeky woman. Damn, she's perfect.

"Let me prove my worth to you right now."

Grabbing the hem of the shirt, he lifted it up and away from her body, leaving her gloriously naked. She gasped, and he took advantage of her open lips, thrusting his tongue into her mouth. Her skin was smooth and soft as he roamed over her bare flesh with his hands, touching, teasing, tantalizing. She met his fervor, running her hands down his back, matching his tongue thrust for thrust.

Their mouths simulated what their bodies would soon be doing. She was so open in her hunger for him. It drove him wild. He needed to be inside her soon or it would all be over much too quickly.

"Bed," he murmured, pulling away from her lips.

"Too far." Tugging the tie from her braid, she shook her head, sending her silky hair tumbling over those perfect breasts. "Here. Now."

Fine with him. He didn't care where they made love. And it *was* making love, because Colton realized something when Maggie was opening up to him. He loved her. Loved her strength, her courage, her independence, and most of all, her heart.

But it wasn't the time to tell her. She had just opened emotional wounds from her past and not all that willingly. Based on what she'd told him, he knew Maggie wouldn't trust his love if he declared it to her now. He would just have to show her and keep on showing her, until she believed it when he finally did say the words aloud.

Colton's thoughts scattered as she found his zipper. The rasping sound hit his ears as she opened his jeans and reached in to find him. The anticipation of what was to come had him painfully hard. He needed to be inside her, to fully connect with her on every level.

She pulled him close. Wrapping her leg around his hip, she guided him to her. Heat radiated from her body to his.

"Maggie, oh God!" It felt so good. His mind was a fog of need, but one rational thought crept in as he felt her warm, naked flesh against his own. "Protection. Sweetheart, wait."

She paused with him halfway inside her. *Damn.* She was so tight and perfect. Amazing. But he knew if they didn't stop, things could happen. Strangely, the thought of Maggie round with his child didn't cause one iota of panic in him. Instead, he saw a little girl with his smile and her bright green eyes. The picture was so real his heart skipped a beat.

"Damn. Where's the box." Frustration laced her words.

He might not be afraid of a more permanent connection, but it sounded like she was.

Regretfully pulling out of her warmth, Colton reached down to his jeans and snagged a packet from his back pocket.

"When did you put that there?" she asked with surprise.

Ripping open the foil, he gave her a wicked grin. "I was a boy scout remember? Always prepared."

Her lips found his in a scorching kiss. The condom disappeared from his hand as she grabbed it and rolled it on his length. Then he was inside her again. Right where he belonged.

It was going to be quick. For both of them. He could already feel her inner walls quivering against him, squeezing him tight. Grasping under her thighs, he lifted her, bracing her back against the pantry door as he furiously pumped into her.

Colton angled her hips so every thrust brushed against her sweet spot. In minutes, she was screaming out a climax. He gave one more hard thrust, and then joined her in ecstasy.

****

They should have closed the curtains. Or at least shut off the lights. She couldn't see much from her vantage point in her car across the street, but she knew what they were doing. All that face sucking and bouncing up and down…disgusting!

Slut! Whore! Bitch!

The foul words she never uttered out loud screamed inside her mind. She hated Maggie Evans more with each day.

The little tart stole what she wanted, what she deserved. *What's rightfully mine!*

Now, the stupid whore was going to pay. Maggie should have left Colton alone. He didn't belong with the LA harlot. Brown-haired bitch should have left town. The shop wasn't hers. Colton wasn't hers. Why did the woman keep taking things that didn't belong to her?

Time to stop messing around. Time to stop attacking the shop and start attacking the owner. Her mother and grandmother should have taught the bitch baker her place in life, but since the dead women hadn't…*guess I'll have to.*

She had to make a new plan. More direct, more painful. Maggie would get the message this time, and if she didn't…

Chapter Twenty-Two

Maggie walked out of the small, brown brick building that served as the police station. In a place as tiny as Peak Town, there wasn't a lot of crime. The place consisted of one very small interrogation room, two small cells in the back, and five desks strategically placed about the rest of the small, one story office.

As she promised Colton, she'd called the sheriff that morning to tell him about Miles. Ryder asked her to come down to the station after work. She had, and after she told him about their relationship and how it ended, he promised to check up on him.

Stupid really, there was no way her ex was behind the problems she was having. When she told Miles it was over because she'd found out about the other women, and her technically being an "other woman," too, he really did just shrug and say, *"Whatever. I have plenty of women to keep me satisfied. I was getting bored with you anyway."*

That was what hurt the most. Yes, she hated the fact he cheated on her and was angry that he made her a part of his infidelity. She never sought out to be a home wrecker. Thinking about his poor wife made her sick to her stomach even now, a year later. She felt stupid for never realizing who he really was. But all that, she could get over. What she could never forget were those words, *"I was getting* bored *with you."*

It had been yet another example of someone she loved leaving her because she wasn't enough. Her father never even tried to get to know her, having run out on her mother before Maggie even existed. It was the ominous start to her life of loved ones leaving. What was so wrong with her that no one stayed?

Then her mother, the person she loved most in the world, left her. She fought the cancer for two years, but eventually the fight was too much to bear, and she left Maggie all alone. Gran had gone not long after. Another person she loved, out of her life forever.

She knew her mother and Gran hadn't chosen to leave her. Everyone died eventually. But still, the women in her life left the earth, and the men just left her. For their booze, easier women, or just because she was boring. She'd just never been enough. Not a great sign of her relationship longevity.

That was why, no matter how wonderful and right it felt to be with Colton, she was keeping her heart out of it. She would have her fun. When he got bored of her and left, she would remember their time with fondness and not a broken heart.

Yeah right. And she had a bridge to sell herself, too.

Maggie made her way down the sidewalk. The station was only a few blocks from the shop, and it was a surprisingly warm spring night. The sun had just started to sink beneath the mountains. Red, purple, and orange hues painted the evening sky. The sunsets were really beautiful out here. Back in LA, you couldn't even see the sun through the smog most days.

The rushed clacking of multiple heeled shoes behind her disturbed the peaceful evening stroll.

"You've got some nerve, Maggie Evans."

Oh crap. Now what had she done?

Turning, she came face to face with Natalie *and* her mother, Deloris Brake. The older woman was a smaller, more wrinkled version of her daughter. She sneered at Maggie, the sour expression a carbon copy of the younger Brake. Crabapple didn't fall too far from the tree it seemed.

"Hello, Natalie. Mrs. Brake. How are you?"

"Don't you 'Hello, Natalie' me! Not after what you did."

"What are you talking about?" With her, it could be so many things.

"You know very well what I'm talking about."

The line free face—thanks to Botox—was red with anger, arms crossed over her very expensive red silk shirt, and a foot tapped away aggressively in her three inch, stark white stilettos. Though Maggie thought it was still too cold out, the perfectly put together former cheerleader wore a short black mini skirt that looked like it was made for a twenty-two year old girl, not a thirty-two year old woman.

Deloris was more appropriately dressed for the weather in a pale blue tracksuit with a light yellow windbreaker. Both women had flawlessly done hair, not a strand out of place. Ms. Brake had thin white gloves on, but Natalie's hands were bare, displaying nails painted the same color as her shirt. Even her jewelry matched her outfit, dangly gold heart earrings with a ruby in the center and a matching necklace.

Maggie couldn't even remember the last time she wore a piece of jewelry, other than Gran's ring. She barely ever wore anything besides jeans and T-shirts.

Maybe a sweater if it was cold out. Her sneakers were well worn and probably in need of replacement. Once, Lizzy had convinced her to wear heels to a bar. She'd fallen right on her face the second she got out of the cab.

She and Natalie couldn't be more different.

Her heart plummeted as she remembered Colton had dated this woman. Probably the type of women he dated all the time. Perfectly polished and put together.

Then why the hell is he with me?

Again, the impending end of their relationship reared its ugly head in her mind. That was why she had to keep her heart out of it.

But she was afraid it might be too late for that.

She was suddenly feeling very snarky. "I'm afraid you'll have to tell me which thing I did this time to piss you off."

"You watch your language, young lady." Lips bracketed with age lines no amount of plastic surgery could help curled back.

Oh great, Natalie brought her mommy along to yell at me. Worst tag team ever.

The younger Brake pointed a long, manicured finger at the police station. "You were in there telling the sheriff more lies about me. Admit it!"

A vein on the wrinkle free forehead started to throb. If the woman knew it did that when she was angry she'd Botox it for sure. Maybe Maggie would get lucky and the poison would freeze her face.

"I don't know what you mean."

Deloris huffed out a sound of disbelief.

Reigning in her temper, Maggie tried to remember the lessons her mother had taught her about respecting

205

her elders.

"Not too bright, are you?"

Respect your elders, respect your elders, respect—

"I can see why that big time LA restaurant fired you."

The old lady was making it really hard to be polite.

"I wasn't fired," she said, teeth clenched, fake smile in place. "I quit so I could take over the shop my grandmother left me."

A dark, ugly look passed through Deloris Brake's eyes. Guess that smile had been a little too fake.

"The sheriff came to my store the other day and harassed me. In front of my customers!" The vein grew bigger by the moment. "He practically accused *me* of sabotaging your store! As if I don't have better things to do with my time."

Maggie was sure Sheriff Ryder had simply asked her some questions, but Natalie was a drama queen. A simple question would be like the Spanish inquisition to that woman.

"Stop spreading nasty lies about me! I don't care about your stupid cupcake store, and I don't care about you and Colton."

Yes she did. She could tell by the way the prissy woman's teeth clenched together on his name.

"I wasn't at the station to talk about you," Maggie offered. "I was simply talking to Sheriff Ryder about other people."

Bright red lips turned up in a smug grin. "I'm not surprised you have a list of people who want to hurt you. You seem to piss people off everywhere you go."

The Brake women shared a harsh laugh. Not hard to see where the daughter got her spiteful attitude.

Maggie would love to give them both a piece of her mind, but she didn't have the time or energy.

"Yes, I'm a horrible person. I got it. Now, if you'll excuse me, I have to get home." The cruel women had pissed her off just enough for her to smile sweetly and add, "Colton's staying at my place, and I'd hate to keep him waiting."

Deloris mumbled something under her breath. An unpleasant observations of her character, no doubt. Natalie's face turned bright red. The vein throbbed so hard, Maggie feared it would burst.

The ruffled woman stepped closer, leaning down to get in her face. Maggie held her ground as hateful words hissed out between bleached white teeth.

"Enjoy your time now, but know this. Colton could never be with someone like you for very long. He's just *slumming* it for the fun. You're sloppy, garish, and pathetic. He will get *bored* with you eventually…and drop you like the dead weight you are."

Tears burned the back of her eyes, but Maggie refused to let these two awful women see them. Turing on her heel, she didn't even respond. As she briskly walked back to her apartment, she could hear Natalie and Deloris making crude comments behind her.

But even someone as dimwitted as Natalie could see the eventual end of her relationship. It took everything in Maggie to push back the tears forming in her eyes. She should just save herself the heartache and end it now.

Except, there was still a crazy person out there gunning for her, and until they were caught, Colton would insist on staying for her protection.

So, for now, she would continue the relationship,

enjoy him while she had him. When the bastard hurting her shop was found…then…what would happen when the threat was gone?

She didn't have to ask, she knew—Colton's reason for being with her would be gone from her life and so would he.

Chapter Twenty-Three

"Today's the big day, sweetheart."

Maggie buried her head in her pillow. It had been a week since Colton started staying with her. A week of wonderful, bliss-filled nights.

They'd settled into a routine very quickly. After closing up her shop, she would head upstairs to her apartment where he'd already be waiting. Most nights, they made dinner together, and afterward, stood side by side in the kitchen washing and drying the dirty dishes. Then they would try to watch a movie or play poker, but inevitably, ended up in bed.

Not that she was complaining.

Her favorite place to be with Colton was in bed, or the shower, couch, floor. Really, anywhere she could feel his warm, hard body against her own.

He seemed to take her disbelief at using the entire hundred-count condom box as a challenge. To his credit, they'd made a sizeable dent in just one week.

The saboteur had been quiet. No more broken windows. No threatening notes. No shop vandalism. It was comforting and suspicious at the same time. She had a sinking feeling in the pit of her stomach. Like she was waiting for the other shoe to drop.

Soft lips grazed her shoulder, sending chills skating along her body.

"Rise and shine, Magpie."

A groan escaped her lips. "I should have been a bartender. They get to sleep 'til noon, and they don't have to worry about impressing critics. Enough alcohol and everyone loves your drinks."

A firm hand stroked her from hip to chest. The large palm cupped her naked breast and squeezed. Her breath caught in her throat.

"You're too sweet to be a bartender. That's why you make delicious, wonderful cupcakes that everyone loves. And so will the blogger today."

Her stomach sank again at the reminder of what the day held.

"You need to relax, sweetheart." His hot breath fanned her ear. "Can't make scrumptious cupcakes if you're all tense."

She laughed when his breath tickled her neck. "Who the hell says scrumptious?"

Rolling her beneath him, Colton rose over her. A wicked smile played on his lips as he pressed himself into her. He was hard. She knew men always had morning wood, but he seems to be permanently hard around her. Kind of flattering.

"Now," he said, moving his hips against hers, forcing all thoughts to scatter from her brain. "Let's see what we can do to relieve some of that tension."

****

After Colton had relieved her tension, he left to go back to the ranch, and Maggie hit the trails for her morning run. Instead of taking the small loop as she normally did, she ran the long trail. Anxiety still racked her. A good long run would help.

She decided to forgo the coffee at Merle's since her run was longer than usual and Jamie was coming in early today to help with the regular orders so she could focus on the blogger. She had decided on three recipes: Chocolate Mint Truffle, Buttercream Vanilla with champagne frosting, and Raspberry Chocolate Torte. All three were Gran's recipes with a little twist thrown in to make them her own.

Sweat coated her body from the run. The days were getting warmer, finally. A shower was in order, but it would have to be a quick one.

Climbing the outside stairs to her apartment, she noticed the door slightly ajar. Had she left it open when she went for her run? No, she always made sure to lock it. Maybe Colton forgot something and came back? She'd given him her spare keys when he started spending the night.

Her heartbeat picked up at the thought of seeing him again—and maybe convincing him to share that shower with her.

"Colton? Did you forget something?" she called as she walked through the open door.

One step into her apartment and her overheated body turned ice cold. Colton had not came back, but someone had.

Breath left her lungs as if punched right in the gut. A cold sweat coated her palms as she gazed at the surroundings of her once cozy and safe apartment. Furniture was turned over. Piles of papers littered the floor. Pillows slashed. Her TV had been smashed. Picture frames broken. Glass was scattered everywhere, and on the walls, hateful blood red words: Slut. Whore. Bitch.

Who would do something like this?

Her saboteur had changed his tactics. He was

coming after her now.

Fear formed a solid lump in her throat. Pulling the cell phone from her pocket, Maggie hit the speed dial. It rang four times.

"Hey, sweetheart, I'm kind of in the middle of—"

"Colton?"

"What's wrong?" His tone went from jovial to concern in an instant.

"H-he was here."

"Who was? Maggie? Maggie, talk to me. What's going on?"

She couldn't stop the tears from flowing as she glanced down and saw the picture of her and Gran baking a cake. It had been her eleventh birthday and the first cake she ever made entirely by herself. Gran declared it to be the best cake ever, even though the bottom had burned. It was one of her best memories. The picture had been slashed, Maggie's face scratched out.

What had she done to deserve such hatred?

"Maggie! Answer me, goddammit!"

She could hear the fear in his voice. *Join the club.* She stepped back and closed the door. "I have to call the sheriff. My apartment's been broken into."

An understatement. It'd been destroyed.

"Don't go inside. I'll be right there. Lock yourself in your shop. Don't go inside your apartment!"

She wouldn't. She would not let this asshole ruin all the hard work she had achieved. They may have destroyed her home and her sense of security, but they wouldn't destroyed her.

"I'll be there in ten minutes."

He made it in five.

Sheriff Ryder arrived only seconds after. Maggie stood on her front stoop, Colton's strong arms wrapped firmly around her. It was the only place she felt safe anymore.

"Colton. Maggie." Ryder tipped his hat. "What happened?"

"I came back from my morning run and saw my door was open. I thought maybe Colton had forgotten something after he left and had come back to get it." A shiver of fear racked her body. Strong arms tightened around her, giving her the strength to continue. "I stepped inside and th—the placed is trashed."

"All right. Stay here, but don't leave. I'm going to need a statement. I'll also need you to come in after I check the place out, to see if anything is missing."

"I don't think robbery was their motive." Moisture pooled in her eyes again as she remembered those hateful words scrawled across her walls.

"All right. I've got a deputy on his way over. I'm just going to make sure no one is inside."

With that, Ryder disappeared into her apartment. He came out a few minutes later with the all clear. A deputy arrived, a young, red-haired man who didn't look old enough to shave. She recognized him from the earlier incident. He carried the same large, gray metal case and had a camera hanging from around his neck.

"I want pictures of everything, Tom. Dust the doors and windows for prints. Let's see if this bastard left us anything to catch him." The deputy nodded and headed into the apartment. Ryder turned to her with sympathetic eyes. "I know this is hard, but I need you to look through the place and tell me if anything is missing. Can you do that?"

With Colton close on her heels, Maggie made her way back into her apartment. Only, it didn't feel like home anymore. Whoever did this had destroyed her sense of safety. How could you call a place home when you didn't feel safe there?

Going room by room, she surveyed the devastation. The bathroom was untouched, as was her small dining area. The kitchen had broken dishes, glasses, and overturned drawers. The living room held most of the damage, but her bedroom had also been wrecked. Her mattress was slashed from top to bottom. Sheets, blankets, and pillows were torn to shreds. Her clothes were strewn about the room. Scissors had been taken to a lot of her clothing.

And blazed above the bed in deep red letters: GO HOME WHORE!

"Who would do this?"

She hadn't realized she asked the question out loud until Ryder answered her.

"Who knows your schedule? Who knew you would be out running this morning?"

"Most everybody in town knows I run in the mornings. I usually go to Merle's for coffee after my run, so lots of people see me. I didn't go today because I ran longer than usual, and I wanted to get ready for— shit, the blogger!"

Colton grabbed her arms when she turned about her room frantically.

"It'll be okay, sweetheart."

"No it won't! The blogger is coming in a few hours. I need to open the shop, make the cupcakes— crap." She looked down at her running clothes then around the room at the scraps of what used to be her

214

wardrobe. "I don't have anything to wear. That asshole ruined all my clothes!"

"Maggie, calm down. Take a deep breath."

Jaw clenched tight, she scowled at him. She was pissed as hell, and he was telling her to calm down?

"Let's look in the back of your closet and see if there are any clothes intact. Is that okay, Ryder?"

The sheriff nodded.

She stomped over to her closet, thankful and angry at Colton for being the voice of reason. Flipping on the light, she saw, however, that he was indeed right. There were a few T-shirts and a pair of jeans on the closet floor that the vandal missed. They were dirty, but at least they were in one piece.

"There, see? Problem one solved."

She turned at the sound of his deep voice so close behind her. Glaring, she replied, "You're not always right, you know."

He grinned, placing a kiss to her lips. "There's my feisty Magpie."

She sighed, arms going around his waist. Taking her frustrations out on him wasn't fair. "I'm sorry, Colt."

"Hey, it's fine. You have a big day ahead of you, and this was the last thing you needed. No one needs this, ever. We're going to find this guy, Maggie. I swear." He growled the last part.

"*I'm* going to find this guy," Ryder corrected from outside the closet door. "You two are going to stay out of it and report anything you know to me. Right?"

"Right," they both answered, coming back into the bedroom.

"You can go about your day. I'll let you know what

we find out. I think it's better if you don't stay here tonight."

"She's staying with me, at the ranch." Colton tucked her under his arm.

She could argue about him making assumptions, but truthfully, she didn't want to stay here. Even with Colton staying with her, she wouldn't feel safe. Someone had violated her home. She felt an intense need to take a shower, wash away the cold dread seeping its way through her.

"I'll stay at the ranch," she agreed.

"Okay. As soon as we have any information, I'll let you know. Now, go wow that blogger's taste buds off." The sheriff winked.

She smiled, clutching her few remaining clothes tight to her chest. "Thanks."

That was precisely what she intended to do. The asshole who did this might have taken away her sense of security, but he couldn't take away her ability to make a kickass cupcake.

Time to keep calm and bake on.

Chapter Twenty-Four

"Oh my God," Stephanie Delany, blogger from Guilty Pleasures: A Cross-Country Food Journey, mumbled through a mouth full of cupcake. "It's times like this when I love my job, sooooo much."

Maggie twisted her hands, watching the woman eat. Stephanie had arrived at the shop an hour ago. The woman appeared to be in her mid-thirties, with short, curly brown hair and a pleasant demeanor; Maggie liked her immediately. Ms. Delany had leapt right in, asking a series of questions about the store and Maggie's history in baking. When she told the blogger about inheriting the store from her grandmother, learning the craft of cooking all those summers ago, Stephanie brightened with interest. When she handed over a plate of carefully crafted cupcakes, the woman's eyes lit with hunger.

The pleasant moan after the first bite set her nerves at ease.

"I'm glad you enjoy them."

"Enjoy them? Maggie, honey, if I enjoyed them any more I'd gain fifty pounds! These cupcakes are delectable."

Things were going better than she could have hoped. Quite a turnaround from this morning. There was her roller coaster luck again. She was just glad her car was at the top of the coaster for the blogger's visit.

"I usually don't tell people how the review is going to go before I write it, but let me just say, you might want to hire more help for the summer. I have a feeling you'll be getting a lot of new business."

Hallelujah!

The blogger loved her cupcakes. She was going to get a great review. Tourists would soon be flocking to her store, spending money. Her till would be full, and Gran's legacy secure. Everything was perfect!

Well, okay, not everything.

She still had a crazy person attacking her. Those crude words flashed in her mind again. She pushed them away. Now was not the time. It was time to celebrate and rejoice in all her hard work. She'd worry about her shattered home later.

"Let me just take a few more pictures for the blog and I'll be out of your hair."

"I'll wrap up the rest of these for you to take with you." She grabbed the plate of cupcakes.

Stephanie's smile widened revealing twin dimples in the woman's cheeks. "Thank you. I always try to bring a sample of food home to my husband, but I doubt they'll last until my plane ride tomorrow."

"If you leave your address, I can ship a box to your home. I have a great Strawberry filled Chocolate Gnocchi cupcake that's perfect for a romantic date night."

"You are an angel." The other woman eagerly wrote down her address, took a few more photos of the shop and cupcakes, then, with a wave, left.

Maggie turned to the counter where Jamie and Colton—who had refused to leave her side after this morning—were anxiously waiting. The bakery was small enough that, even though she and Stephanie had been at the far corner table, she was sure they heard every word. Still, they waited for her to speak.

"I think she loved them!"

Jumping up and down in excitement, Jamie let out an ear-piercing squeal. Colton jumped over the counter. Picking her up in a bear hug, he swung her around, kissing her soundly on the lips before setting her down.

"I knew she'd love them. You are amazing, Magpie."

"Do you really think we'll be as busy as she said?" Jamie asked. "I can work full-time this summer if you need."

If the review was as good as Stephanie hinted at, they might be. It was one of the highest followed food blogs on the Internet. People showed up in droves to the high-rated eateries on Guilty Pleasures. Hiring extra help might become necessary.

A name popped into her head: Tony. He showed a great talent for cooking. He could work part-time in the summer for her, and if he enjoyed it, he could continue in the fall. Much to her dismay, she had to think of a replacement for Jamie when the young woman went off to college.

She'd bring it up with Colton later. If the young man wanted to, he could split his time between the ranch and her shop. If he found he enjoyed baking, maybe he'd let her help him apply to culinary schools. He had such talent. She'd hate to see it go to waste.

"We need to celebrate," Colton said.

"I still have some champagne in back from the frosting." She glanced at Jamie. "Oh, but—"

The teenager rolled her eyes. "Don't worry boss,

I've got a soda in my bag. It's got all the bubbles with none of the booze."

He retrieved the bottle of champagne and they toasted—the underage girl toasting with her soda—to a successful review. After they closed up. Her young employee gave her a giant hug goodbye, squealing with delight once again. She really was going to miss that girl.

"Ready to go home?" Colton's deep voice whispered in her ear.

Home.

He said it as if she belonged there. As if it was their home and not just a place she was staying because hers was in shambles. It was lovely to imagine it being true, but she knew she couldn't. As wonderful and caring as Colton was, she couldn't let herself fall so far for him. It would just destroy her when he left. And he would leave—

No. She couldn't think like that now. For now, she would enjoy her success, enjoy Colton. She deserved a little happiness before the inevitable happened, and she planned to take it.

Chapter Twenty-Five

A week passed before Maggie got a call from the sheriff. A week of working at her shop, then heading out to the Denning ranch to stay with Colton. They'd fallen right back into their routine. Cooking dinner—sometimes with Dade's help—watching movies, playing poker, making love.

Not being alone anymore, the routine had altered a little. She insisted on their lovemaking being confined to Colton's room. She would die of embarrassment if Dade or one of the ranch hands walked in on them in a...compromising situation. Some nights they would saddle up a few horses and go for a ride. While the horses grazed, Colton would put down a blanket and make love to her under the stars.

It was pure heaven.

When Sheriff Ryder called asking her to come down to the station, the high she had been on for the past week died. He told her they had no leads, but were ready to release some property of hers that had been taken for DNA and fingerprint testing.

Colton insisted on accompanying her to the station. She didn't argue. Having him around was calming. She was coming to rely on it. That was the problem.

They stepped into the small building that housed the police station and headed toward the back to the sheriff's desk.

"Thanks for coming," Ryder said with a nod, standing to shake both of their hands. "Have a seat."

She took a seat beside Colton across from the sheriff's desk and started twisting her hands together. Grasping her palm in his own, Colton squeezed reassuringly. Her nerves calmed immediately. How did he do that to her with just a touch?

"I'm sorry I don't have more information for you." The sheriff's face was grim. "The perpetrator was good. He didn't leave a hint of himself in your place."

"You did your best. Thank you."

Ryder rubbed a hand across his tense jaw. "Have there been any more incidents? At your shop? Your home?"

She shook her head. "Nothing has happened in over a week. I'm still staying with Colton at the ranch, for the time being."

Sky blue eyes slanted her a look she couldn't decipher.

"Well, then I'm afraid for the moment there's nothing more we can do. I don't think this is over though, so keep a wary eye out."

She nodded.

"I have some things we took from your place for testing. We're done, so you can take them now." He handed over a small box with some picture frames, silverware, papers and jewelry...all coated with powder. "We were hoping to get some prints, but the bastard must have worn gloves."

She rifled through the box, looking at the broken remains of her home; sadness and anger welled inside her.

At the bottom of the box, something caught her

eye. A gold chain.

She didn't wear gold.

Jewelry wasn't really her thing, but when she did wear it, she preferred silver. Digging out the chain, she held it up. A gasp left her lips, and her heart started to race. She recognized the necklace, had seen it the other day. The pendant matched a set of earrings. A very specific set of jewelry. A gold heart with a ruby stone.

"Oh my God!"

"Maggie?" Colton gripped her hand tighter. "Sweetheart, what is it?"

"Where did you find this necklace?" she asked, ignoring the question.

The sheriff scanned the papers in the open file on his desk. "It was found on the floor by the bed. We thought the perp might have grabbed some of your jewelry, but dropped this on his way out. We hoped there would be a partial fingerprint on it, but no such luck."

"This *isn't* my necklace." The clasp was broken. It must have fallen off when—

"Then it could belong to the person who ransacked your place." Ryder smiled, a triumphant gleam in his eye. "Now, we have something to go on."

"Wait," Colton interrupted. "But that's a woman's necklace. Are you saying the person who did this to Maggie is a woman?"

"Look's possible."

"It's not only possible. It's a fact. I know whose necklace this is."

Both men turned to stare at her.

She swallowed past the lump in her throat. "I saw this necklace on Natalie Brake just last week."

She should have known. The woman hated her. Hated her shop, hated she was with Colton. Had that hatred pushed Natalie to throw a rock through her window and destroy her apartment?

It appeared so.

"Tom," Ryder called to his deputy two desks away. "Call Judge Harper. Get me a warrant to search Natalie Brake's home. Now!" The young man grabbed the phone on his desk, eager to follow his sheriff's orders. Ryder rose, tugging his hat and jacket on. "I'm going to pick up Natalie."

Anger and disbelief warred inside her, making her gut turn sour. "I want to talk to her."

The sheriff paused. "Maggie, I can't let you do that."

Rising from her seat, she pleaded, "I have to know why she hates me this much. Please."

Those words. Those ugly, red words, flashed in her mind. People had disliked her before, even flat out hated her. But no one had ever resorted to violence. She needed to know why Natalie did this. What was it about her that caused people to leave her, attack her, want to get rid of her? She needed to know.

Ryder sighed. "I can let you watch the interrogation. As the victim, you have that right, but you can't be in the room. You can't talk to her. Otherwise, the case could get thrown out."

She nodded. It would have to do.

The sheriff placed a comforting hand on her shoulder before hurrying out of the station to pick up her attacker.

Natalie Brake.

She sucked in a deep breath, desperate, but

determined to discover why the woman hated her this much.

****

Colton stood with Maggie in the small observation room. It wasn't really a room. More like a tiny closet. Through the one-way mirror, they could see Sheriff Ryder questioning Natalie. The woman did not look happy.

Good.

Natalie had terrorized Maggie, broken her window, and destroyed her home. The woman *should* be unhappy. She should also be scared, because he was going to make sure she paid for what she did. He was going to ride ass until she was locked up for a good, long time. When he thought back to how his ex had tried to hurt the woman he loved, his blood began to boil.

"We have proof that you were in Maggie Evans' apartment." Ryder's voice came through the small speaker attached to the wall.

"You don't have crap, because I was never there. I told you, I didn't do anything to Maggie. That stupid bitch is just trying to blame her problems on me because she's jealous." Long, fake fingernails tapped on the metal table. "I bet no one is even after her. She probably did all this to herself just to get attention."

That was Natalie. Always someone else's fault. Even after he discovered she was cheating on him, she blamed *him*, saying because he didn't follow her to college she got lonely. Hell, he had gotten lonely, too, but never thought that gave him clearance to find company elsewhere. The vain woman only thought of herself and her needs.

"We have proof," Ryder repeated.

"Oh yeah? What?" the woman shot back with heat.

The sheriff pulled out an evidence bag containing the gold heart necklace. Natalie's eyes went wide with recognition. She touched her throat where, today, she had on a silver necklace with a blue teardrop pendant.

"I believe this is yours. It was found in Maggie Evans' bedroom. You said you've never been to her apartment before, so how did it get into Maggie's bedroom? My guess is that it fell off your neck when you ransacked her place. The clasp is broken. It would have slipped right off without you even knowing."

He watched from behind the glass as she reached out to touch the bag then caught herself, closing her hand into a fist.

Her gaze darted back to Ryder. "I want a lawyer."

Her voice was cool, but he knew Natalie. He could hear the fear behind those words. Something was off. She sounded worried, but not worried because she had been caught. Worried about something else. What else was there to be worried about? What was worse than getting caught? Something was definitely wrong here.

"I know my rights, and I want a lawyer."

Ryder put the necklace back into the small box he had with him. "I'll get you a phone."

"Let's go." Maggie turned to him.

She was hunched in on herself. The fear that he had seen in her eyes the past few weeks replaced by sadness. It killed him. He wished Natalie were a man so he could kick her ass.

They left the station and got in his truck. He didn't ask her where she wanted to go, just drove back to the ranch. He was beginning to see it as their home.

Hopefully she was, too.

"I always knew Natalie didn't like me, but I never thought she hated me this much. What did I do to make her so angry?"

He gripped the wheel so tight he thought he'd rip it right off. Damn his ex for doing this to Maggie.

"You did nothing, sweetheart. Natalie Brake is a mean, selfish person. Trust me. She fabricated some slight in her mind and ran with it. When she wants something and someone is in her way, she doesn't care who she hurts to get it."

She turned to him, bright green eyes dim. "But what did she want? My store? My absence? You?"

His jaw clenched. "It doesn't matter what she wanted, she's not getting it. The store is yours, you're not leaving, and she already had me. It's her fault we broke up. Not yours."

"If she hadn't cheated on you, would you two still be together?"

He heard the apprehension in her question. She still didn't fully grasp how deep his feelings went for her. Showing her wasn't working. Maybe it was finally time to tell her.

He pulled into the driveway. Turning off the truck, he reached across the seat to grab her hand. "Listen to me, Maggie. Natalie and I were done even before she left for school, we just didn't realize it at the time. We tried to make the long distance thing work, but it didn't. We would have broken up eventually, because we weren't right for each other."

She gazed up. His next words were very important. He had to say them right.

"I didn't care for her. Not like I care for you. I

didn't love her."

Her breath hitched. Those dim eyes brightened like two glowing emeralds. Her lips parted as she edged closer.

"Maggie, I—"

"Hey, you're back! How'd it go?"

Worst timing ever. He was going to kill his brother.

Maggie slipped from his grasp, opening her door. She hopped out to meet Dade, who was walking toward them. "Not well." She accepted a hug from him. "I'll let Colt tell you about it. I'm pretty worn out. I think I'll go lie down before dinner."

Getting out of the truck, he shut his door and watched her walk into the house.

"What happened?"

"You have shitty-ass timing, that's what happened." He glared at his brother.

Dade widened his stance, crossing his arms over his chest. Giving his best big-brother look, he stared him down. "And just what does that mean?"

Colton placed his hand on the warm hood of the truck and recounted the story. Going to the police station, discovering the necklace was Natalie's, watching the interrogation.

"Damn. Natalie Brake? I never would have thought. I mean, I know the woman can get a little crazy sometimes, but I never would have pegged her doing all this. Did she say why she did it?"

He pushed away from the truck, running a frustrated hand over his head. "No, and the thing is, when Ryder showed her the necklace, she recognized it, but...I don't know. It wasn't a look of guilt, more like a look of fear."

"Jail time is a scary thought for most people."

"I guess. It's just so—so—"

"Frustrating, because she's not a man so you can't kick the crap out of her for terrorizing Maggie?"

His head rose, eyes going wide.

Dade smiled. "Who do you think you're talking to? I know my little brother."

"Yeah, well, too bad you don't know me a little better or you would have stayed in the damn house for five more freaking minutes."

"Ah." His older brother walked over to lean against the hood of the truck with him. "Is this my shitty-ass timing part?"

"Yes." He glared. "I was just about to tell Maggie how I felt about her, and you had to go and ruin the moment."

His brother's large palm smacked him on the back of the head. It didn't hurt, but was surprising. "What the hell was that for?"

"Idiot! You don't tell a woman you love them for the first time in your truck right after she just went through a traumatizing ordeal."

"And exactly how many women have you confessed your love to?"

Dade went silent.

Huh? Had his big brother loved someone at one point in his life? He knew he'd dated a few girls in high school, but nothing serious ever came out of those relationships. There was a woman a while back who lived down in Aspen, but that only lasted a few months. He always assumed his brother was single by nature. Had some woman broken Dade's heart?

"Women like romance, Colt. Do something special,

a nice dinner, a horseback ride. Set the mood, then tell her you love her."

"And what makes you the expert on women?"

"Are you kidding? No one is an expert on women. Not even other women. I'm just trying to give you some brotherly advice."

Realizing he was just taking out his frustrations on his brother—who was only trying to help—he sighed. Clasping a hand on his shoulder, Colton gave it a small shake. "I know, thanks."

"Anytime."

"I better go check on Maggie." He headed toward the house.

"Want a little more advice?"

Colton stopped and turned around. "Lay it on me, brother."

Dade bent down to pluck out a wildflower from the ground. "Flowers and food make everyone feel better after bad news."

He grinned. "Then I better get cooking."

Chapter Twenty-Six

Maggie stood at the window in Colton's bedroom, gazing out across the ranch. The sun was still an hour away from setting. Already the sky was turning dusky hues, painting the dwindling, sun-filled sky like a watercolor canvas. It was beautiful here. She wished so badly she could stay, but couldn't.

Before his brother interrupted them, Colton had been trying to tell her how he felt. Her heart had jumped up into her throat. She'd been sure he was going to say those three magic words. Hopeful anticipation had lodged deep in her, waiting, wanting, eager for the words to come out.

Too eager.

The fact she wanted him to say the words *so* badly only proved she was in over her head. Like an idiot, she'd let her heart get too involved. With no more danger, no more stalker, there was now no more unnecessary obligation on his part to protect her...or stay with her.

She had to get out now before she got in any deeper. When he did end this, there was a good chance she would shatter.

She just had to leave first. That's all there was to it. Maybe if she ended things on her terms, she could keep her heart from breaking. Yes. Better it be *her* doing the leaving than him. Less pathetic that way. Then, at least, she could say she ended it her way.

That Frank Sinatra song took on a whole new meaning.

The bedroom door creaked open.

"Magpie?"

Okay, time to be strong. Determined, she chanted to herself, *I can do this. I can do this.*

Taking a deep, fortifying breath, she turned. Colton held out a tray with a steaming bowl of soup and a mug filled with brightly colored wildflowers. They looked suspiciously similar to the ones growing in his front yard.

"I thought you might be hungry, so I made you some soup."

He made her food and picked wildflowers for her? The sweet gesture brought tears to her eyes. *Gah.* When did she become such an emotional mess? Oh right, when she decided to be a complete idiot and let Colton Denning into her heart, again.

"Thank you," she said, her voice barely above a whisper. She could hardly talk; how was she going to end things?

Setting the tray down on his dresser, he made his way over to her, wrapped her in his strong arms, and brushed his lips across her forehead. "Everything will be all right now. I promise."

His lips continued a path down her face to her ear, her cheek, her jaw, and finally her lips. He kissed her with such an overwhelming tenderness…

Her strong determination broke.

One more night, just one more night in Colton's arms.

One more memory to last the rest of her life. One

more moment of heated passion before she went back to her cold, lonely existence. She needed this tonight.

Tomorrow would be soon enough to be strong.

Colton had sensed Maggie pulling away from him. That's why he set the food and flowers aside. Dade's idea was nice, but it hadn't worked. Time to try things his way. Time to show Maggie how much he loved her the best way he knew how.

By loving her.

Slowly, taking his time, he made love to her lips. Kissing, tasting, savoring them. Tonight, there was nothing else, only them. No shop, no ranch, no problems, just him and Maggie. He was going to show her how much he cared for her, by loving every single inch of her delectable body. He would imprint himself on her, so whenever she thought of love, she thought of him. She was his and he was hers.

He just had to make her see that.

Stroking his hands down her back, he pulled her closer. He was already hard, but he didn't grind himself against her. Tonight was about connecting on a deeper level. Instead, he massaged small circles on her lower back with his fingertips. Keeping his touch light, he worked his way down to her spectacular ass.

A soft moan escaped her lips, and he swallowed it with his mouth. She arched her hips against him, rubbing that sweet, sexy body of hers along his. *Damn*, what she did to him.

"Colton, please," she begged, pulling away from his lips. "I need…"

"Shhhh." He gentled her with his touch. "I know, sweetheart. I know."

Backing her toward his bed, he moved them until

her thighs hit the mattress. Instead of throwing her down and ravishing her like he desperately wanted to do, he gently laid her on the soft, quilted covers. Tonight was about her. About showing her how much she meant to him. He could do slow. He would take his time. For Maggie, he would make everything perfect.

Grasping the hem of her T-shirt, he slowly lifted the material up and away from her body. Tossing the garment aside, he nibbled the side of her neck, right at the sensitive spot that turned her to mush. She arched off the bed, making it easy for him to unhook and dispose of her bra.

Leaning up on one arm, he gazed down at her unfettered breasts. "Beautiful," he whispered with reverence.

She blushed at his compliment. So endearing, he kissed her again. Her nipples pebbled, the hard peaks rubbing against his chest through his shirt. If he took his clothes off, all his good intentions would be gone. So they would remain on.

For now.

Her breathing became erratic as he slid a hand down her body, pausing to focus on each perfect breast, then continuing the path to land on her hip. Reluctantly pulling away from her lips, he followed the trail his hand made. Sucking a ripe, firm nipple into his mouth, he stroked over the bud with his tongue and bit ever so slightly.

"Colton!"

A chuckle rose in his chest. He continued to focus on her breasts while slowly undoing her jeans. He started to tug, and her hips rose in assistance. The jeans joined her shirt and bra on the floor, leaving her in only a pair of cream-colored, lace panties.

"So pretty." He stroked her softly.

Colton could feel her readiness through the tiny scrap of cloth, but he didn't remove it. With one hand, he gently petted her, while the other joined his mouth in worshiping her magnificent breasts.

Her hips moved in a silent plea. Slipping one finger beneath the lace, he obeyed, stroking her. She groaned loudly. With his thumb, he found that tiny bundle of nerves and began rubbing, slow, easy circles.

"Oh God!"

Her eyes closed, and her mouth opened, and he took advantage, leaving her breast to claim her lips once again. Her body trembled. Sinking first one, then two fingers inside her, he pumped them in and out. Deep, slow, maddening strokes. All the while gently circling her with his thumb.

Her mouth ripped from his. "Colton, you're killing me."

"No, sweetheart. I'm loving you."

Her eyes snapped open; those deep green orbs locked with his. He saw the questions, the fear, the hope. It was the hope he latched on to.

Quickening his thrust, he added a third finger, increasing the pressure of his thumb. Her head fell back, eyes closing once again. Her inner muscles tightened around his fingers, then...

She screamed, her entire body going taut. He kept up the rhythm until the tension left her and her body went limp.

His control almost shot after watching her come so beautifully, Colton shucked off his clothes in seconds. Reaching to his nightstand, he grabbed a condom and sheathed himself. He was so hard, even the slight touch of putting on protection was almost too much.

"Maggie, look at me," he commanded.

Her eyes flew open. Slowly, he entered her. Because of her earlier release, he slid in with ease and buried himself deep. He wasn't going to last long, but he refused to go without her. Angling his hips so that every thrust would hit her in just the right place, he pulled back until only the tip of him was inside. Gazes locked, he thrust hard and deep. Her hands flew to his shoulders, clasping him tight, holding on for the ride.

It wasn't a long ride. Only a few moments, and she was coming again, tightening against him, gripping his shaft like a fist. He gave two more deep, penetrating thrusts and joined her.

They fell to the bed together. He rolled them so he wouldn't crush her. A pleasant sigh left her lips.

Colton kissed her forehead, tucking her to his side. "You are magnificent, Maggie."

Eye still closed, she grinned. "You're not so bad yourself."

"Ready for round two?"

One eye cracked open. "There's more?"

"We've got *all* night." *And the rest of our lives.*

"Give me ten minutes to recoup."

"Anything you want, sweetheart."

And he meant it, too. He would give Maggie Evans anything her heart desired. He just prayed that desire was him.

Chapter Twenty-Seven

The blare of the alarm was an unwelcome sound. Waking up with Maggie's soft, warm body wrapped around him, heaven. Slapping the off button, Colton burrowed into her silky brown hair, inhaling the unique fragrance that was hers alone.

"Good morning."

Her voice was still husky with sleep. It turned him on. Then again, everything this woman did turned him on.

"Yes it is." A chuckle escaped as he pressed his morning wood against her.

She groaned, half-lust, half-exasperation. "Much as I'd love to make this a great morning. I really need to get to my shop."

"Spoilsport." He kissed the side of her neck. "Let me get dressed, and I'll drive you into town."

They had left her car in town yesterday as she'd been in no condition to drive after the incident at the police station. He'd planned on driving her into town today anyway; a chore he didn't mind because it meant they got to spend more time together. He was finding he wanted to spend all his time with her.

"Thanks."

"We should go out tonight. Celebrate."

"Actually, I think I should focus on cleaning up my place tonight." She sat up, placing her feet on the floor in front of her. Her back was to him, but he could feel her hesitancy.

"I'll help."

"There's no need." She didn't look at him. "I'm sure you're eager for a night alone anyway. I know I've been kind of horning in on your space."

She was pulling away.

He wasn't going to let her.

Sitting up in bed, Colton gently grasped her chin with his hand, turning her face. She kept her gaze down on the bed.

"Maggie. Look at me."

That mossy green gaze rose to meet his. So many emotions flickered in their depths: fear, sadness, longing. What the hell? Why was she trying to push him away? Hadn't he made it clear last night how he felt about her?

"You are not a bother. We have plenty of room on the ranch. I like having you here. I thought you liked being here, too."

"I do, but it's time for me to go home."

Here it was. The moment he laid it all out for her.

He took a deep breath, going for broke. "This could be your home."

She sucked in a breath. Eyes wide, she stared at him.

"Move in with me, Magpie. Live here with me."

Her mouth opened, but it took her a moment to reply. "That—that's not necessary, Colt. Natalie is in custody. There's no one after me anymore. I'm safe. You don't need to protect me anymore."

She thought *that* was why he wanted her to live with him? Anger began to burn, slow and deep inside.

"I'm not asking you to live with me so I can protect you. I'm asking you to live with me because I want you to."

She rose from the bed, tugging the comforter around her bare body. "There's no point."

He rose as well, not giving a damn that he was naked as the day he was born. "What the hell do you mean by that?"

"I move in here and things go great for a while. Then one day, you'll get bored of me or find someone new and I—I can't take that again, Colt. I can't."

"Shit, Maggie. I'm not your freaking ex. I don't cheat. I know how shitty a thing that is to do to someone. I would never hurt anyone like that. Don't you know me at all?"

She ran a shaking hand through her sleep-rumpled hair. "Yes, I know you. You're kind, and sweet, and sexy, and the most amazing man I've ever met."

If she thought he was so great why didn't she want to be with him? For the life of him, he couldn't follow this woman's crazy logic.

"Then move in with me," he practically shouted.

"Why?" she shouted back, her temper rising with his.

"Because I love you, goddammit, and I want to spend every moment I possibly can with you!"

She gasped, slapping a hand over her open mouth.

Okay, maybe yelling wasn't the most romantic way to tell a woman you loved her. She had him so riled up. Did she really think herself so unlovable? How could she not realize what an amazing woman she was? The men in her past were jackasses, and he wished he could punch every single one of them right in the face.

"You—you say that now, but—"

"No, Maggie." He sliced a hand through the air. "I say that now and tomorrow and forever. I love you. I love you! I have never said that to another woman before. Ever."

Tears were pooling in her eyes. He could see her fear, but there was also a glimmer of hope in her eyes. It was what he needed. Just a small bit of her to believe what he was saying.

Latching onto that, he continued to plead his case. "I know you've been hurt in the past, hell, we all have. That's just part of life, but you can't let your past dictate your future or you'll miss out on something amazing."

Taking a chance, he stepped forward and tried to steady his trembling hands as he reached for her. This was probably the most important moment of his life, and he could not afford to screw it up. When she allowed him to take her hands in his, he sent up a silent victory cheer.

"Don't miss out on us because you're afraid, Maggie."

Tears ran down her pale cheeks. "I don't know if I can do this."

"I'm not asking you to love me." Not true, but he wouldn't force her to say anything she wasn't ready to say yet. "I'm just asking you to give me a chance, give *us* a chance. We're good together, Magpie. I love you, and I know you care for me, too."

A sob racked her body. It freaking killed him to see her cry, but he had to break down this wall of fear surrounding her heart.

"Oh, Colt. I more than care for you. I…"

She stepped into him, pressing her face against his chest. He dropped her hands to wrap his arms around her. He could feel her resistance crumbling. She was accepting his truth. Now, she just had to see her own.

"It's okay, sweetheart. You don't have to say it until you're ready. But…" He hesitated, the words sticking in his dry throat. "Will you at least agree to keep seeing each other? Maybe consider moving in with me?"

Never in his life had he been so afraid of an answer. Breath froze in his lungs as he awaited her reply. If he hadn't been holding on to her, he would have sunk to his knees. He wasn't above begging. Not when it came to Maggie.

She lifted her face out of his chest. That cute button nose sniffled one last time. Her hands pressed against his bare skin, steady, no nervous twisting in sight.

A shy smiled crossed her face. "I…think I would like that very much."

It felt like the sky broke open and the heavens themselves shined down on him. A gush of frozen air left his lungs. Before he got too excited, though, he needed to know. "Which part?"

Her emerald gaze bore straight into his own, determined, yet still vulnerable. If he had to, he would spend the rest of his life proving to her that she had no reason to doubt him or his love.

"The staying together part."

Hell yeah!

"And, um, also the moving in thing." Her gaze dropped to his chest as she fiddled with his hair there. "You're right. We should give this thing between us a chance."

She hadn't said she loved him, but she did agree to move in and continue the relationship. A big step for her. He knew she cared for him, and as much as he wanted to hear those three little words returned, he could wait. He would wait forever as long as she never left him.

Colton bent down, scooping her up in his arms. She let out a surprised yelp.

"What are you doing?" A big grin spread across her face.

Warmth filled him. Like the damn sun was burning right in the center of his chest. Leaning his head forward, he pressed a loud, smacking kiss to her lips. "We have to celebrate this momentous occasion."

Her eyebrow quirked. "Momentous occasion?"

He laid her gently on the bed, following her down until he was stretched over every inch of her.

"Yeah. Maggie Evans just admitted I was right. Doesn't happen often."

She smacked him playfully on the shoulder before sobering. "I was afraid last night was going to be it for us."

He leaned down, brushing his lips across hers. "This is just the beginning, Magpie."

The beginning of their life, together. And he intended to enjoy every delicious moment of it.

Chapter Twenty-Eight

Maggie still couldn't believe it. Colton loved her. The words kept ringing in her ears, but she still felt like it was all some magical cupcake induced dream.

Colton loves me!

Sitting in his truck as it rambled down the bumpy road, she glanced at the man beside her. He insisted on driving her into town after their morning, ahem, celebration. She was so happy she didn't even mind the knowing grin Dade had given them when they'd emerged from the bedroom. She knew there had been a big goofy smile on her face—still was—but she was so happy she didn't care.

Last night, she'd feared the end of her and Colton. The end of the most wonderful relationship with the most amazing man ever. But this morning, her whole world had turned upside down.

When Colton admitted he loved her—albeit not in the most romantic way—her head didn't want to believe it, but her heart almost burst with wanting. There was still a tiny nugget of fear inside telling her this wasn't real, that it couldn't last. But, it was time she started letting go of her past, letting go of the men who had hurt her, and start trusting her heart. And her heart was saying, *Go for it!*

As they pulled up to her shop, Colton put the truck in park and turned to face her.

"How about I come by after you close and help you pack up a few things to bring to the ranch?"

Most of her clothes had already ended up there over the past week, but if she was going to be staying full time she needed to bring the rest and a few things like her laptop and cooking supplies. The stuff at the ranch was okay, but her utensils were higher quality.

"You don't have to, Colt. Besides, I have to get my car out there somehow."

He leaned over to place a soft kiss to her lips. Heat rushed through her body from that small touch. Would his touch affect her like this forever? She'd bet all the cupcakes in the world it would.

"You can drive your car back, but my truck has a lot more room. We can fill it with whatever you want to bring over, and then I'll follow you home."

Home. It sounded so wonderful coming from his lips.

"Okay."

His arm snaked around her waist, pulling her closer so he could nuzzle his lips across that sensitive spot that drove her wild.

"Mmmmm, you're being so agreeable today. I like it."

A shiver ran up and down her spine. One corner of her mouth quirked. "Yeah, well, don't get too use to it."

"Wouldn't dream of it." His words were muffled as he gave her a small love bite on her neck. "You know I love it when you get all feisty on me."

There he went using the L word again. It was so strange to hear coming from his lips. Strange, but wonderful.

"Okay, cowboy. Cool your jets." She pulled back,

giving him a small push. "I have a business to open, and you have chores to do."

"There's that feistiness. Love it. And I love you."

His sky blue eyes gazed into hers with such raw emotions she had no doubt of his words. As much as she wanted to return them, though, there was still a small part of her that held on to her past and doubted, feared saying them out loud. Instead, she placed a hand on his whiskered cheek, leaning in to deliver one scorching hot kiss.

"Now who needs to cool their jets?" he chuckled as she pulled away.

She shook her head, opening the door and hopping out of the truck. "Goodbye, Colt."

"See ya later, Magpie."

He waited until she unlocked the door and was secure in her shop before waving and driving away. After a morning like today, she needed two things: cupcakes and a gleeful, tell-all call to her best friend.

The cupcakes she got started on right away because she had to. She started baking the morning batch and before she knew it, time to open.

The day was busy. Everyone had found out about her visit from the blogger and wanted to know how it had gone. Jamie had the day off, so Maggie was busy baking and answering questions. She barely had time to think about Colton, but he was always there in the back of her mind.

By closing time, she was exhausted, but the thought of him coming to help her pack up her stuff to move in with him put a bounce in her step.

She'd just finished her end of day cleaning when her cell phone vibrated. Pulling it from her pocket she smiled, reading the incoming caller's name.

"Boy, you must be psychic. I was just about to call you."

"Call it best friend intuition." Lizzy chuckled. "So tell me, how was the blogger? Did she just die from fantastiliciousness after eating your cupcakes?"

A laugh bubbled out of her chest. "That's not a word."

"Well, it should be. Come on, give me some good news."

"Why? What's wrong?"

She might be riding on cloud nine at the moment, but she could hear the dejection in her best friend's voice. Lizzy was never dejected; sarcastic sure, but never dejected.

"No. I called to talk about your rousing success, not my descent into destitution."

There was that sarcasm, but there was something real behind it. Elation momentarily forgotten, she pushed her friend. "Lizzy?"

"Oh fine! Things aren't going great at the restaurant at the moment. Bill is pissy as hell, but not like that's anything new."

Bill Collins, owner of Le Central, was a high stress kind of guy. Some of the wait staff had a running pool on when the tyrannical owner was going to keel over from a heart attack. It seemed cruel, but the guy was an ass. He screamed at everyone, especially Lizzy. Every little thing seemed to set him off, even when nothing was wrong. Maggie always figured the guy got off on making people cry. It was one of the reasons she'd been willing to move to Peak Town and take over her grandmother's shop.

A horrible thought sparked her mind. "Oh no. It's not because of me is it? Because I left and the new guy isn't quite up to par yet?"

A very indelicate, but Lizzy-like, snort came across the line. "First of all, I fired the new guy two days ago. The man couldn't reach the par of a cake maker for a kiddie party place, let alone achieve your culinary status. Second, Bill always has a bug up his butt about something. You leaving was just another thing he could complain about. If you hadn't left, he would have blamed me for the dishwasher quitting or the hostess getting poached by Antoine's. Seriously Maggie, the guy will use any excuse to call me a shitty manager."

"He said what!" If she wasn't four states away, she'd go kick Bill's pompous butt. "You should quit. He doesn't deserve you."

Her best friend laughed sadly. "I know, but we can't all inherit the family business. Some of us have to take what we can get."

Lizzy could get better, but the job market was hard. Quitting a good paying job without another on the horizon was career suicide. And there was no way the proud woman would take money from her parents. It would inevitably come with strings. Lizzy hated strings.

"Aren't we a pair." She let out a sad sigh. "You dealing with a jackass of a boss and me being too chicken to say—"

She cut herself off, but not fast enough.

"Whoa, what was that?"

Dammit it. She hadn't meant to say anything. Yes, she had been going to call later and relay her giddy excitement over Colton and her stupidity at not being able to say three little words, but now it didn't feel right. She didn't want to brag about her amazing morning when her best friend was obviously struggling with problems. What kind of shitty friend would that make her?

"Nothing. Forget it."

"I don't think so, Maggie Marleen Evans."

Why had she told Lizzy her middle name? It made her feel all of six years old when someone used it. As her friend intended, she was sure.

"You were too chicken to say what to whom?"

"I'm sorry. I didn't mean to bring it up. You called to talk about your problems."

"Bill is a jackass! There, my problems are done. Your turn."

No bullshitting with her bestie.

When she remained silent her friend prompted. "Does this chickenness have anything to do with a certain cowboy?"

She rolled her eyes. "Chickenness isn't a word."

"Stop avoiding the question."

There was no stopping Lizzy when she wanted answers. It was better for everyone just to give in. "Yes, it has to do with Colton."

"Hold on. Let me grab some ice cream. I feel this is going to be an ice cream type of conversation."

It so was.

She heard some shuffling on the line, a freezer door open and shut. Then her friend was back.

"Okay. I'm ready. Go."

"Elizabeth Audrey Hayworth, are you eating out of the carton?" Two could play the whole name game.

"Yes, and stop changing the subject. You, Colton, chickenness. Go!"

She sat in her desk chair and proceeded to reveal the morning that should have ended in tears, but instead made her heart soar in the clouds.

****

She stared across the street at Cupcakes Above the Clouds. Never before in her life had she been so angry. That bitch, Maggie Evans, had accused the *wrong* person. It was just one more thing to add to the list of why Maggie had to go. Time to force the bitch cupcake maker to leave.

Slipping her hand into the deep pocket of her coat, she fingered the .44 magnum revolver. It had been her husband's. The only useful thing that bastard had left her after he died.

Now, it was going to fix her problems. Maggie would be leaving town tonight…one way or another.

She'd watched the shop from across the street all afternoon. The young woman had locked the door about an hour and a half ago. Not that it mattered. She'd stolen a spare key to the bakery from the upstairs apartment when she trashed it. The stupid whore never even noticed.

The streets were quiet. Everyone was heading home for the night.

It was time.

Crossing the deserted street, she kept one hand in her pocket firmly gripping her gun.

This ends tonight.

Maggie Evans had been a thorn in her side for too long. Time for that cupcake-making slut to leave. She was going to give the bitch two choices: leave Peak Town forever or stay forever.

Six feet under the town.

Chapter Twenty-Nine

"So, let me get this straight. Natalie was the one attacking your shop because she hates you for dating Colton, who is her ex, but he's totally in love with you. And now you're moving in with him, but you didn't say 'I love you' back?" Lizzy spouted off the facts like a bullet point list.

A large sigh escaped Maggie's lips. "I wanted to, but I just couldn't get the words out."

"I'm going to start calling you Chicken Little."

Her grip tightened on the phone. "Don't you dare."

"I think it's clever. You're only five three, and you don't even have the balls to say 'I love you' to a man who protected you, poured his heart out, and basically worships the ground you walk on." Her friend paused before adding. "Which he should do, by the way."

"I don't have balls at all, Lizzy." But her friend was right. She was being a coward by not responding to Colton's declaration. There was still a tiny part of her too afraid to believe it.

"Fine, ovaries then. They're way tougher anyway. Considering what we go through every month."

She couldn't hold in the laughter at her friend's apt analogy. "Be serious."

A shuffle came over the phone, sounding much like an ice cream carton being placed on a table. Uh oh, Lizzy was putting down her food. Things were about to get real.

"Okay, you want my honest opinion?"

That's what best friends were for.

"I think you love this guy, but you're too scared to say it out loud because that makes it real."

Duh, she figured that out all herself.

"You've been hurt by almost every guy who's ever been in your life, starting with your dad and ending with Miles. This Colton guy sounds like the real deal. He loves you, which makes him smart, and he's been good to you. Right?"

She thought over the last few weeks. The cabin, her gas leak, the many times he came rushing to her side. Then there was all the encouragement and support he had given her. He believed in her. Always told her how amazing he found her. Last, but definitely not least, the sex. No. Scratch that. The love making. Because that's what it was. Every time he touched her, she could feel Colton's love pouring out of his body into hers. Even in the simplest of kisses, it was there.

"He's been more than good to me." A warmth spread over her, and her lips tilted in a smile. "I've never felt more loved in my life." She let out a long groan. "So, why can't I just say it?"

"That you love him, too?"

"Yes."

"Because you're scared that the moment you admit your feelings, this whole thing will come crashing down on you."

Leave it to Lizzy to hit the nail on the head.

"If you don't say it, you can pretend it's not real. But sweetie, it *is* real. Even I can see how much you love this guy, and I'm a thousand miles away. Now, put on your big girl panties, stop being such a chicken, and tell the poor cowboy you love him."

A snort of laughter burst out of her. "That easy is it?"

"That easy."

Her best friend made it sound so simple, but…

"What if you're wrong? What if he stops loving me?"

"First of all, I'm never wrong."

She could almost see her friend ticking off points on her fingers.

"Second, not loving you is impossible. And finally, Maggie, there are no guarantees in life. Sometimes, you just gotta grab the bull by the horns and go for it."

"Grab the bull by the horns?"

"Hey, you're in Podunk Town. I thought the analogy would fit."

She chuckled, but her friend was right. Time to stop being scared of what might happen and just go for it. She'd already agreed to move in and keep seeing Colton, how much more was she risking by saying she loved him?

Just my entire heart.

"It's Peak Town. And…you're right."

Her friend yelped in victory. "Duh, didn't I just tell you I'm always right?"

She started to laugh when a sound at the back door caught her attention. Was someone trying to get in? Only she and Jamie had a key for the store. Had Jamie forgotten something in the shop? No, she'd been off today.

"Maggie? Are you still there?"

"Hang on a second."

She rose from her chair. There was definitely someone coming in the back door.

"Jamie, is that you?"

The sound of a key turning the lock tumblers echoed in the quiet air. The doorknob moved. She could hear Lizzy calling her name through the phone at her ear. A familiar person stepped though the back door, but it wasn't her young employee.

"What are you doing here? How did you get a key?"

"Maggie! Answer me!"

Lizzy's voice screamed through the phone, but she couldn't respond. Fear had frozen her vocal chords when a large, very lethal looking, gun pointed right at her.

"Hang up the phone and toss it to me now, or I use this gun to make your insides, outsides."

Ignoring her best friend's frantic screams over the phone, Maggie pressed the end button on her cell and tossed it to the deceivingly sweet looking, older woman standing in front of her.

Chapter Thirty

Colton had been in an amazing mood all day. Like he won first prize at a bull riding competition. He'd never ridden a bull before, but according to his buddies who had—one a national bull riding champion—the high he was feeling came pretty damn close.

No, it's better.

The woman he loved had agreed to move in with him. True, she hadn't said those three little words back to him yet, but he was confident she would. She just needed to get there. Get over her fear. She loved him…

He hoped.

After dropping Maggie off at her place, he came back to the ranch to find Thunder, their prize-winning stud, had escaped his pen and run up into the hills. Trekking his ass all over the mountainside looking for a wayward horse was not the way he wanted to spend his day. He'd rather spend it with Maggie, but since he was a responsible adult—most of the time—and had a business to run, he put thoughts of the woman he loved to the back of his mind and concentrated on finding the wayward horse.

Molly and Thunder had a thing going on lately. The mare's cold had gotten better, so he saddled up the cream colored Palomino and headed out.

The horse's coloring reminded him of the panties he peeled off Maggie last night. He smiled as he thought of those undergarments soon joining his in his dressers. He still couldn't believe she said yes. This morning, he'd wanted to toss everything of hers into his truck and drive back to the ranch. Get her moved in before she had a chance to change her mind. But he held off, knowing this evening was soon enough. Patience. He couldn't push her or she might run scared. It was why he didn't force the whole "I love you" issue. Though, he desperately wanted to hear those words.

The first fissures of doubt began to creep in. Maybe he was wrong. Maybe she didn't feel as deeply for him as he felt for her.

Wouldn't that be ironic?

He finally got serious about a woman, and *she* wanted to keep it casual.

Life could be a cruel bitch sometimes.

Molly paused, raising her head; her ears flicked back and forth. Most people didn't know horses had an excellent sense of smell. Colton did.

"What do you smell girl? Is it Thunder?"

That or a mountain lion.

He moved his right hand from the saddle horn to his rifle, tucked away in its hanging scabbard. He wasn't a big hunter, but a loud shot in the air would scare away any wild beast. Unfortunately, it would also scare his horse. Bringing the rifle to his lap he sat and waited.

Movement stirred in the tree branches a dozen feet away. Colton tightened his grip on the gun, but didn't raise it yet. The branches cracked as something moved through them. Something big, something dark, something that was not a mountain lion.

"Thunder, you great big pain in the ass!" He swore

at the horse as the large animal came into view.

Thunder pranced up to Molly, as if he hadn't wasted Colton's entire morning, and touched his nose to the other horse's. They did their sniffing routine, nuzzling necks before moving to smell each other's flanks.

"All right, all right. You guys can sniff butts later. Whatever turns you on, I'm not gonna judge. But right now, we have to get back to the ranch."

The horses were so close together it was easy for him to slip the extra halter onto Thunder. He kept a firm grip on the lead rope and gave Molly a little kick, turning her back toward the ranch. Thunder followed.

It was well past noon when Colton got back with the horses. He wasn't particularly hungry, so he opted to skip lunch. After he got Thunder and Molly settled back in their pens, he went in search of his brother, but Dade was nowhere to be found. Eventually, he did find Juan. The ranch foreman told him that his brother was inside on the phone in his office. Talking with some lawyer.

A rider had fallen from a mount a few weeks back. It was the rider's fault. Colton had told the guy not to kick his horse, but the balding, self-important jerk had fancied himself a Wild West cowboy. The guy kicked, the horse bucked, wannabe cowboy fell flat on his ass. The only thing he hurt was his pride, but he'd been ranting and raving about contacting his lawyer and suing them into the ground.

The guy had no case. Safety was top priority at the ranch, but accidents happened. They had every rider sign a waiver before they could even come within ten feet of a horse. Still, he was glad his brother—with his even temper—handled situations like this. He'd probably threaten to throw the lawyer and his asshat client in the pen with Thunder and let the stallion use them as a tap dancing mat.

Dade emerged from his office just as the sun was going down. It must have been some call, because his cool-headed sibling looked livid. Being the little brother, he had to take the opportunity to tease.

"Have a nice chat with the attorney?"

"Don't start with me, Colt." His brother stalked toward him. "I've been on the phone all afternoon with that guy explaining to him about the waiver his client signed. He's trying to bring up all these chump charges against us, but he has no case. His lawyer knows it, but the guy is a big cash cow so the law firm is trying to find anything to bring us down."

Dade removed his Stetson, running a hand through his short, dark hair.

Colton held up his hand in surrender, knowing when to stop. "Hey, I gotta talk to you about something."

His brother raised a brow. "This have anything to do with the goofy grins you and Maggie were wearing this morning before you drove her home?"

Said grin tugged at his lips. "Maybe."

"Congratulations."

"You don't even know what you're congratulating me on."

His brother slapped his hat back on his head. "No, but judging by the stupid expression on your face, I'd wager it's good news."

He resisted the urge to flip his brother the bird. "My expression is not stupid, and yes, it is good news.

Maggie agreed to move in."

Only now did it occur to him that he probably should've discussed it with his brother first, considering Dade lived there, too.

"That's great, Colt." His brother's strong hand slapped him on the back. "So, you told her you love her?"

"Yup."

"And she loves you, too?"

He rubbed the back of his neck, wincing. "Uh, well, she didn't exactly say it, but she did agree to move in."

Dark brows furrowed before blue eyes went soft. "Don't worry. She does. Love you, I mean. I think she's loved you since we were kids. Sometimes…women have their reasons for holding things back." Dade slapped him on the back once again. "She'll say it, little brother, don't worr—"

The sound of a phone interrupted his brother.

"I think your pants are ringing."

Startled, Colton pulled his cell out of the front pocket of his jeans. No one called his cell except for his brother or Maggie, and since his brother was standing right here…

Elation turned to disappointment followed by confusion as he realized the call wasn't from Maggie. It was an area code he didn't recognize. Solicitor? He didn't think they had access to cell phone numbers. If it was someone trying to sell him something, they were in for a rude awaking. He was in no mood to be polite to someone who wanted him to buy crap he didn't need.

"Yeah?" Rude right off the bat, that ought to deter them.

There was a beat of silence, then. "Is this Colton, Colton Denning?"

It was a soft feminine voice. She didn't sound like a solicitor. In fact, she sounded scared.

"Who wants to know?"

"My name is Elizabeth Hayworth. I'm a friend of Maggie's."

"Lizzy?"

"Yes." This time her voice held a note of relief. "She gave me your number in case of emergencies—"

"What's wrong?" He cut her off, concern superseding suspicion in a heartbeat. "Is Maggie okay?"

"That's the thing," Lizzy said, voice shaky. "I was talking to her on the phone. She was in her shop, and then someone came to the door, I think. I kept screaming her name, trying to get her to tell me what was going on, but she just hung up on me."

He could hear tears in the woman's voice.

"Maggie would never hang up on me. Never." She sniffed loudly. "And there's more. I'm pretty sure I heard someone else there with her. I couldn't make out what they were saying, but it didn't sound friendly."

Shit, shit, shit!

"I'm really worried. I would have called the cops, but I don't have the local number. Please, can you go check on her?"

"Dade, call the sheriff. Send him over to Maggie's shop. Right now!"

Bless his brother. He didn't ask what was going on or who was on the phone, just whipped out his cell and dialed Sheriff Ryder.

"Lizzy, I'm heading to Maggie's right now. My brother called the sheriff."

He ran, full sprint, to his truck. The ranch hands glanced at him, jaws wide open, but he didn't care. He had to get to Maggie. That was his only concern.

Had Natalie been let out of jail? No, Ryder wouldn't do that. Unless she made bail…or she wasn't the attacker. He'd thought something was off when his ex clammed up in the interrogation room.

"Hurry, Colton. Please, she means the world to me."

"Me, too," he said, ending the call.

He put pedal to the metal as he hauled ass out of the driveway. This would be the fastest he ever made it into town. He wasn't slowing down for anything, because Maggie didn't just mean the world to him.

She *was* his world.

Chapter Thirty-One

"What's going on Mrs. Brake?" Maggie tried to keep the tremble out of her voice as she spoke.

Natalie's mother sneered. "What's going on is that you can't take a message unless it's spelled out for you."

Her cell phone started to vibrate again, but she kept her focus on the older woman. Kind of hard to pay attention to a phone when you had a gun pointed at your head. There was always the possibility the gun wasn't loaded, but she wasn't taking any chances.

"I tried for months to get you to leave town. Little hints, subtly. Should have known that wouldn't work on a girl like you. No manners, no class, a selfish bitch just like your grandmother!"

Now that was too much. Gran had been a wonderful woman. She'd be damned if she let this crazy old loon talk poorly about the woman who'd taught Maggie her passion in life. Gun pointed at her head or not.

"Gran was a good woman."

"She was a liar!" Deloris screamed, eyes going wide with rage.

The wrinkled, frail looking hand holding the massive gun started to shake. This was not a stable woman.

"Okay, Deloris. Why was my grandmother a liar?"

If she wanted to get out of this alive—and she really, really did—she would have to be smart.

Gray brows drew together. "She promised me a job for as long as I needed. She said the store would be mine after she was gone. She lied."

Deloris had worked for Gran? It must have been after Maggie left. She didn't remember anyone working at the shop. Her grandmother never mentioned anything about needing help when they had talked on the phone. Guilt, for the way she abandoned her grandmother, swamped her. She shook it off. Now was not the time. She had to stay focused if she wanted to stay alive.

"You worked here, for Gran?"

Deloris huffed in irritation. Her mouth pinched, giving her the expression of someone who had just tasted a sour lemon. "Of course I worked here, you idiot. When you decided not to come out for the summers anymore, like the selfish brat you are, your grandmother needed help during the busy season."

There was that guilt again.

"After my Carl died, I needed to bring in some means of living. The old bastard didn't leave us a dime. Jackass liked to bet on the ponies. He was an idiot, too. Never won. Gambled away our life savings. The life insurance was gone after a few months. With Natalie off at school, I had to do something. Your grandmother offered me a job working for her. She promised to leave me the shop when she retired."

"I'm sorry. I didn't know. Gran never said anything about you working for her or leaving you the shop. Her will left everything to me. I would have kept you on if I knew you were an employee when Gran died—"

"*I wasn't*," Deloris interrupted. "That bitch fired me two years ago."

That's why she knew nothing of the old woman's employment. Gran's record keeping was not the best, and it only went back a year.

"Why did she fire you?" Her grandmother would never fire anyone without good reason.

Shuffling her feet, Deloris lowered her face. But not before a flicker of something close to shame fill it. "Money was tight. Natalie's tuition was more than I figured on and I—I would have put the money back, once I got it. I was just borrowing it. Like a loan."

"You stole money from the shop." Yeah, that was a good reason to fire someone. "You could have asked Gran for a loan. I'm sure she would have given it to you."

Her grandmother had been a very generous, caring woman. Gran tried to help everyone, but Betty Browning didn't suffer liars. Once, Maggie lied about breaking a mixing bowl. When her grandmother discovered her fib, she had been grounded for a week. Not for the broken dish, but for the lie. Her grandmother had been nobody's fool.

Wrinkled hands, shaking with anger, raised the gun. "I am not a charity case!"

She ducked her head, not that it would help. She was pretty sure she couldn't dodge a bullet. "Okay, okay. I'm sorry."

Deloris took a few deep breaths. Once the old woman appeared to have her outburst under control, she continued. "Betty fired me on the spot, even though she promised I could have my job until I didn't need it. I still *needed* it."

You probably shouldn't have stolen money then. Not a wise comment to make, so she kept it to herself.

"I had to sell my home, my land. That land had been in my family for *three* generations! It killed me to sell it, but I needed the money. There was tuition to pay, and then Natalie wanted to start up a spa in town. I was able to put a down payment on the shop right next door." The old woman sneered. "I figured when Betty died, we could expand into this place. I thought your grandmother would at least make good on her promise to give me the shop. But then *you* came to town." Cold, dark eyes raked her with an ugly sneer.

A sickening thought occurred. "Deloris…did you—did you kill Gran?" She could barely get the words past her dry throat, but it was a valid question. If this crazy old woman was willing to pull a gun on her, then it stood to reason she may have done something to get Gran out of the way. In order to get what she thought was hers.

Mrs. Brake laughed, cruelly. "No. Mother Nature did that for me. Old women like us have death following us every day. I was content to wait her out. I knew with all those sweets around her, Betty would kick the bucket before me."

Since her grandmother died of heart failure, she wasn't sure that was entirely accurate. As far as she knew, sugary treats didn't give you heart attacks. But Deloris was out of her mind, so logic wasn't really the old lady's forte.

"I was sure the shop was coming to *me*. I was going to give it to Natalie as a present. She always talks about expanding her spa. I even put in an offer with what little savings I had left."

She had no idea Mrs. Brake had been the one trying to buy Gran's shop. Not that it would have changed her mind.

"I could finally give my baby girl something worthwhile. More than that sorry excuse for a father ever gave her." The older woman looked around, as if envisioning her daughter's store in the cupcake shop. "But then you came to town and snatched away what was rightfully mine!"

She could say it had been Gran's shop to leave to whomever she pleased. She could point out that Gran's promise was broken when Deloris betrayed and stole from her. She could also mention Natalie's store was hardly a spa. Bringing up all those points would more than likely get her another hole in her head—and not the kind you could put a piece of jewelry through—so she kept her mouth shut.

"After you rejected my perfectly reasonable offer to sell, I tried subtle hints to get your attention. Calling Pansy's and changing your orders, switching delivery times, things like that."

She owed Pansy's an apology, big time.

"But you didn't take the hint. So, I tried to be a little more obvious. I started attacking your equipment next, thinking you'd see how troublesome this all was and give it up. Move back where you belong."

It had been Deloris the whole time? She never would have guessed. And now...

"When you were too stupid to grasp even that hint, I decided to go on full attack."

The rock through the window. Her trashed apartment.

"But you just wouldn't leave! Can't you see no one

wants you here?"

According to her, maybe. "Some people want me here."

Cold eyes edged with crows' feet narrowed. "Yes, I know. You've sunk your claws in that Colton Denning boy. Spread your legs for him like the slut you are, and he fell for it like a puppy dog."

That was rather crude imagery for an eighty-some-year old woman. Did she kiss her daughter with that mouth?

"He's not yours either, but you don't care about that do you?"

"I never claimed Colton was mine."

"But you took him anyway didn't you? Took him away from my sweet Natalie."

That did it! Time for this nasty woman to learn about the consequences of actions.

"Natalie cheated on him. That's why Colton broke up with her. She was unfaithful. It had nothing to do with me. I wasn't even here when they broke up. Besides, that was years ago."

"They would have gotten back together, if you hadn't shown up!" Deloris screamed with fury, waving the gun around. The woman was out of her mind. "But with you out of the way, I can buy the shop for Natalie, and then she and Colton can get married. Everything will be as it should."

Change that to flat out delusional. Even if Maggie weren't in the picture, Colton would never go back to Natalie. He didn't love Natalie. He loved her. He told her so. Colton was a good man, a solid man. A man who meant what he said. A man who protected her, respected her, loved her. And she loved him, too.

Standing in front of a mad woman with a gun pointed at her face, she could finally admit that she loved her sexy cowboy with every fiber of her being. They could make it. They would make it. All she had to do was get out of this situation alive so she could tell him that.

Piece of cake, right?

"I was going to give you a choice to leave on your own, but I've changed my mind." One winkled hand clenched into a fist. "My precious girl is in jail because of you. That requires punishment."

Natalie, the necklace, it must have been—"It was *your* necklace?"

"A matching set," Deloris said with a sniffle, her eyes tearing up. "Natalie got them for us on my last birthday. She's such a sweet girl."

Yeah, so sweet the other woman clammed up the second she knew it was her mother attacking Maggie. She could understand wanting to protect your mother, but Natalie had left the door wide open for another assault by withholding information from the police. And here they were. The wrong Brake in jail, and the other pointing the business end of a gun in her face.

"I'm sorry, Deloris."

"Not as sorry as you're going to be."

That was such a movie line; fear gave her a momentary lapse in sanity, and she laughed.

Mrs. Brake took a step forward raising the gun higher. "You think this is funny?"

Maggie shook her head. Nothing about this situation was funny. In fact, it was pretty damn sad all around. She and Colton were just starting their life together, just admitting how they really felt about one another. Would she even get the chance to tell him she loved him?

Her phone vibrated again. Lizzy? Probably wondering why she hung up. Hopefully, she lived long enough to call her best friend back and explain.

No, she *would* live long enough. She wasn't done with life yet. She had things to do, and a man to confess to. Leaving this earth without telling Colton she loved him was not an option. Deloris would have to be disappointed yet again, because Maggie refused to die today.

When the phone continued to buzz, Deloris grabbed it off the desk and threw it across the room. It slammed into the wall, shattering into pieces at the force of impact.

There went her lifeline. *Guess I'm on my own now.*

The old woman placed both hands on the gun, bracing to take the shot. Maggie knew she had to do something, quick, or she was done for.

"No one is going to miss you when you're gone," the crazy lady taunted.

"*I* will."

Maggie's gaze flew to the back door. As did Mrs. Brake's.

"Colton!" She was equally happy and terrified to see him standing there. "Colton, get out of here."

"Not a chance, Magpie." He slowly made his way toward her. His gaze remained fixed on Deloris and her freaking huge gun. Which was now moving back and forth between the two of them.

"You," the old woman hissed. "You broke my sweet baby girl's heart. How could you?"

"Now, Deloris, you know that's not true. Natalie

and I were never right for each other. She and I both know that."

"She still loves you." Wrinkled lips frowned in protest.

"She just wants what she can't have. Always has."

Must be a family trait.

"No, no, no! This isn't fair! This wasn't how it was supposed it be!"

"Life often isn't fair," he said calmly, still making his way to her side.

She was so happy he was here, but at the same time, she didn't want him getting hurt.

"I wanted to give Natalie everything, but I see now you don't deserve her." The older woman raked Colton with an unpleasant glare. "I'll just have to get rid of you, too."

Maggie's heart raced. This was what she feared. Colton Denning was the love of her life. She would not be responsible for his death. She had to diffuse this situation before he got hurt.

Colton stood close enough to touch.

"Colt," she said softly.

"Yeah, sweetheart?"

She kept her gaze focused on the mad woman with the gun and took a small step forward, preparing for what she knew she had to do.

"I'm sorry I couldn't say it earlier. I guess I was just scared of admitting it out loud, but I'm not afraid anymore. I love you, Colton Denning. I always have."

She could sense some tension leave his body.

"You don't know how happy I am to hear that, but you picked a hell of a time for declarations, Magpie."

"Will you two shut up!" Deloris shrieked. The

woman's hands grip the gun harder. A wrinkly snarled finger tightened on the trigger as it aimed toward Colton.

Now or never.

"I love you," she whispered, then jumped in front of him.

It all happened in an instant. Colton yelled, trying to grab for her. Reacting on an instinct she didn't even know she had, Maggie lunged at the crazy woman, knocking her down to the hard, tiled floor. Startled, Deloris fired the gun wildly into the air.

Burning pain lanced through Maggie as she fell. *Ow! That hurt.* Should a tiny fall hurt that much?

"Maggie!"

She heard Colton screaming her name, but he sounded like he was in a tunnel. Why was he in a tunnel? That didn't make sense.

"Maggie!"

He wasn't in a tunnel. He was at her side, holding her.

"Oh God, no!"

Why was he so upset? She saved his life. *Jeez, you think the man could be a little grateful.*

Ouch! Why did her side hurt? Had she hit something when she knocked Deloris over?

"Hang on, Maggie. Help is on the way."

Help for what? Deloris was down for the count. She could see the old woman lying on the floor a few feet away. She hoped she hadn't killed her, but wouldn't feel too bad. After all, the crazy old lady had tried to kill them both. Self-defense was not murder. Still, she wasn't keen on taking human life. Even if it was to save her own and Colton's.

Sirens wailed in the distance. No, not the distance, they were close. Really close. Had someone called the cops?

Her side was really hurting. She was also, suddenly, very cold. That wasn't right. It had stopped snowing days ago. *Stupid Colorado weather.*

"Maggie, stay with me." Colton sounded far away again.

Well, of course she was staying with him. Where did he think she was going?

"Stay with me, Magpie."

Had someone put a blanket on her? Because now she felt warm and wet.

Footsteps and shouting suddenly filled the room. She could barely make out the voices.

"Hurry, she's been shot!"

Who was shot?

Me? Have I been shot?

That might explain why her side hurt so much. She had been shot. She was bleeding, maybe dying. Deloris must have hit the mark with one of those wild bullets.

At least Colton was safe. That's what mattered. He was all right, and she had gotten to tell him she loved him. She could die knowing that.

"Don't you even think of leaving me now!" he growled at her, making her wonder if she had spoken out loud.

Everything was fuzzy and painful. The lights dimmed. The last thing she saw before darkness took over was Colton's face. A good image to leave with.

Chapter Thirty-Two

Colton paced the hospital hallway. He had never been this scared in his life.

When he arrived at Maggie's shop and saw the back door slightly open, fear had gripped him tight. She would never leave the back door open. Which meant someone else had gone inside. And had still been inside he'd discovered once he entered.

The sight of Maggie being held at gunpoint had almost been enough to stop his heart. The blood-pumping organ had skipped a beat or two, he would bet on it.

He caught enough of the bullshit speech to realize Deloris Brake was off her little old rocker. He'd *known* there had been something off with Natalie. It hadn't been his ex attacking Maggie and the cupcake shop, but her mother. And the woman had known it the second Ryder showed her that necklace. They all thought Maggie was in the clear. The attacker was in jail. There was no more threat. Boy, were they wrong.

And now the woman he loved was paying the price.

He still couldn't believe she jumped in front of him like that. What had she been thinking? When she got out of surgery he was going to…to…to fall down at her feet and beg her to let him take care of her for the rest of their lives.

He couldn't lose her. Not now. Not like this.

She admitted she loved him, but it could have just been a heat of the moment type thing. A "holy shit I'm going to die, better just tell him what he wants to hear" kind of confession.

He glanced at the clock on the wall. What the hell was taking them so long?

After Ryder and the EMTs had arrived, they whisked Maggie off to the hospital. Thirty miles away. She lost consciousness and blood. So much blood. It still coated his hands and shirt, but he refused to wash it off. Not until he knew she was going to be okay.

They let him ride in the ambulance with her, but once they arrived at the hospital, the medical staff had taken her back to surgery. He wasn't allowed to follow, so here he paced the hallway just outside the waiting room.

"Colton!"

He turned to see his brother hurrying toward him, concern etched deep in the lines of his face. When Dade reached him, his older sibling pulled him into a fierce embrace.

"How is she?"

Tears clogged his throat, but Colton refused to let them pass. He needed to stay strong now, for Maggie. She would make it out of this.

She has to.

"I don't know. They took her into surgery over an hour ago. No one will tell me anything."

Dade glanced around. "Let me see if I can find anything out."

If anyone could, it would be his big brother. His calm demeanor and diplomatic ways could get a confession out of a preacher.

While his brother went over to the nurse's desk to inquire about Maggie, Colton turned to do another lap around the hallway. For the millionth time, he sent up a silent prayer she would pull through.

Light footsteps sounded on the tiled floor. Hope rose as he turned toward the sound, but it wasn't the doctor. Dejected and angry, he watched as sheriff Ryder made his way down the hallway.

"How is she?"

Question of the hour.

"I don't know. Dade is trying to find out."

Ryder nodded grimly as he removed his hat, gripping the dark brown Shepler tight. "Deloris is in custody. She bumped her head pretty good in the fall, but nothing serious."

"Too bad." It might have sounded callous, but the old woman shot the love of his life. He didn't care if she got a tiny bump on her head.

"Natalie is still in custody, too. Withholding information and conspiracy," he added at Colton's questioning look.

"Good."

"There's a solid case against both of them. I need your statement, though. It will help."

"Later."

Ryder looked for a moment as if he might argue, but then nodded. The sheriff was a smart man. He knew there was no way Colton was leaving here until Maggie was in the clear. Even then, he wasn't leaving without her. The statement could wait.

"If Maggie pulls though—"

"*When.*" He shot the sheriff a dark look, fists

clenched.

"When," Ryder corrected, looking abashed. "I'll need her statement, too. I just came to let you know we've got Mrs. Brake in custody, and she's not getting out. Maggie's not in danger anymore."

He said nothing. They both knew she was still in danger. She had a bullet tear through her gut. At the moment, she was in the most danger she had ever been in.

Dade joined them, looking irritated.

"Nurse Ratchet over there won't tell me a damn thing."

Colton swore.

"I'm sorry, but she says I'm not family and it's against hospital procedures."

Screw hospital procedures. He needed to know what was happing.

Fists still clenched, he started to storm the nurse's desk. Ryder put a firm hand on his chest, stopping him.

"With all due respect, Sheriff, I'd remove that hand if I was you."

"Colton, I know this is hard, but you causing a scene and trying to scare the daylights out of some poor nurse just doing her job isn't going to get you anywhere."

No, but it might make him feel better.

"Maggie is going to need you to be there for her when she wakes up. How are you going to do that if I have to haul your ass in for public disturbance?"

The bastard was right, but that didn't mean he had to agree.

"Let me go talk to the nurse," the sheriff offered. "After all, I have to check and see how the victim is doing, right?" Ryder gave his brother a look that said, *keep him under control*, before he turned and headed toward the desk.

"How you holding up?"

His brows drew down as he glared at his sibling.

"Right. Stupid question."

Colton sank against the wall in defeat. "I can't lose her, Dade," he said softly. "I can't."

A comforting hand squeezed his shoulder. "You're not going to. If anyone is stubborn enough to pull out of this, it's Maggie. Right?"

Laughing, he nodded. "Yeah."

Though he knew it was only said to make him smile, it was true. Maggie was stubborn. It was one of her most endearing qualities. He just hoped she used that stubbornness to fight for her life. He needed her to…or his was worthless.

Colton stood next to his brother in the hallway, leaning against the cold hospital wall. He watched Ryder talking with the stern looking, gray-haired nurse at the desk. She started to shake her head until he pulled out his badge. Her attitude changed immediately.

God bless the sheriff.

She searched her desk, pulling out a yellow folder and opening it on the counter. She pointed to a few things, making motions with her hands. He had no idea what those motions meant, but Ryder nodded his head, so he guessed it wasn't too bad.

Please let it not be too bad.

The sheriff put his badge away, tipped his hat to the nurse, and turned toward them.

Finally!

Colton pulled away from the wall. He wanted to

sprint across the room to discover what was found out, but the tight hand his brother had on his arm prevented him from doing just that.

"Easy, Colt. Let him come over here." Dade motioned with his chin.

Nurse "Hospital Procedure" glared at them. She saw where Ryder was going. Yeah, she'd just been played and realized it.

Well, too bad, lady.

He was going to find out what was going on, one way or another.

Turned out, he didn't need Ryder to divulge what he learned. As soon as the sheriff joined them, the hallway doors burst open. A middle-aged man and a young blonde woman, both in green scrubs, came into the hallway.

"Are you all here for Maggie Evans?" the young woman asked.

He stepped forward instantaneously, anxious for news.

"How is she? Is she awake? When can I see her?"

The bald man eyed him. "Are you family?"

"I'm her fiancé."

A little lie, but he wasn't dealing with this "only release information to family" bullshit again. As long as Maggie lived, he'd make sure it wasn't a lie much longer.

Please be alive, Maggie.

When Dade and Ryder said nothing to counter his statement, the doctor nodded and continued.

"The bullet was a through and through. She was lucky. It missed all major organs, but there was some small damage to her intestines. We were able to patch everything up. Ms. Evans is still sedated, but she should be awake soon."

Colton almost fell over in relief. *She's alive! She was going to be okay.*

"There won't be any lasting damage that we can see," the younger doctor said. "But she'll need to take it easy for a few weeks. It would be best if she stayed with someone until the stitches are ready to come out."

"She'll be staying with me."

The woman nodded. "I'll go over her medications with you and the procedure for keeping her stitches clean. Then I'll take you in to see her."

At last! He was going to get to see Maggie. She was alive and okay.

Once the doctor gave him the run down, she showed him to Maggie's hospital bed. An ugly white gown with a faded flower print covered her. The blood had all been clean off, but he could still see it in his mind, red and dark. She'd lost so much, and there had been nothing he could do to help her. There were wires coming from her and hooked up to beeping monitors that displayed numbers. He wasn't even going to begin to guess what they all meant.

She could have died. He could have lost her.

Colton felt so many emotions right now, relief, anger, happiness, but most of all love. Only at that moment, seeing the woman who held his heart and knowing she was going to make it, that he sat in the chair beside her bed and finally let the tears fall.

Chapter Thirty-Three

The Sahara was wetter than her throat right now.

Maggie scraped her sandpaper dry tongue over the roof of her equally dry mouth.

Gah!

Never in her life had she wanted water more than right now. What had she done last night, eaten a pile of sawdust?

Cracking her eyes open, she glanced around.

This isn't my room.

Where was she?

A beeping sound came from somewhere, and everything smelled like bleach and sickness. It looked…like a hospital room.

Everything came rushing back to her. Deloris, her shop, the old woman raving about Maggie stealing what was hers. Or some such nonsense. A gun. A big *freaking* gun. Colton and gunfire.

Oh God, Colton!

"Col—" She tried to get the words out, but her throat was so dry. She could barely croak out a syllable before a hacking cough racked her body.

"Maggie! You're awake."

Suddenly, enveloped in his strong arms, she inhaled his musky, warm scent. Colton was here. He was okay.

"How are you feeling?" he asked, as he pulled

back. Those beautiful sky blue eyes roamed over her body, checking for injuries.

"Throat...hurts."

He smiled, gently cupping her face and stroking her cheek with his thumb.

"They had to put a tube down your throat during surgery. It's going to be a little sore for a while, they said." He turned, grabbing a cup from a side table. "Here."

He placed something on her tongue. It was cold and square and began to melt immediately. Ice chips.

"They won't let me give you water just yet, so you'll have to make do with these. Sorry, sweetheart."

The ice chips were cool and did quench some of her thirst, but not fast enough. She'd kill for a giant pitcher of water.

The synapses in her brain fired again. More memories came rushing back. Jumping in front of Colton. Slamming into Deloris. The sound of a gunshot and both of them falling. Had she killed Deloris?

"What...happened?" She grimaced at the pain those two words cost her.

His smile turned into a scowl. "What happened is that you nearly got yourself killed. What the hell were you thinking, Maggie?"

"Save...you." Stupid man, what did he think she'd been doing, seeing if she could dodge a bullet for fun?

His forehead dropped to hers. Firm lips brushed against her own in a soft kiss. She wanted more, deeper, longer, but he pulled away. Those sapphire gems glittered with anger, fear, and best of all, love.

"Thank you for saving my life, but don't you *ever* do anything that stupid again. My life is worth nothing if you're not in it, Magpie."

Tears welled in her eyes. He was alive; she was alive. They were in love, and their future hadn't been taken away by some crazy old woman.

"Owed you…saved me…few times."

Deep laughter rumbled from his chest. He gave her another kiss.

A longer one this time.

Still not enough.

"Let's just call it even okay?" he whispered against her lips.

She nodded.

"I see the patient is awake."

Peering around Colton, she saw a bald, middle-aged man in green scrubs and a white doctor coat. If not for the outfit, she would have thought her doctor was Patrick Stewart.

He approached the bed. "I'm Dr. Simmons."

Colton moved to make room for the doctor, but he stayed close by. She was glad he wasn't leaving. Everything was still a bit fuzzy, and it helped having him nearby.

"Do you remember what happened?"

She nodded. "Mostly…bit fuzzy, but I remember— I think…shot?"

The doctor nodded, pulling a penlight out of his coat pocket. He shined the light in one eye then the other. "Yes, in the abdomen. You were very lucky though. No major organs were hit, and there should be no long-term damage. But you'll need to take it easy for a few weeks."

That might be difficult.

"She owns and runs a bakery," Colton answered

for her when she tried to speak again.

She sent him a soft smile of thanks.

"I would suggest you have your employees run the shop for at least a month. Exertion and standing for long periods of time will slow down the healing process and may cause more damage."

School was almost out. Jamie did say she could work full time, but she didn't want to spoil the girl's last summer before moving away to college. Plus, with the blogger's review coming out, she was expecting more business to come in this summer. What was she going to do?

"Don't worry, sweetheart. I can send a hand or two down to the shop to help out. I'm sure Jamie can boss them around just as well as you."

She glared, but he did bring up an idea she had been meaning to talk to him about. She grimaced as she shifted and started to speak. Colton immediately shushed her and placed another piece of ice on her tongue. The cool, frozen chip started to melt immediately and helped ease her painful throat.

"Save your voice, Magpie." He smiled, looking far too sexy for the bedridden position she was in at the moment.

He was right. They could talk about Tony and the young man's culinary talents later.

The doctor continued his examination. Checking her limbs for reflexes and noting whatever was going on with all the machines beeping around her.

Colton leaned down to brush his lips against hers. "Don't worry about the shop. We'll figure it out." He kissed her again, lingering longer this time.

Dr. Simmons cleared his throat, reminding them he

was still in the room. Colton straightened, with a shameless grin on his face; her own cheeks heated.

Damn man wasn't embarrassed about anything.

"Well, you seem to be coming along nicely. No complications that I can see. We want to keep you another forty-eight hours for observation, and then you will be released. You'll need to stay with someone until the stitches are ready to come out." The doctor glanced at Colton. "Your fiancé has offered. The nurses will explain your recovery process to him before you leave."

Fiancé?

Maggie gave a sideways glance to the man standing by her side. When did that happen? She was still a bit groggy from the anesthesia. Did he propose while she was unconscious? There was a part of her, a bigger part than she wanted to admit, that reveled in that word "fiancé." They may not have been dating long, but they'd known each other forever, and she had been in love with him since the day she met him. There were more than a few times, in her youth, when she'd planned out their wedding in her mind.

The doctor made a note on her chart then left the room.

"They wouldn't let me see you unless I was family," Colton offered in answer to her unspoken question. "Some hospital procedure bull."

Oh.

She shouldn't be disappointed—after all, every woman wanted to be conscious for their proposal—but she was. The word "fiancé," had made her heart soar in her chest. Now, it fell to her toes.

Stupid.

Tired, she closed her eyes. Just because Colton said

he loved her didn't mean he was ready to marry her. Guys took their time with things like these. Especially guys like him.

She already agreed to move in with him. Marriage might come later, down the road. Until then, she decided that every day with her sexy cowboy was one to be cherished. The future could take care of itself. No use worrying about what might happen. From now on, she would only focus on what was happening at the present.

Amazing how almost dying could change a person's perspective.

Maggie opened her eyes at the sound of footsteps entering the room. A nurse came in then and gave her a glass of water approved by the doctor. She greedily drank the cool liquid, her throat feeling a million times better. The silver-haired woman checked her vitals and smiled at them both before leaving.

"I know you said you'd move in with me before, but we can stay at your apartment if you prefer."

"I think the ranch is better." She took another sip of water before continuing. "If I'm not going to be working for a month, there's no reason for me to be at my apartment. If I stay at your place, your day won't be interrupted as much."

He scowled. "Forget the ranch. I'm taking care of *you*, Maggie."

She rolled her eyes. "I won't need twenty-four seven care, Colt. Besides, you can't take off all day just to sit by my side. You need to help your brother. I'll be fine."

He eyed her suspiciously as she took another sip.

"I'll sit on the porch swing all day reading books.

That way, you can see me lazing about. I have a stack of novels I've been meaning to read anyway." She held up a hand to swear to it, but winced as the motion pulled on her wound.

He moved in until their noses touched. "If you move that sexy ass of yours one inch off that swing without calling for me, I'm locking you up in my bedroom with no clothes. And I'll make sure you stay in bed. All. Month. Long."

She gulped. "Sexy ass, huh?"

"Damn sexy."

Maggie grinned, then his mouth descended on hers. The kiss was deep and hot. His tongue stroked along hers, making her burn and ache in private places. His kiss held all the love he professed.

One of the monitors in the room started to beat faster. It must have been connected to her heart because at the moment, it was racing so hard it felt like it would burst from her chest.

"Jeez, Colt, she was already shot. What are you trying to do, give the poor woman a heart attack?"

Colton pulled away, but didn't turn. "Go away, Dade."

"Can't." His voice held amusement. "Someone's here to see the patient. That is if you're done mauling her."

He sighed. Her face burned hot, probably beet red again. Colton, however, seemed more put out than embarrassed to be caught making out in a hospital bed.

"Gee, boss, you look like crap."

Glancing at the door, she saw Jamie standing next to Dade, a tentative smile plastered on the young girl's face. She clutched a bright yellow teddy bear to her

chest that held a sign stating, *Feel better BEARY soon!*
Her eyes glistened with unshed tears.

"Oh, sweetie. I'm okay, I promise."

The youthful face appeared even younger as the
girl burst into tears and her sobbing employee ran
across the room.

She bent to give Maggie a gentle hug. "I was so
scared when I heard you had been shot."

Maggie braved the pain to hug the girl back,
stoking her hair and murmuring softly to her.

"Good to see you awake, Maggie." Dade stepped
fully into the room, placing a hand on his brothers
shoulder.

She saw the two exchange a glance—they had both
been worried for her. Jamie had been worried for her,
too. She had so many people who cared for her.

Happiness filled her. Deloris was wrong. People
did care. People *wanted* her here. She was home, and
no one could ever make her leave.

Ever.

Chapter Thirty-Four

Two days was an eternity in a hospital. Maggie's throat was fine, and the painkillers took care of all the aches. Now she just wanted to get out of here and go home. Well, to Colton's ranch technically, but it would be home for her now.

Thinking of Colton and home in the same sentence made her smile. It was nice to think of sharing a place with the man she loved.

"Hey, sweetheart. You about ready to go?"

There he stood, leaning against the open door jam, the man who held her heart. He had on worn jeans that hung low on his hips, a blue button up open over a white T-shirt that hugged his deliciously chiseled chest, feet covered by his standard cowboy boots, and black Stetson in his hand. He looked yummy enough to eat.

"I was ready two days ago."

He chuckled. The sound was a caress right between her legs.

"Let's get you home then."

Home. She liked the way he said home. It felt right.

"I need help changing." She gave him a naughty look.

Dade had brought a change of clothes yesterday. The clothes she'd been brought in with had been ruined beyond salvage. Not that she wanted to keep them. There was no way she could ever wear those particular

287

items of clothing ever again.

Colton stepped into the room, shutting the door behind him. With a wicked gleam in his eyes, he stalked toward the bed. She was thankful they had detached her from the heart rate monitor that morning. With the way her heart was racing, she would have broken it for sure.

"Let's get you out of this hospital gown to start with."

He stood in front of her as she sat on the bed. Reaching around, he pulled the tie on the back of the gown. It slowly released, falling softly, causing the back to gape open. The cool air hit her skin, sending shivers up her spine.

"Cold, Magpie?"

She nodded her head.

"Let me see what I can do to warm you up."

He leaned in, his lips brushing hers. Gentle was nice, but she was done with gentle. She needed him and she needed him now. Thrusting her hand into his hair, she pulled him to her, taking over the kiss.

He let out a muffled sound of surprise, but happily obliged her fervor. When her tongue pressed against the seam of his lips, he opened enthusiastically for her.

This was what she needed. Colton, hot and wild, pressed against her. It'd be even better if he were naked.

At that moment, two voices could be heard shouting out in the hallway. They paused as the voices got louder. It sounded like a man and a woman, and both very familiar, too.

"She's changing, you can't go in there now."

"Don't tell me what I can't do. I need to see her."

She did know that voice. "Is that—"

Colton turned to face the door just as it burst open.

"Maggie!"

"Lizzy?"

Shocked at the sight of her best friend, she could do nothing except stare. Thankfully, Colton had a little more brainpower. He stealthily moved behind her and pulled her gown closed, retying it for her.

"I told you she would be happy to see me." Lizzy sneered at Dade, who stood behind her and appeared very put out.

"She looks more confused than happy."

Her best friend growled, actually growled. "Stow it, cowpoke."

"Cowpoke?" Dade looked confused by the insult.

"Lizzy, what are you doing here?"

"My best friend gets shot, and you don't think I'd drop everything to come see you?"

The tall strawberry-blonde rushed to the bed, arms open. Maggie welcomed her friend's embrace. She'd missed her so much, and only wished her friend had a better reason to come see her. But Lizzy was here now, and that was all that mattered.

Soft arms squeezed her, causing her stitches to pull slightly. She winced, and her friend immediately pulled away.

"I'm sorry, are you all right?"

"She just had a bullet rip through her gut. What do you think?" Dade crossed his arms over his chest, scowling at Lizzy.

What was wrong with him? Maggie had never seen him act this way toward anyone. Dade was kind and stoic. She had never seen the man get riled.

Her best friend sent him a glare over her shoulder. "Was I talking to you, cowpoke?"

He glared right back. "It's Dade."

"Hi, I'm Colton Denning," his brother said from behind Maggie. He gave Lizzy his friendliest smile and stretched out his hand. "You must be the famous Lizzy I have heard so much about."

She returned his smile, accepting his outstretched hand. Maggie was glad he was good at diffusing tense situations, though she was still confused as to why Dade and Lizzy seemed to be at such odds.

"Oh right. Colt, this is my best friend in the whole wide world, Elizabeth Hayworth."

"Lizzy, to my friends," she said releasing his hand. Jutting her chin over her shoulder, she scowled at the older Denning brother. "You may call me Elizabeth."

Dade narrowed his eyes.

"You'll have to excuse my brother." Colton grinned. "He's just grumpy because he hasn't had his morning coffee yet."

"Colton." The big man narrowed his gaze in warning.

"Lighten up, big brother. We're almost ready to go."

"The nurse says the discharge papers need to be signed," Dade said, now glaring daggers at Lizzy's back.

Colton kissed the top of her head. "I'll go take care of the paper work. Let you two catch up. Be back in about ten?"

She nodded, giving him a smile. "I'll be ready to go. Lizzy can help me change."

He leaned down to place a soft kiss on her lips.

"*This* time. She can help you into your clothes. *I'll* help you out of them when we get home."

Her cheeks heated at his words, so full of sensual promise.

The men left, and once the door was closed, Lizzy fanned herself with a hand. "Good gravy girl, you didn't mention he was scrumdiddlyumptious!"

She laughed. "I'm pretty sure I did, and that's not a word."

"It should be."

"Help me get dressed, will you?"

Her best friend helped her stand and retrieved the long maxi dress Dade brought for her. It was one of the few dresses she owned. She requested it, specifically, because it was easy to slip on and wouldn't put pressure on her stitches. No jeans for a while, that was for sure.

As Lizzy helped her get out of the hospital gown and into the dress, she inquired about how long her friend would be staying.

"Well, you see…the thing is…it's kind of open-ended."

Dress on, she lowered herself into the wheel chair the nurse had brought in earlier. It still took a lot of energy to stand for too long.

"What do you mean? Did you get fired?"

"No, I quit. I couldn't take working there anymore." Lizzy absently folded the gown and placed it on the bed. "It's just no fun if you're not there, Maggie." She leaned against the bed, arms crossed. "I have some savings and time on my hands, so I thought I'd come out here and help you until you're back on your feet."

She really could use the help, and Lizzy already

knew about managing a business. She could take over for Maggie while she recovered. But it would be a lot of work; she couldn't do that to her friend.

"Stop that right now."

She glanced up in shock.

"I know what you're thinking, and you're not forcing me to do anything. I'm offering. You can't very well run the shop after being shot. I'm here to take over as long as you need." Her friend thought for a second then added, "As long as someone else does the baking."

Lizzy could burn water. The woman's go to meal was ordering take-out. Maggie laughed out loud, wincing when the action pulled at her stitches. "Okay, okay, you win. Actually, I really do need you. I have the bakers, but having someone to run the business side would be extremely helpful."

Bright red lips smiled. "Then it's settled." Her friend's eyes misted over as her smile dimmed. "I was really scared I might lose you, Maggie."

Her own eyes started to tear. "Me, too."

Lizzy grabbed her in another tight embrace, being careful of her stitches this time. "I'm so glad you're okay."

That was how the men found them when they returned, locked in a hug of happiness. It was a bit awkward since she was still sitting in the wheelchair, but it felt good to be with her best friend when there was a moment in time she thought she might never see the other woman again.

"You ladies ready to get out of here?" Colton gave them his trademark grin.

Lizzy stood, wiping at her eyes. She smiled at Colton, but sent Dade another glare. He didn't respond to her look. Just stood there with a grim expression.

What's the deal there?

Colton walked over and grabbed the handles of the wheel chair. He leaned down to whisper in her ear. "Ready to go home, Magpie?"

Home. A home she could share with him.

"I'm ready."

She really was.

Epilogue

The June sun hung high in the midday sky. The weather had finally warmed up enough to break out the shorts. It was strange, but now that all the snow was gone, Maggie kind of missed it. She knew she'd be regretting that thought come mid-January.

The sounds of the ranch buzzed around her as she sat on the porch swing. A few horses neighed. Birds sang in the trees. The ranch hands chatted and called out tasks to each other. It was nice, comforting.

It had been almost two weeks since the shooting. Natalie had actually called her and apologized for her mother's actions, as much as Natalie could apologize. The woman said her mother had some mental problems since her father died and sometimes forgot to take her medication. It wasn't an excuse, but it was something.

She'd accepted the apology, but had a hard time forgetting the fact Natalie neglected to mention the necklace the sheriff had found was her mother's and not hers. If the woman had spoken up, Maggie would never have been shot.

Lizzy was living at the apartment for the time being, running the shop with the help of Jamie and Tony—who was coming along quite nicely according to Jamie's updates. Colton had agreed with her idea of letting the young man work for her while he worked toward his citizenship. These days, the man agreed to anything she said.

Her shop was running so smoothly with her best friend in charge, she was starting to think about what it would be like if she and Lizzy ran the place together. Her baking and Lizzy doing all the boring business stuff. It would be wonderful to have her best friend around.

Her recovery was coming along nicely, too, thanks in part to Colton waiting on her hand and foot. The man even insisted on carrying her to the bathroom. That's where she'd drawn the line, however. She was not so feeble she needed assistance in the restroom, thank you very much.

He barely let her lift a finger, though. Even when he was working, he would check in with her every so often, either by phone or in person. It was sweet. She had never felt so loved in her life. He was, by far, the most wonderful man she ever met.

Speaking of the sexy devil.

Colton walked up the porch steps, a huge grin on his face as he ambled toward her. He removed his hat and smacked the Stetson against his thigh, causing a dust cloud to billow up, then used it to motion to the laptop on her lap.

"Hey, Magpie. What cha' doing, sweetheart?"

Him and his nicknames. They were so endearing now, she had forgotten why she was ever annoyed with them.

She made room for him as he came to sit beside her and showed him the screen. "The review is coming out today. I can't bring myself to read it."

"Stephanie already implied it was going to be good, right?" His lips brushed her temple.

She shivered at the contact. Every touch from him set her body ablaze, no matter how small.

"Yes. But what if she changed her mind, or the cupcakes made her sick later, or—"

He held up a hand to stop her paranoid tirade. "Maggie, she loved the cupcakes, and she loved your shop." He turned the screen back to her. "Now, read."

Taking a deep breath, she braced herself and typed in the website address. The review was right there on the front page.

Oh, boy. Here goes.

She began to read:

Guilty Pleasures: A Cross-Country Food Journey

I recently went to a charming little town in the mountains of Colorado, just outside Aspen. Peak Town, Colorado is home to "Cupcakes Above the Clouds," an enchanting cupcake bakery run by the wonderful Maggie Evans. Forget your diets, people, because this place is delicious sugary heaven!

"She likes it!" She glanced up at him, unable to keep the smile from her face.

"I told you." He turned her chin back to the computer. "Now, keep reading."

Stephanie went on to say how much she loved the cupcakes and added a lovely sentimental touch when telling the story of how Maggie got the shop from her grandmother.

It is a wonderful little bakery that had been passed down through the generations. I hope Ms. Evans continues with the tradition and passes it down to any future children she may have. So, go visit "Cupcakes Above the Clouds" in Peak Town, Colorado. The owner says she makes everything from everyday treats to cupcake wedding cakes. Something tells me she'll be making one of those for herself very soon.

Confused by that last sentence, she glanced up to see Colton down on one knee in front of her. In his hand, he held a red velvet cupcake with frosting...and a beautiful diamond ring placed on top.

Her breath caught. Tears blurred her vision.

"Stephanie called me after she heard about your shooting."

It seemed the small town gossip mill extended to visitors of Peak Town now, as well.

"I let her in on a little secret." He cleared his throat. "I love you, Maggie Evans. You are my best friend, my better half, my everything. As a kid you were fun, as a woman you are amazing. When you left it hurt, but when I almost lost you forever, it nearly killed me. I don't ever want to feel like that again. Will you please put me out of my misery and promise to never leave me again, and marry me?"

She could barely speak past the tears of joy, but she managed. She needed him to know how much she loved him, too. "I have loved you since the moment you rescued me from a bunch of kids who knew a horse sneeze couldn't kill you. I never want to be without you either, Colton. You are the most amazing man I have ever known."

"So, that's a yes?"

He looked worried. As if she'd say no. *Silly man.*

Nodding her head furiously, the tears of joy still streaming down her face, she cried, "Of course that's a yes!"

"Wahoooo!"

He jumped up, lifting her from the swing in a

jubilant embrace. Spinning her around, he kissed her soundly. Then, as if just remembering her injuries, he stopped spinning but didn't let her go.

"Just so you know," she said, adding a feisty smile. "Marrying me will not get you free cupcakes."

He kicked open the front door, making his way down the hallway toward their bedroom. "Spoilsport. That's okay, though. I know something that's much sweeter than your cupcakes." He winked as he placed her softly on the bed.

Maggie shivered with anticipation. As he began to peel their clothes off, she wondered at how blessed she was. Her shop was successful, her best friend was in town, and the man she loved more than anything in this world wanted to spend his life with her. Her roller coaster of bad luck was over.

Colton leaned down, whispering against her lips, "You and me, Magpie. Forever."

He was right; those words were sweeter than all the cupcakes in the world.

A word about the author...

Mariah began writing at the tender age of five. Her first book *George and the Green Glob* received high praise from her mother. Many years, and green glob stories later, Mariah recieved a playwriting degree from the University of Wyoming. After a few years in Hollywood, working in "the biz," she came home to the beautiful rocky mountains.

When she's not writing Mariah loves to read, crochet, and play her ukulele. She loves to hear from readers.

You can contact her through her website www.mariahankenman.com or on twitter @MAsbooks

Made in the USA
Middletown, DE
28 October 2018